THE CRYSTAL SEDUCTION

Novels by Dennis Bowen

THE WATER DIAMONDS
Book 1: International Thriller Series

THE BLACKSTONE PERFECTION
Book 2: International Thriller Series

THE CRYSTAL SEDUCTION
Book 3: International Thriller Series

THE CRYSTAL SEDUCTION

Dennis Bowen

The Crystal Seduction is a work of fiction. Names, characters, places, and incidents are the products of the author's imagination or are used fictitiously. Any resemblance to actual events, locales, or persons, living or dead, is entirely coincidental.

ISBN: 978-0-9960412-0-1

FIRST EDITION

www.DennisBowen.com

www.twitter.com/DBowenThrillers

www.facebook.com/Dennis.Bowen.90

Book Interior Design by 52 Novels

ACKNOWLEDGMENTS

I would like to thank the readers of my *International Thriller Series.* It is still true that readers give writers a gift of immeasurable magnitude. As with *The Water Diamonds* and *The Blackstone Perfection*, numerous people offered suggestions and encouragement during the writing of *The Crystal Seduction*, and they also deserve my appreciation.

I wish to express my continued appreciation to Laura Taylor, my mentor, editorial consultant, and colleague. Her knowledge, skill, and consistency have helped make this series a source of great pride for me. Any errors or omissions in *The Crystal Seduction*, I claim as my own.

And finally, I wish to express my gratitude to family, friends, and former colleagues whose presence in my life has made the *International Thriller Series* possible. Thank you.

—*Dennis Bowen*

CHAPTER 1

"It looks fabulous in your hands." The tall young man, having given the football-shaped object to the older man, stepped back.

"It rightfully belongs to the both of us, my Son." The older man pushed in the ends, as if to plump up a rugby ball.

"Please don't do that," admonished a third man. "Five megatons, you know."

"I'm sorry, General. I thought these miniature nuclear devices were only unstable in the hands of Muslims."

The men laughed. A fourth, a second Chinese, spoke. "The world is only in danger when we possess one of these." He raised the CIA's version of a universal TV remote.

The men laughed again.

"I, Chin Yao-wu, next emperor of China, propose a toast." He raised his glass. "To better bombs. To better governance. To mutual success." He glanced at the general.

General Li inclined his head. "And faster horses."

"Boom!" teased the young Frenchman.

The older men glared.

The young man's father supplied redirection. "The castle you have chosen here in the elegant town of Victoria, British Colombia, is quite beautiful."

"Hong Kong is my home. I purchased Craigdarroch as my home away from home, where I visit my offshore wealth."

"The stained glass windows are legendary, are they not?"

"The finest in North America, Sylvain."

"The structure, positioned atop this hill, commands the area. I'm sure the general appreciates its defensibility." The bandaged Frenchman glanced at the uniformed man seated opposite.

"Yes, easy for my small force to protect."

"And protection is key, gentlemen." An unexpected participant strode into the room.

"You!" cried the Frenchman. "What are you doing here? I never expected you to leave your subterranean lair."

"Manassas? As you said, home away from home."

"This is Canada. Your specific role is to be our, Illuminé's—"

"My role, today, is to provide secure transportation for you and your football to the European continent. While Interpol and the rest of the world's forces stand down, believing you are quite dead. We mustn't disappoint them."

"What we must do is attack before the nuclear bombing of Marseille loses its effect. It has been three weeks."

"Had you not gone terribly rogue," Neil Wohlford added with typical arrogance, "we would not find ourselves in this awkward situation."

"I had to attack America. New York was perfect. The Americans, one of which you are, Neil, have withdrawn support for my France. That was essential. Now, *I* can return with *my* bomb and finish *my* work."

"Gentlemen, we are on the same team. We are the necessary components of the American's master strategy, are we not?" Chin asked, diffusing the escalating interplay. "Sylvain, it has been too long since our first face-to-face meeting in Scotland."

Lalumière came back to Earth. "Yes. The Scottish name of your castle brings to mind that Elite Single-Malt gathering."

Apropos of that comment, two young women dressed in black and red cheongsam dresses wheeled in a cart that bore a 30-year-old Scotch and five crystal glasses. They poured three fingers each.

"To our success in China!" Chin beamed.

They drank.

"To our success in France!" Lalumière tilted his chin upward.

They drank.

"Then Europe."

They drank.

"We'll require more mini-bombs, General," the Frenchman advised.

"I now own, in all respects, the People's Republic military forces and their collective resources. You shall have bombs."

They drank.

Chin Yao-wu, swept up in the moment, turned somber. "Gentlemen, my country continues to reel from the Beijing explosion. General Li and I must, regrettably, depart your company to deal with the chaos. But we shall gather again soon … when France is ours."

"Here, here," Neil declared.

Lalumière sipped his drink. *Sharing* France appeared no where on his mental map.

Li stood. "Well, we must be on our way."

"You will return to Manassas, Neil?" a concerned Lalumière asked.

"My movements are, of course, classified. Need to know, and all."

Lalumière sucked in a breath. The arrogance of this man rivaled that of Parisian waiters.

"Dad! You must see this!"

"What, my Son?"

"A gorgeous Rolls-Royce, maroon over beige, just pulled into the porte-cochère. Royalty incarnate."

"Impossible!" gasped Li. "My sentries—"

"Jean-Marc, push me to the window."

The son complied.

"That automobile is perfect. I want it for my coronation."

"Dad, we're far from any coronation. You've survived an atomic blast, for Christ sakes. It will take months to recover. Well into the Spring. Out of sight of Interpol—"

"Look, Son!"

The front window of the Roll-Royce opened, revealing a black-clad figure, an MP5 machine-gun, and a face.

"Crayle!"

CHAPTER 2

Crayle's fierce blue eyes fixated on the Frenchman. The man was a nemesis he had created by his own hand. His jaw clenched as he twisted his head over his shoulder. *"Take 'em!"*

The elongated sunroof rotated to reveal a multi-barreled weapon modified with special silencers by Crayle associate Mick Mackay. Known as Micmac by the team, he controlled the M134. Calibrated to the 4,000 rounds per minute rate recommended for unrelenting fire, it could reduce the Washington Monument to dust in a matter of minutes.

The beveled antique glass windows exploded. Two of Chin's daughters, trained only in covert forms of warfare, became the first castle casualties.

Ornate deer carvings adorning the walls exploded into toothpicks. Marble and golden frames, likewise. Priceless paintings were shredded in an instant. Cries of agony and fear sounded from the dining room.

Guards, who rushed in to the front-facing rooms with weapons at the fore, were pulverized.

The weapon spewed rage at the occupants of the old castle, exploding window after precious window. Those inside dove to the floor, trying to escape the wrath of their former target, Crayle.

Splashed in blood, the men who hoped to rule the world in the near term hugged the floor beneath the heavy dining room table.

Hekka Poppi and Phoebe Bransfield jumped from the limo, taking up positions left and right.

Crayle had stashed the usual variety of weapons that "project manager" Jack Sommers supplied and had replaced them with the ultra-reliable HK MP5's.

Crayle now circled the castle. More explosions of windows and devastation of Chin's priceless treasures followed Micmac's aim.

While the silenced mini-gun continued its back and forth drone, General Li surveyed the damage inside Craigdarroch. "Chin! Black and Red daughters are down, both likely dead. Our defense force has failed us. We must leave."

"No!" cried Chin. "Not Black! No!"

For the first time, Li understood the depth of the old man's love for the nineteen-year-old. "Chin, calm yourself!" He steadied his voice. "The fate of our country is at stake."

"No!" Chin continued.

Li took another look. "Wait! There are no golden embellishments. They are the understudies. Follow me."

Chin wiped his eyes on the black napkin that lay next to him. He crawled after the general, away from the violence.

Outside, the mini-gun continued its assault, pulling ammunition from the trunk and kept cool by the Micmac-extended air-conditioning system of the limo.

Through the dining room doorway, on hands and knees, Neil, who had previously reconnoitered the castle in inimitable CIA style, led Chin, Lalumière, Jean-Marc, Li, and the remaining daughters through a covert doorway into the castle galley.

To the east of the castle, Phoebe Bransfield crouched behind a short wall next to the demolished gated entry. On indefinite loan to

Jack and the Crayle team, her FBI creds meant nothing in Canada. Still, the spatter from the building pinged and ponged off the wall, causing her to pull into a ball.

Hekka Poppi, positioned to the west, also sought refuge from the storm of violence just fifteen yards away.

With the castle between them, they avoided any crossfire risk. Micmac had reached back into his Navy special forces background to create the umbrella of death. As Crayle had directed, there would be no prisoners taken.

"Take down the building! They'll have to run!" Crayle yelled over the din.

As Micmac exercised the joystick, the gun raked the building from side-to-side. The heavyweight 7.62 millimeter rounds exploded the charcoal gray blocks like dynamited watermelons.

One of Li's guards, a sniper who'd survived the first onslaught, had climbed to the top tower of the castle. From the balcony, he peered down at the offending vehicle. He flipped his AK-47 to full automatic and leaned against the railing for the perfect shot. He would kill them all. He would be rewarded.

The raking of the building finally took a structural toll. It started to shake. The castle crumbled, the sniper falling directly into Micmac's line of fire. Flung into the rubble, he exploded like a shotgunned tomato.

Inside, the CIA mole, the Chinese, and the French were subjected to a crumbling ceiling and then falling support timbers. The structural integrity compromised, the upper floors began to collapse on them.

"This way!" shouted Li.

Silence.

Hekka and Phoebe's heads popped up as the limo completed its circle.

"No one survived," Hekka surmised.

"Not in that mess."

Phoebe peeked over the wall. She spoke into her boom mic. "There they are! Out the back!"

She watched the five intended victims scramble into a set of earthmovers, backhoes, and pickups, ostensibly there for modifications to the back yard. The vehicles trundled off toward the Strait of Juan de Fuca, which separated Victoria from mainland America.

Phoebe opened fire with her brace of .45's. Hekka let loose with her MP5. Their withering fire cut down the remainder of Li's defense force, but the principals were escaping.

"This is Phoebe. They're getting away on tractors. Pick us up at the gate. Hekka, get your Indian ass back in the assault vehicle!"

Micmac ceased fire. Crayle cranked the limo into a K-turn. Hekka jumped into the shotgun seat next to Crayle. At the gate, Phoebe hopped in back with the gadget man.

The chase would have posed no problem if the moving equipment had not been enhanced by Li's Gao Bo-da and Chin's Red daughter.

Driving southwest through residential streets, the large powerful machines crushed parked cars and toppled decorative trees. A team of bicyclists, practicing for a race, turned tail and pedaled for their lives.

"Be judicious with the mini-gun, Micmac!" shouted Crayle. "This area is residential."

CHAPTER 3

Within minutes, the yellow fleet of escape vehicles mounted a huge grassy knoll known as Beacon Hill Park. Fans and players of baseball and soccer stood frozen in place.

Three helicopters soared into range and provided fire support against the Crayle team. Crayle swerved the Rolls-Royce left and right while Micmac reasserted his weapon. The first helicopter exploded into a fireball. The other two landed amidst the panicked throng on the park-like knoll.

"Take your baby down, Micmac. We'll have to use light weapons on the ground. Be ready, though, if either chopper takes off. At that point, they're yours." The thought of Ling perhaps being aboard one of them spiked his conscience.

With no doubt that an urban combat situation was in full swing, the screaming crowd switched from fright to flight and opened a path.

The fugitives bored through and parked their large vehicles in front of the helicopters, providing protection for themselves and their means of escape. Their action impeded sight lines for all combatants, providing a sense of safety. A false sense.

Just then, an ambulance screamed up the driveway. Jack and his lieutenant, Lenny Lipschitz. They popped out, using the doors as cover, and fired over the heavy equipment at the helicopters' engines.

One of Li's snipers yanked a pilot from his seat, and searched for a target.

Within ten seconds, Jack took a hit. He rolled over the knoll's edge. Lenny chased after him.

The sniper sought another victim.

Crayle scrambled up behind a backhoe, using it as cover. Li's door gunners rained bullets down on his position.

Hekka, seeing Crayle in a compromised position, skirted the periphery of the knoll. She ran through a copse of trees, firing as she went. Her weapon clicked empty. She stopped to change magazines.

The sniper spotted her. It was next to impossible to acquire the target with the trees moving in the wind, the characteristic helicopter vibrations, and his coffee-induced shakes. However, he was good.

The bullet slammed Hekka's head back. She fell sideways, and over the knoll's edge. Her body bounced and rolled down the rough terrain before becoming airborne and landing in a deep drainage channel. It hit hard. It lay still.

Crayle ran to the plateau's edge. He couldn't see her. He heard a *pfft*, reminiscent of a silenced weapon. His last vision was of Chin's Black daughter Ling beside a tree, holding a tranquilizer gun in a two-handed combat grip.

One of Chin's oversized eunuchs tossed an unconscious Crayle into a helicopter. Ling and the eunuch climbed aboard. Both choppers lifted off, veering east across the water.

They soared away, almost out of range.

Not realizing Crayle's status, Micmac picked one and took aim.

His aim was true. Eighty rounds slammed the aircraft in the next two seconds. It exploded in flames, destroying any visual of the third and final machine. That one was gone. Its occupants had escaped.

Shaking his head, Micmac flipped the sunroof back to safe. "Phoebe. We're done." He hopped over the partition and into the driver's seat.

"Hang on! I'm looking for Magus and Hekka! They're not here!"

"Then we boogie. Safe house."

CHAPTER 4

Daylight waned. Sirens fell silent. Victoria's tactical teams stood down. The television stations had scrapped their coverage of a quilting contest and afternoon teas to cover the *What Just Happened* affair in the typically staid community.

Phoebe and Micmac scuttled the limo and exfiltrated via a faux Medevac helicopter to their home base—the upscale Sutton Place hotel in central Vancouver.

When they'd arrived the day before, Micmac had noticed a camera placed above the emergency exit. He'd turned, taken a cell phone picture, mounted a bracket of his design, and clamped it onto the camera, showing hotel security what the hall looked like empty. Now he led the way up the stairs, comfortable that they would not appear on the security system. He smiled.

Time was of the essence. Inside their room, they swapped clothes and donned disguises. The former short-cropped UDT man was now a bearded, long haired rock star. His groupie sported short shorts, a chartreuse tank top, and a pair of lipstick-red cork heels. Her lips sported lip gloss to match.

Micmac stopped to retrieve his cell phone contraption as they proceeded out the way they had arrived. On the street, they assumed relative anonymity amongst the British Colombians.

Phoebe, now a brunette with decidedly darker skin tone, spoke first. “Mick, we lost them all. What are we going to do?”

“I saw Jack take one and fall over an embankment. Lenny ran after. I didn’t see either one again. As for Magus and Hekka, I just don’t know.”

She squeezed his bicep. “I loved them, Mick. All of them.”

“Lenny, too?”

She sighed.

A bus ride later, the two remaining agents caught the early evening ferry from an otherwise picturesque Horsehoe Bay, as planned. Dark now, they observed the shore lights as the boat sailed to their rendezvous. Jack had provided them with exfil intel that Bowen Island encompassed twenty square miles, sported a central height of about 600 feet, and contained a population of 3,400. Less formal, but laid back like Victoria. That could change in an instant if they were discovered.

“The lights would be pretty if …”

“If we had succeeded?”

Phoebe didn’t respond.

In twenty minutes, their craft was tied up at Snug Cove landing. They departed the tiny port past shops and restaurants, watchful for undue interest. Micmac stepped to an overhead light and viewed his phone display.

“GPS points us past those shops up what seems to be Main Street.”

As they proceeded inland, a school playground appeared on the right.

“The thought of innocence and laughter seems so remote.”

“Here. We turn left up this path. Be extra watchful. It’s steep and looks like a winding corridor through a forest. Our visibility will be quite limited, but no one behind or below will see us.”

As soon as she was out of view, Phoebe transferred her compact Glocks from their lower back holsters to her parka's pockets.

In twenty minutes they reached the top level of the flattened hill. Exhausted from the firefights and the climb, they located their three-story safe house on the verge of a small, isolated village. A figure in a top floor window waved. Jack.

"Jack, you son-of-a-bitch," Micmac muttered under his breath.

Before he could knock, the door opened. Lenny, with a sweep of his arm, motioned them inside. "It's okay. I don't mind being the doorman. I see it as a promotion. Jack's lieutenant."

A roaring fire prompted the new guests to strip off their parkas. For the first time since daybreak, they felt safe.

In obvious pain, Jack rode a mechanized chair down a wood-railed stairway. He winced as he moved. An unfashionable sash tightened around his waist indicated his wound site. Then, a brief smile. "Welcome to the *eh*-hole. Home away from home. It becomes a safe house whenever we need protection from the Mounties." He forced a smile.

Lenny didn't see the humor. "The RCMP doesn't like their favorite towns shot up. Given what we did in Victoria, they'll be searching for us with extreme prejudice. How do we get the hell out of Dodge, kemosabe?"

"If we were First Nation, we'd put on native garb … it'd be that easy. But we're not. We speak American, which makes Canadians suspicious right off the bat."

Phoebe couldn't decide if Jack was telling the whole story. "How'd you two get out?"

"Lenny helped me back up the hill to the ambulance. He was a little excited. I gave him a couple shots of whiskey. I looked around for team members. Local justice was closing in. We boogied."

"Where are Magus and Hekka? We hoped they'd be with you."

"Don't know, Phoebe. We got separated at the park, what with helicopters full of shock troops firing at us. Chin and his general got away. Lalumière and—"

"Lalumière? He's dead. He went up with the Queen Mary 2 bomb."

"Not so, Phoebe," Micmac interjected. "Magus spotted him just before we dismantled the castle. Major surprise."

"I'll be damned."

"There's more. Magus spotted someone inside the castle he said matched your description of your boss, Jack. Three-piece suit in French-blue …"

"Impossible."

"It would explain a lot. It would explain why his life is just a step from being over." The FBI agent massaged the receivers of her .45's.

"You mean as in *traitor*?"

Phoebe and Micmac nodded.

Jack raised his hands. "Alright, alright. I need to bring this down a notch. What I'm about to tell you is Top Secret, and the security compartment, you don't want to know. Understand that I don't officially work for Central Intelligence any longer. They can't fire me if they get pissed." He let that notion sink in. His intensity garnered attention. "He said my ass'd be in a sling if I told anyone."

"Nice sling, boss," Lenny noted.

"Neil's under cover. He's pretending to be the Illuminé's man in Central Intelligence. I didn't expect him to be there, but needless to say, if word gets out, he's dead … along with our chances of preventing that nuke from doing its thing."

"But Jack, he went with them. He's deep. You may not hear from him again," said Phoebe.

"What do you suggest?"

"Simple. Rorschach. Last time, before we trouped off to Taiwan, he restored Magus' Chinese memories. We need the rest. Restore the French memories."

"Excellent idea, Phoebe." Lenny's eyes went to the ceiling.

"And for that, we need Magus." Jack glanced at the fire. "What of that third chopper? Did either of you see who went aboard that one?"

Phoebe shook her head. "Negative. It looked different from the others, like a police helicopter. It landed behind a bunch of trees. Magus and Hekka headed that way. When they rendezvous here, they can fill us in." Her eyes closed. When they reopened, they were wet.

Jack moaned. "Guys, today was a tough one."

"We screwed up, huh?"

"No, Phoebe. The screw-up was mine. Or Neil's. I'm not even sure right now."

"With three choppers at a moments notice, they were ready. If I hadn't witnessed what we did and the numbers we took down, I'd suspect we were set up." The former UDT man looked Jack straight in the eyes.

Phoebe shook her head and stepped into the bathroom.

"What now, Jack?" asked a visibly tired Micmac.

"The best we can do is give the other two time to make their way here. Then we'll exfil to an offshore oil platform and hopscotch our way out."

"And then?"

"From there on is classified."

"And if they don't make it?"

Jack took a deep breath.

"And in the meantime?"

"We wait."

CHAPTER 5

"Here, boss. That's gotta be painful." Lenny stepped over to assuage his boss' pain. "Maybe we should adjust—"

"Don't touch me. I'm fine. But these nerves don't help. I'd be pacing without the wound." He seemed to experience an epiphany. "Okay. You can pace for me, Lenny. Just walk back and forth. Emit no sounds and look concerned."

The P.I. turned spy did as instructed. He walked back and forth for twenty seconds. He stopped, took his chin in his hand, and peered up at the ceiling for guidance.

Jack closed his eyes and massaged his temples. "We're missing Crayle and Hekka. Lenny, check the Web news. I'm fearing the worst."

"I was just getting into—"

"Check the frikkin' Web!"

Lenny brought up local news on a widescreen. Next, he set up international and Seattle news, side-by-side and with closed caption, on his computer. "The Canadians are screaming bloody murder about the destruction of a landmark, JS. Oh, that can't be right. A cute blonde journalist says it might have been a gas leak. Another blames the Conservatives in Ottawa. Another says global warming is causing people to behave irrationally."

"What's irrational is the news. They rarely get it right."

"Change of subject, boss. What about Magus and Hekka?"

The wall clock chimed midnight. "We've waited long enough. Time's up." He placed a call on his cell-sat. "I just hope they're together. They do quite well in that configuration."

"Where are we going, boss?"

"We'll hop out to the platform."

A half hour of silence passed, broken when someone knocked at the door. Another ride.

Jack held himself together by pressing on his abdomen. He winced each time he spoke. "Everyone. Mount up. We're outta here."

They piled into a GMC Denali for transport to a helipad.

"Where to, boss?"

"Daisy Chain Two," Jack said, referring to the second in a line of offshore rigs. "Step one is out of Canada. We were supposed to vector over the Arctic to Europe. With this wound, I can't make it. You three will have to go."

"Bullshit," Phoebe declared. "We need to know what comes next. They've put another mini-nuke into play. And you don't really know where to go next, do you?"

Jack considered the insubordination, and then its content. "Rorschach."

Phoebe's irritation boiled over. "Yeah. Maybe he can restore the rest of Magus' memories. The French ones. Oh, we'll need Magus."

"But maybe he can restore them to me. I'll see if I can reach Neil. Privacy, please."

It was easier for the three team members and driver to exit the vehicle than the wounded project leader. In five minutes, he signaled them back.

"It's just me, boss," Lenny said from the back seat.

"What!" Jack turned. Phoebe and Micmac were missing. "Get your ass outside and tell them we've got an exfil to catch!"

"Uh, don't shoot the messenger, but they decided … Micmac said … uh … UDT—like the SEALS—don't leave folks behind. They're history."

"Back to Victoria? Shut up … that's rhetorical."

"What's—"

"It's done then. Back to the States." He settled back and let his mind drift to his missing team members. Hekka, the Serrano native, had proven a major asset. No challenge too big or too unknown for her. Crayle seemed, by all accounts and all he'd seen, to have been a sorcerer of strategies. Fighting his former magic seemed to be a fools game. He peered at his mental scoreboard. The team had been successful in stopping the eradication of New York City, but thwarted in Kaohsiung and Victoria. In addition, following the set-up detonation in Iran, they had failed to prevent subsequent nuclear bombings in Marseille, Xinjiang, and Beijing. He wondered for the first time whether his team was merely a pawn. And, if so, who was moving the pieces.

• • •

It took the pair gone rogue two hours to find their way back to the seaside resort city called Victoria.

"This is our impromptu Plan B. If things go wrong, our best route of escape is across the straight to Port Townsend."

"Washington State."

"Then south. Back to Big Bear. If they've been wounded, that'll be a problem."

"FBI plus UDT spells get the job done, Mick."

"Roger that. We can't afford to lose them, not with a nuclear device in play. We need to make certain that bomb is not used."

"The good news is that we changed clothes at the hotel. We won't match up with surveillance."

"Except for face recognition. Here, plant a couple near my cheek bones. Lotsa lipstick."

"Altruism abounds," Phoebe said as she kissed him twice.

"All for the cause." He held up papers. "Good thing you grabbed these. I just know they'll come in handy."

They left their rented vehicle and proceeded along the coast. A quarter mile later, they approached the knoll. Beacon Hill.

"They'll be recovering shell casings for weeks. You never know which one'll have that lucky print."

"Forensics? I had the training. When I started putting government issue .40 caliber rounds into the same hole …"

"So it was always guarding those government witnesses."

"I don't want to talk about the rock star."

"It was big news. The cruise line tried to cover it up."

"I heard it was a Bowie knife. Hard to cover up," she observed.

"They found his people. A man and a woman. They'd been with him since before you guarded him."

"Some would call it karma."

Micmac shook his head. "Justice."

With the large contingent of Canadian law enforcement putting on a light show up in the park battleground, the area resembled a Fourth of July celebration.

"Phoebe, there's no one along the base of the knoll. They're all up on top, so let's try there."

"Hold my hand, sailor. We're lovers on a stroll."

"Don't move!"

They froze.

Two officers and a man in a tight brown coat surrounded them.

"Officers, what's going on?"

"There's a police action up on the hill. What are you two doing here?"

"We're looking for a little privacy, eh. We started at Clover Point." Phoebe pointed behind them. "For a moonlight walk."

"Let me see what you have in your hand, Sir."

Micmac handed him the items Phoebe had snatched on their way out of Snug Cove.

"Hmmm. A BC Ferries schedule, a Bowen Island Sea Kayaking brochure, and a copy of the local Undercurrent newspaper. Alright. Stroll elsewhere, please."

Micmac acquired a deferential expression. "Officer?"

"Hmmm?"

"We'll have to head back across soon. My mother is quite ill. She lives in Sequim."

"Oh, I don't know. They're checking everyone. Mother, eh?" He scribbled on an official note pad. "Here. This'll get you across." His smile didn't break his lips, but it told that he'd once been young and in love. A good deed. That's what he'd done.

"Come on, guys. Let's check the other side again."

The two police officers and the Mountie left in short order. In fifteen seconds, they disappeared from sight.

"*Eh?* Did you say *eh*? Phoebe, where did you learn Canadian?"

"A close relative spent some time in a city back east. Took in some schooling and learned the language."

"Montreal?"

"Toronto."

"Never been."

"And you knew how to pronounce *S'quim* like a native. What's that all about?" she asked.

Another story, another woman. "Come on, Phoebs. Up above is crawling with cops. We'll check the perimeter. It's all we've got."

Half a minute later. "Nothing. Nothing. Wait."

"Find something?"

"Let's check this drainage ditch."

CHAPTER 6

Increasingly, his mind cleared of cobwebs. He started to think like himself. With a semblance of clarity. A woman, just a blur, stood nearby.

"Please, bend close. Tell me his plans," the groggy man whispered. He attempted to lift himself from the gurney to a sitting position. "Tell me—"

He was cut short by movement to his right. Two Asian men, dressed in black tactical gear, stepped in and grasped each arm with a grip that hurt. A third held his feet.

Then, a woman's voice he recognized. "The tranquilizer dart barely penetrated his light Kevlar. Too little of the drug was absorbed."

He looked up just as a fourth person, a female dressed in red, plunged a needle into his neck.

The three men restrained the former spy until the drug rendered him, once again, docile. They carried him from the forged *Police* helicopter and loaded him into the hold of a huge jet transport.

The thrum of the huge jet engines returned him to consciousness, although it seemed the liquid that normally lubricated his eyes had turned to goo. He attempted to wipe it free, but his hands didn't move. Through the blur of red night-lighting, he saw large yellowish shapes. Nothing definitive. He felt warmth to his side as someone gently wiped his eyes with a damp cloth. Then his forehead.

"It's okay, Mr. Crayle. We are taking you on a little trip."

Once the giant nose door fully closed, the red hue gave way to soft white. His vision cleared. A scan revealed that he was in the belly of a large cargo plane. Aft, he could see the source of the yellow-orange images. Several earthmoving tractors with the word CAT painted on each in stark black lettering. He scanned left. Next to him, also in black, he now recognized Annie Ling—Chin's Black daughter—sporting a guarded smile on her perfect, rounded lips.

"Those aren't all the machines that Father wanted. Because of the actions of you and your team, he had to leave some of them in Canada."

"There are machines just like these in China. Surely—"

"The machines we have appear similar to these, but are underpowered. The fools who cloned them painted the word DOG on each one. A joke. Punishment was severe. In any event, Father used his trip to Victoria to acquire the real thing." She smiled as if remembering happier times. "He often uses terms he learned from you … during your stay with us. I was just sixteen …" Her smile faded. "In any event, he has specific and very important plans, and these machines will play a major role."

The plane, supplied by Li and piloted by trusted military pilots, had been U.S. Air Force surplus. The C-5, one of the finest and largest American military transports in history, had been re-outfitted to Chin's specifications and upgraded to the new M-series engine and avionics specifications. Instead of cream-colored canvas bulkheads, these combined burgundy and alabaster—framed in carved wood and covered in 24-Karat gold leaf. The deck under foot was a dark teak and the overhead dangled with clanging crystal chandeliers.

A man dressed in green slacks and a beige IZOD golf shirt descended a ladder some twenty feet distant. So attired, Chin Yao-wu appeared more like a member of the new upper middle class in China than one aspiring to reinstate its former empire.

"Black daughter, you are required to re-inject Mr. Crayle for the duration of the flight. Every four hours. Here are the syringes." He handed a zipped leather case to her. "Should you forget …" He laughed. "… or require their use as weapons, Mr. Crayle will suffer a severe withdrawal—he might die." Chin knew that Black daughter would be quick to understand the ramifications of a Crayle death. He left to examine and admire the enormous earthmoving equipment.

One of the three specially-designated guards, a last minute replacement for one who had died in the battle of Beacon Hill in Vancouver, did not comprehend the relationship of Black daughter to Father Chin. He stepped to her side, and touched her thigh.

Black daughter completed the placement of the syringes on a table attached to the bed. She turned. In two lightning fast moves, she rendered the Chinese special forces man to the floor, immobile. "You must address me with respect." There would be no further dialog. She glanced at the other two warriors, returned to her seat, and began her vigil. The obviously educated young woman—pretty and quite deadly—fastened her seat belt.

The cargo plane lumbered from the Vancouver runway. The insulation from noise, plus other creature comforts, indicated that it belonged to an upper echelon of the military.

In precisely four hours, the important passenger began to rouse. Black daughter, as instructed, prepared the next syringe. The injection acted quickly. Crayle's eyelids closed in three seconds.

"Take care, Black," said Red, standing behind her. "Too much of the special medicine, and Mr. Crayle dies. Father would throw you to the fishes."

"I gave him the precise amount. He'll be fine when we reach Hong Kong. You should join the others. Sleep will be precious. I'll stand watch over him."

Red considered the suggestion. Yes. When they arrived home, she would be well-rested, and Black, vulnerable. Perhaps then would be the time to move. From a bulkhead thirty feet away, she rotated a day bed into position. Soon, like the others, the hum of the aircraft put her into a deep sleep.

Minutes passed. Black released the belt and moved silently to the gurney holding America's strategic spy.

"Mr. Crayle," she whispered, placing her face next to his. "I gave you a placebo. We must talk."

Crayle, still dazed, nodded.

"Father vacillates, Mr. Crayle. In one moment, he seeks to have you dead. A removal of the ominous threat that you pose. In the next, he seeks your continued counsel as he implements the final aspects of your Blackstone Strategy."

"What threat?" a bleary Crayle asked.

"You know the entirety of the strategy he utilized to overthrow the Party government. That information, and the tens of thousands killed in Beijing, would cause yet another revolution. And how he caused the mass deaths in Xinjiang would cause a religious war, a jihad, if it were ever made public."

"Is that all?"

"Not quite. You are the lone person on this planet who possesses the intellect and skills to take him down. He is ever aware of that fact."

"And the other side of the coin?" he mumbled.

"The other side … relates to his colleague."

"General Li?"

"No. The Frenchman. Father will elaborate when we arrive at home. Now, get some sleep." She emptied the second hypodermic.

CHAPTER 7

Having escaped the mayhem in Victoria, Jean-Marc Lalumière landed safely at the Estonian capitol's airport. The weather was typical for this time of year, a cold 38 degrees Fahrenheit made worse by a chill wind from the north. Fortunately, the aircraft carried a large wardrobe in his sizes for all occasions. A gray, houndstooth overcoat and a charcoal-colored sweater kept his top half warm, and wool slacks over cellophane thin silk thermal underwear and socks took care of the rest. Still, the biting cold stung his face and ears until he donned a bright yellow wool scarf and matching watch cap. He stood out as a foreigner.

Without incident, he was whisked into Tallinn proper to the five-star Hotel Telegraaf and shown to its finest suite. Upon removal of a boogie-bag from his large suitcase, he extracted the most important component. A quick elevator ride to the lobby, he stepped into a waiting SUV. He observed that the seat belts were aircraft quality and a quick examination of the window edge showed the door glass to be double thick. A quick smile, a short ride later, and with a polished walnut gift case under his arm, he stood at Tallinn Bay's edge, peering up at a thirty-foot high monument. As if conversing with an old friend, he spoke to it.

"Tell me, Rusalka, why did your battleship sink in this harbor? It surely possessed great power, such as my dad and I wish to acquire. If we fail, will there be a monument for us?"

The green-hued statue said nothing. Her wings pointed at the heavens as if the sunken ship had somehow achieved victory.

Behind, a guitar player and a violinist played *The Tennessee Waltz.* Perhaps they mistook his use of American English as an indication that he was an American. He concluded that his accent was top notch. He dropped a 100-Euro note in the violin case left open for such purpose. As he walked away, the duo launched into the Australian bush anthem, *Waltzing Matilda.*

Jean-Marc continued inland along a manicured dirt pathway until the magnificent Kadriorg Palace came into view. Created by Russian Czar Peter the Great for his wife Catherine, the three-story white and coral structure was surrounded by lakes, streams, fountains, trees, and carefully manicured *parterres*. It was a castle of baroque architecture with no parapets. No towers. No ramparts. Indefensible. He glanced up at a balcony that ran the length of the building. Men with coats, doubtless hiding submachine guns, patrolled. The days of an out-front, uniformed and mounted Imperial Guard seemed like so much history.

The young Frenchman, at six-foot-six, towered over the Estonians he passed as he took the palace steps two-at-a-time. Preoccupied by his thoughts, he perceived little of the grandeur of a past age. The large wooden doors already stood open in anticipation of his arrival, and a smiling much shorter man greeted him.

"Ah, *Monsieur Jean-Marc*. So nice to see you again."

The young man had no time for small talk. "*Bonjour, monsieur.*"

"Please, follow me. Your guests await."

The man took his outer-garments, placed them with care on a garment rack, and led him along a mirrored hallway with no further comment. They stopped just outside a room known as the Festive Hall.

"Here." The man straightened Jean-Marc's bow tie. He whispered what he perceived to be critical details of engagement before pulling open two twelve-foot high doors.

From where Jean-Marc stood, walls embellished by ornate plaster trim and figures with light gray wall inserts that curved into a ceiling painting worthy of Michelangelo set the tone.

Inside, an entourage flanked an older woman, who sat in the middle of an otherwise sparsely-decorated room on a regal-appearing chair—gold with maroon seat and back inserts. Her auburn hair was arranged to complement her black satin dress, and with the elegant refined jewelry, she certainly looked the part. By the nature of his invitation, Jean-Marc expected her to be the distant offspring of Russia's final Czar, Nicholas II.

"Please stand, Mr. Lalumière. I am, by all accounts that matter, still a czarina."

"Of course." Not quite sure how to address Russian royalty, he notched up his choice of words. "Might I summon a drink for your relaxation, Your Highness?"

"You're right." She smiled. "We'll skip the crap." As she moved to stand, an assistant provided aid. "To the sofa?"

They proceeded to an 18th Century sofa to begin their mutual journey. A servant placed two bottles of beer with blue and cream-colored labels on a coffee table that matched the walls.

"Soku," the young man observed. "One of my favorites."

"Yes. I am aware. Do you visit Tallinn often?"

"Please call me Jean-Marc—everyone does."

She tilted her head. "I'm not everyone … Jean-Marc."

"Forgive me, Your Highness. These are both troubling and changing times. Poverty and joblessness have hit all countries. The promises of democracy remain unfulfilled dreams."

"Yes, young man. As you are aware from our Communist experiment, ours is a nation of unfulfilled dreams. Now that the unrest has turned violent, the politicians who made the promises are nowhere to be found. In my country, shouts of "Remember Mussolini" evoke an image of him hung upside down—dead—at a fueling station by countrymen who'd finally had enough."

"The socialists who would steal from the rich to give to the poor have stolen from rich and poor alike."

"And those between."

"Amen."

Jean-Marc appeared shocked. "You are religious?"

"Russian Orthodox. Like my great-grandfather, Czar Nicholas. And my grandmother, Anastasia. Mostly to honor them. Too much harm has come from organized religion. My plan, should an upheaval—a renaissance—come to pass, is to do good. To solve problems."

"That simple?"

"I'm afraid it is. It must be."

"Then, amen to that. You have precisely described the goals of myself and my father."

"Ah, yes, your father. Tell me of his current state of affairs."

Jean-Marc laughed. "It's a long story."

"I'll have the Reader's Digest version."

Sylvain Lalumière's son cleared his throat. This was a one-time opportunity. It required that every word count. Each word needed to be perfect. His father, his own life, depended upon it.

"My father fought the system for years, finally exceeding the government's tolerance. They captured him and put him behind bars, a political prisoner in the bowels of the old Bastille. With help, he escaped."

"With help?"

"An organization I cannot name. It has positioned its members in very high places. It has a grand strategy for the remake of Europe." He carefully omitted the Chinese component and that the Illuminé would try to extend itself to the entire world. He regained focus. "As I mentioned, my father escaped."

"Then?"

"It was brilliant. He invoked the Man In The Iron Mask personage of old. Even down to the genuine mask. He embodied the captive French spirit. He became the *cause célèbre*. He parlayed the role into a huge following by a disaffected French public."

"We have heard. The media is saturated with news and sightings of this man, Mitim. The name implies royalty. It was an inspired invocation of a legend."

Jean-Marc felt in control. He was prepared for the next step, he thought.

"Did he have help?"

Oh. This was problematic. In fact, the CIA had caused his escape, invented the role-playing notion, provided the mask of legend, and, most beneficial to the cause, orchestrated extensive social media publicity. That, though true, would be too much information for the czarina. It was time for a little bastard son redirection.

"You called me Lalumière. You should be aware that I am his son, but not by marriage."

She smiled. "Another bastard French crown prince … that is, *dauphin*, as you say. We can handle that."

The two now felt comfortable in each other's presence. Relaxed.

A second later, a side door burst open. Two men dressed as workmen, but sporting shotguns ran at the czarina. When they halted in front of her, the elder woman gasped in fear.

"This is from Vladimir!" one of them shouted.

The two shots that rang out were not from their shotguns. Both men crumpled to the floor. The woman turned to the source of her salvation.

Jean-Marc held the brace of smoking Russian dueling pistols he had brought as a gift. He replaced them in their presentation box and turned to her. "These are for you, Your Highness."

Guards, in the aftermath of the gunshots, arrived in time to clean up the mess.

"We have a deal, *Monsieur Lalumière*. You can count upon my support. I'm sure you are aware of my wishes for the future of my country. And the part I shall play."

Jean-Marc stood, produced a half-bow, and left the room. He located the nearest restroom and lost his breakfast. Once he recovered, his mind went back to the rush of adrenalin at the moment of truth. He now felt certain, for the first time, that he could, and would, go the distance.

With his mouth rinsed, face washed, and head properly screwed back on, he followed his handler to a succession of rooms where he met with royal representatives from Finland and Estonia. While the results were far less dramatic, he achieved their cooperation after he offered assurances that the New Russia would never again invade and occupy either country. Estonia, in particular, still had a sub-population of half-Russian citizens to remind them of earlier years. Any sign of interest by the Russians in adding Tallinn back to an array of Baltic ports would change the game in its entirety.

CHAPTER 8

The patient opened his eyes to a whirling blade overhead and the glare of a totally white room, even in the dim light. He saw no curtains or furniture, other than his bed, from which to draw location intel. The cold room, plus the absence of outside sounds or window visuals, enhanced his sense of isolation.

"Good morning, Mr. Crayle. Despite the circumstances, it is good to see you. As you can tell, you are not at present in control of your limbs, but your mind is unimpaired. You can speak and hear, and that is all that will be required of you during your stay. Are you comfortable?"

Crayle, strapped into a wheelchair, demanded, "What do you want, Chin? Where's Hekka? If you've harmed her ..."

"Rest easy. She is, as we speak, receiving a spa treatment fit for such a goddess." The lie came easily. The drugs inhibited Crayle's short-term memories, and he needed to believe that she was alive. "Assisted by my daughters. Do you remember Black and Red? And White?"

"Memories of my time here, planning the Blackstone, are intact. I recall that your daughters are dangerous. If you—"

Chin waved a dismissive hand. "Don't worry. She will be safe … as long as I have your cooperation."

"The assault in Canada was my tactical design. She only came to support me."

"Yes. Your assault was quite effective. It transformed my new castle-away-from-home and its antiquities into dust and powder. Clearly, your ability to plan and execute is no longer impaired."

Crayle was in no mood. "Sorry about your castle."

Chin took a moment. His jaw tensed, and then relaxed as he pressed a button. The lights came up. "It's quite okay. I'm building a new one." A curtain parted. "There, Mr. Crayle, is China's new tomorrow."

The view from the Dragon Building's penthouse was of Hong Kong's Victoria Peak at the island's center. "It is the highest point on the island. A dozen yellow land-shaping vehicles reconfigure not only the mountain top, but our history."

"I can see that they're flattening the top. You're going to build your palace there, aren't you? You've leveled Beijing—there'll be no possibility of governance there for decades. How does it feel having murdered tens of thousands of innocent people?"

"They've been necessarily sacrificed," retorted an angered Chin. "It was your doing. The situation had to be dramatic, you said. It had to be irreversible, you said. The leaders had to be deleted, as you advised, permanently. The public, though shocked at the devastation in Xinjiang and Beijing, had already demanded radical change. I removed the intransigent leadership and shall fill the void. Me, Mr. Crayle. They want *me*." He strode to the window. "Do you see that? On the left? The foundation blocks for the bastion are being laid as we speak. I am having them fabricated from a quarry once used by China's first emperor. Truly, a man of inspiration to me."

"You should choose your heroes more carefully."

"I shall not fence with you, Mr. Crayle." He turned once against to view the Peak. "The clay adhesive comes from a mine in Hainan. My country's former rulers—those who remain—are working off their sins. I hope you approve."

Chin's Blue daughter, her eyes lowered, brought him a leaded crystal glass containing a perfect three-finger pour of 40-year-old Scotch.

"You should consider joining me. I will require a master strategist, a sort of personal Sun Tzu. Hmmm, Mr. Crayle?"

"The man you model yourself after aggregated the first China, the first empire, by conquering what he called warring states, one-at-a-time. He then slaughtered their armies. Slaughter is the common thread here. Ch'in was labeled a callous tyrant—an accurate description. Exuberant spending was his trademark, and I see the beginnings of a parallel on the mountain. And then, as I expect will happen to you, he became paranoid. It's a common trait of megalomania, Chin. A psychosis."

The stock market mogul gave thought, sipped the expensive liquor, then turned. "Are you ready to die, Mr. Crayle?"

Crayle's saw through the ruse. "You didn't kidnap me and bring me over six thousand miles to kill me. You want something."

"Ha! Of course. You obtained the mileage in order to calculate my travel time to Canada."

"I'm good with numbers."

"Your mind is quite unimpeded, even after Dr. Rorschach."

"How do you—"

"Relax. I've known about his work all along."

"How?"

"When you came here last, you wanted answers. So did I. Your CIA sent a copy of the doctor's computer so that I might attempt to extract the Frenchman's plan. So I could stop him."

"Why would you do that? You are his partner-in-crime."

"It's quite simple. Lalumière is a pawn. Manipulated by someone else, but useful to me. His role has been to make France vulnerable." He took a sip.

"So you find out from me, by means of my French memories, what he will do next. Then—"

"I *have* what I want. What I require. Sylvain Lalumière is a liability."

Crayle thought. "Here's the deal."

"You are in no position to deal."

"It's a confluence of goals, Chin. You're finished with the violence. You're no longer my problem. Lalumière is. I find him. I take him out. I save all the people he would otherwise kill with his final bomb. So, Hekka and I leave Hong Kong alive."

"Hmmm."

"Deal?"

• • •

Chin had Blue administer a sleep-inducing injection while he pondered the possibilities of Crayle's offer. Naturally suspicious, he hadn't expected an agreement in principle so quickly. Crayle's mind remained brilliant, the former strategist and spy already steps and layers ahead of anything he himself could conceive. He made up his own mind, but he ordered the genius revived and sent him out into town with Black. If anyone could, she would ferret out his true motives.

• • •

It seemed a long time since they had strolled into the Monday Club. In fact, it had been just under two months. Annie Ling was recognized within seconds.

"Hey, Ling," yelled an early twenties man from the bandstand. "Sing me a song."

"Boyfriend?" Crayle queried.

"Father does not allow boyfriends until we are no longer teens. But you know that from your memories."

"You were only sixteen when I came here to create Chin's strategy. And then I returned without my memories. You knew me from before, but you said nothing. Why?"

She made no more comment, but led him, once again, up the stairs in back.

The view from the rooftop was one Crayle only remembered in its nighttime incarnation. As dusk approached, the lights of the grand city flicked on. Their position allowed a modicum of escape from the street din below. They could talk.

"About the sex," Crayle began. "In the château garden?"

"I've seen a news clip of your former President Clinton. We didn't have intercourse so, technically, we didn't have sex. I merely assisted you with the blonde Agent."

"I'm aware from my restored memories that you and your 'sisters' are not allowed normal sex."

"Most of your English words have clear definitions, Mr. Crayle. Yet, the word *normal* does not. Its meaning is quite subjective. Wouldn't you agree?"

"You've got me on that one, Ling."

"What if circumstances changed?"

"I've got someone." He glanced up at the flurry of activity on Victoria Peak. He had yet to actually see Hekka. "At least, I hope I have someone."

"Magus, he has to let you go. We—I mean, you—must escape this place. How can you get away for good?"

"You and I can't go anywhere. He provided an antidote to wake me up, and then informed me that these bracelets around my ankles are not only to track my movements while I'm with you, but to detonate should we exit the city."

She looked shocked. "He would blow us up?"

"No. He knows I wouldn't put you at risk, but that's not even relevant. He must keep me alive. To cooperate."

She looked up into his eyes. "I believe you would give your life for me."

"Of course. Chin's letting me spend time with you so I won't forget how important you were in my life."

She hugged him. "I remember what you said to me at the château, after the battle. You came to my room. You said I should not be one of Chin's daughters. You said I should be your sister. Alright, then. We are brother and sister as you suggested."

He smiled. "Phoebe remembers you. I think she would want to be your sister, too. And Hekka. He will let her go, won't he? Tell me she is alright."

Ling stepped back. "I can't say that."

"You must say that."

"At the hill, in Victoria … I saw it." She looked away.

"What did you see?"

"Magus, I am so sorry."

"Tell me now … or else."

"Father didn't do it. She was hit by one of Li's snipers. In the head. She died."

"No! No!" He fell to the graveled roof.

Ling knelt beside him. No words. She pulled his head to her breast. They sat that way, not moving, for several minutes. She broke the silence.

"Even though I am still quite young and have lived my years emotionally confined, I can feel your grief. It is most sad when you have found the right one, and she is taken from you."

"You're right. You can't possibly know. But I feel she's still with me." He pressed his fist to his heart.

"Mr. Crayle … Magus … look into my eyes."

He did.

"While that part of your life has been decided, you must continue. You must prevent the agonies that you foresee. The deaths. The horrors. You must do this to honor her."

Crayle pulled away. He stood and peered up at the peak being leveled, and at the stones being laid. "I did this to her. I'm responsible." He waxed morose. Devastation. Moments passed where even the cacophonous street noises below lessened to a drone.

"Please remember. You can't change what has happened, only what *could* happen."

He looked at her again. So young. So intelligent. So feeling.

"Come. Father wants us back by noon. He'll agree with what you've proposed, and feel like he had a modicum of control over the outcome."

"A modicum?"

"But he didn't, did he?"

"No."

Having descended from the rooftop, they strolled the busiest street of the Wan Chai. Vendors, pedestrians, cars, bicycles, rickshaws—their deafening noise characterized the lifeblood of this Hong Kong neighborhood. Life continued. Regardless.

Crayle stopped. He turned and took Ling by the shoulders. He looked deep into her eyes. "No matter what happens, remember this always. You are very important to me."

They stole enough time for a long embrace, then pushed their way through the teeming throngs back to Chin's special residence.

Once inside the Dragon Building, Gold, and her younger "sister" Blue, awaited them, and ushered them to the penthouse.

"Ah, you have returned." Chin smiled.

Gold and Blue seated them at a table and retreated into the shadows.

"You know, Mr. Crayle, your attack at Kaohsiung—to separate me from my finances—was inspired. Deftly, you removed a pound of perfect diamonds." He hefted a ballistic nylon bag. "As it stands—and I'm sure that you are aware—I have China's extensive fortunes in my hands now." He set the bag in front of Crayle. He tilted his head to the side, as if to reinforce what he was about to say. "I am no longer interesting to you. You can have my word. I will initiate no further nuclear implementations. But as you realize, I have delivered to Sylvain his final device. You and your fine team may wish to stop him in his personal quest."

"You say that as if I have a choice, Chin. I don't. My conscience is full of dead bodies. There is no room for more."

Chin nodded to Blue and Gold, who stabbed Crayle and Ling with needles. Light transitioned to black.

CHAPTER 9

He awoke to the roar of engines. He opened his eyes to a cavernous transport aircraft interior the diametric opposite of the one that had carried him out of Canada. Obviously insulated, the interior was sumptuous. He glanced left to find an American admiral and, next to him, a three-star general. He peered over his shoulder. More high-level U.S. military. His head whipped right. The owner of the hands holding his arm was the only one on board he recognized. Ling.

"You are awake. Magus, you are safe," she whispered. "You are going home."

He moved his arms to be certain that he had control. Then, it hit him. He was attired like the others in a military uniform. Silver oak leaves atop his shoulders proclaimed him a lieutenant colonel. Like his father.

The admiral turned to him. "Good to see that you're awake, Colonel. We'll touch down shortly. Dropping you off. First time on the Embassy Flight?"

"Uh …"

"It's okay. I'll leave you alone, but congratulations on the top honor," he said, nodding toward Crayle's neck.

He turned to Ling. Her sunglasses still in place, he saw the reflection. A blue ribbon with a starred centerpiece in front. A medal dangled.

Ling whispered, "The Congressional Medal of Honor. It belonged to your father."

• • •

On final approach, the pilot engaged the in-flight-operational thrust reversers on the inside engines. He dialed down the four Pratt and Whitney engines. He knew it would be tight, but his orders had come from the highest source.

The aircraft landed on Jack's business jet runway. Once on the ground, the reverse-assist component of twin JATO bottles deployed, doubling the slowing power of the giant C-141's thrust reversers. Because the Air Force always faced its passengers backwards, they were pressed heavily into their seat backs by the additional force. The pilot stopped the plane. After the two special passengers deplaned, the JATO thrusters rotated 180 degrees and assisted the Embassy Flight back into the skies. They watched as the pilot tipped his wings.

A man that neither Crayle or Ling recognized limped toward them. Dressed in civilian khakis and a dark brown bomber jacket, he extended a packet marked *TOP SECRET*. "Here are your new orders, Colonel." He tipped his fingers to his forehead and turned to Ling. "Ma'am." With that, he walked to a waiting black Hyundai Equus and drove away.

Crayle open the packet and withdrew a three-by-five inch card. He showed it to Ling.

Quarry—Light Bulb—JAS.

They walked to the only building at the airstrip, an old Korean War Quonset hut. It was locked, bolted, and barred. An arrow in a wired and tempered window pointed right. Despite the late time of year, there was no snow in the valley, just dirt and dust. Beside the building sat what appeared to be an ordinary, extended-cab pickup.

"I'm betting this is another one of the gadget man's creations."

"The one who created the lethal logging truck at the Lalumière château? The one you call Micmac?"

"Yes. Additional shock absorbers, wide wheels, and knobby off-road tires are nothing unusual out here. Even the arctic white air conditioner over the cab appears normal in the deserts north of Big Bear. A few men can heft a camper shell onto the back—"

"Only men?" The woman also known as Black daughter inspected her nails.

Crayle avoided the gender minefield. "And, like the logging truck, weaponized to the hilt."

Ling suppressed a grin.

"Listen up," Crayle admonished. "We're 500 yards out. Fasten your mental seatbelts."

"We are going to the hospital, aren't we?"

"Beneath these foothills lies the only means we have of understanding, finding, and removing the Lalumière threat."

"Mr. Crayle, we are only two. What could we do? And how can you trust this man, this doctor after all that has happened?"

"I have to trust him. In my previous consciousness, I created a master strategy that led to the deaths of tens of thousands. I can't go back and prevent that. But I must, with Rorschach's help, preclude any further mass murder. Further destruction."

"It all falls on *your* shoulders?"

"Yes. Look, I'm not going to suggest I drop you off for your own safety. You wouldn't allow it. You're with me all the way. I get that."

She stayed silent.

Crayle drove the pickup from the county highway into the Quarry's entry, turned left before the huge piles of gravel, and pulled up short of the ingress garage. He pressed a button on the visor above his head. Nothing.

"Can you honk?"

He honked. He tried the headlights and turn signals. Nothing.

Ling remembered the message. "Light bulb."

Crayle turned, reached up, and removed the dome light cover. He unscrewed the bulb, and pressed his finger into the socket. His fingerprint verified, a clunk sound emanated from the building. The corrugated door slid sideways. As soon as the truck settled inside and the doors closed, the elevator rocketed in normal fashion more than 300 feet into the bowels of the mountain.

The two exited the vehicle. It was eerie. No one met them. They proceeded along a familiar, chartreuse-colored hall. Only the whispered sounds of ventilation tubes broke the silence.

"This place is so large. And complex. How can we find this man?"

"I know this place, Ling. It's not large. We'll grab Rorschach and force him to restore the rest of my memories, from France. It will be up to you to see that we're not disturbed."

Crayle turned them into an office. "Hello, Doctor."

"Crayle!" The old man with the white-bermed pate lunged for his phone.

Ling ran to him, forcing her knuckle into the back of his hand.

"Ahhhhh!" he yelled as he tried to jerk his hand away.

She released.

Slowly, the doctor withdrew. "If you do not harm me, I vill tell you verr she iss."

"I'm not here for—" He grabbed Rorschach by the arm. "She? Who?"

"Why, your woman, of course."

A confused Crayle shook his head. The cobwebs persisted. His cold blue eyes snapped to the doctor. "Hekka? Hekka's here?"

"Release my arm, and I'll take you."

Crayle dragged him into the hall. "Now!"

The doctor led them three doors down. The shades were drawn, but the door was ajar. A moan escaped.

Crayle burst into the room. There, on a bed with blood-stained pillow case she lay. Not with the usual drips, but with a wired cap on her head. He rushed to her side.

"Oh, my God! Rorschach, what have you done?"

"She made a request …"

"She wouldn't want what you can do. Undo it!"

"I can't—."

Crayle gripped him by the throat.

"Vait, vait. You don't unterstand!"

"I'll kill you if you don't return her to herself."

"She vas vorried. She vanted to safe her memories … of you."

"What?"

"As I did yours … after the crash."

"But I lost them *in* the crash. Amnesia." He re-squeezed the old man's throat. "Amnesia, right?"

"You did not come for her," the doctor gasped. "Vy are you here? Haff you killed zem all? Vill you kill me, too? I am chust a scientist. I—"

"You!" Crayle yelled into Rorschach's face. "You restored the memories of my work with Chin. The plotting, the scheming, where did you get those memories?"

The doctor was clearly shaken. "Vell, I—"

"You got them from your files, didn't you? Saved memories. Those I was supposed to have lost in the crash. My crash. Remember?"

"Ja, but—"

"I don't have much time, but here are the three possibilities. One, my memories were archived prior to the accident. Two, they were invented as a form of misdirection. Three, the most insidious, you extracted them from me *after* the crash—under orders. Then you wiped them from my mind." He wrested Hekka's Bowie knife from the computer table. "Which was it, Doctor?"

"I haff no idea vot you speak off. You—"

"I want France. You will restore my French memories now. Hekka and my colleagues will question me after. If I don't have the full set from my work with the Lalumière aspect of the Blackstone …" He thumbed the edge of the Bowie. "I always wanted to be a surgeon, Doctor."

The door swung open. All eyes riveted on it.

"Hi, guys." Micmac and Phoebe entered. "Hold up with that blade, Magus."

The muscles of Crayle's jaw displayed maximum tension. "Dr. Rorschach was just about to restore my plans for the conquest of France."

Phoebe tried to dial down Crayle's emotions. "We sent McDonalds and Burger King to France. Battle's almost over."

"Have you seen my new toy, Doc?" Micmac poked a cattle prod into a glass of water and pressed a button. The glass exploded. "I can make things more exciting."

Clearly terrified, the doctor trembled.

"Oh, look." Lenny walked in. "A computer."

"Leaf my computer be. You haff no right—"

"Let's see. Control … Alt …"

"I'll do it! I'll do it!" the doctor wailed. "Look, look. See what I have accomplished since your last visit."

He brought up his signature application and everyone took a step back. Desktop icons moved out from the screen. In HD3D. Among others, Crayle saw his own visage.

"Votch," the doctor panted. He tapped the Crayle image. It divided into sub-images. "Ah, here iss France." He grasped the Eiffel Tower icon with his hand. "I now hold your memories. I could move them to you if you wore the cap, or …" He moved his hand toward a Trash Can image. "… I could delete them."

Taking a lesson from Ling, Crayle grasped the doctor's hand and dug his knuckle into its back. As if for its own safety, the iconic image flew back to the screen.

The doctor had lost any leverage in a roomful of killers. He began to hyperventilate.

"Calm down. You'll be safe. You've agreed to assist. There will be no more threats on your well-being."

Crayle needed the doctor to be calm enough not to make a mistake. He knew from experience that it would be safe to continue when the man no longer spoke a broken dialect of Swiss-English.

Once Rorschach caught his breath, he spoke. "I must contact Dr. Rikki. Herr Sommers must contact Herr Wohlford. Everything must be in order."

"Stop! You're driving me crazy. Once again. You saved my memories?"

"*Ja, ja.*"

"So, I didn't have amnesia from the crash?"

"Mr. Wohlford authorized it—with Dr. Rikki. You were perfect for my experiment."

Crayle pulled the knife back. "So … I'll be damned. That's how you were able to restore my Chin memories."

"*Ja.*" The doctor smiled.

"The experiment was to save, and later implant, but Wohlford used it for his plot, whatever that is. He had you remove any memories of him, didn't he? He covered up his involvement." Crayle thought for a second. He turned to the team. "It was he who assigned me to Chin and Lalumière." He turned back to Rorschach. "Where'd they find you, Doctor, the Mengele Memorial Home?"

"But Mr. Crayle, the experiment is a success! You were the perfect subject!"

"And the thousands who have died? And her father?" He nodded at Hekka.

"I—"

"What did you do? Here. Fix her. Your life depends on it."

The doctor stroked her brow. "I copied her memories, all of them. They are on this." He detached a memory stick and handed it to Crayle. "I can remove the memories of her father's death."

Crayle yanked him away from Hekka. “The memories in her head, the original ones, they’re intact?”

“Of course. I verified them.”

“How?”

“I saved them to the stick, read them back, and compared them to the original. A perfect match. No changes to her brain. I swear.”

Hekka moaned as she regained consciousness. “I had to, Magus.”

“We’re leaving. I have my memories of France and Lalumière’s strategy on this stick. Be careful with your wound. The rest of the team is outside.”

“Magus, this life is so difficult.” She exited the room.

“Goodbye, Mr. Crayle. *Aufwiedersehen.*” The doctor waved.

Crayle’s left hook knocked him out. The doctor fell back onto the bed. In seconds, Crayle had administered the memory cap and downloaded the doctor’s memory banks onto the stick and removed it once again. He touched an image of Rorschach’s brain. It drew out in apparent 3D. Then Hekka’s. He right-clicked and a menu appeared. He migrated the cursor down the menu and, “There.” He clicked. He took several purposeful breaths.

Hekka’s brain icon was still before him. By wafting his hand through the air as if demonstrating a martial art, he selected her memory icon of discovering her father with his neck slit, bathed in blood. Of her horror at the sight. He transported the icon to Rorschach’s brain image. And opened his fist.

The doctor’s eyes fluttered just as his body began to undulate. He winced. He cried out.

“There, Doctor … feel her pain.”

He exited the room. All that escaped the open door was "Ahhhhh!" from the wailing doctor.

“You done with the Doc?” Lenny asked.

“Yes.”

CHAPTER 10

Rorschach screamed, but couldn't be heard above the din outside. He leapt from the bed, grasping his throbbing head. He staggered across the room, slamming the wall with his elbow. Breaking the security alarm glass, he punched a code with twitching fingers. The wrong code.

From above, there was a rumble.

The doctor's head spun in every direction.

The hospital room shook, followed by more rumble.

The sounds took shape. Gravel bits fell from the fresh-air tubes that descended from the surface three hundred feet above.

One … two … then more. Then, a shower.

Outside, in the hallway, Magus Crayle yelled, "Out! Now!"

Armed guards dashed around a far corner.

The team made for the elevator as Micmac and Phoebe laid down covering fire.

The level of gravel in the hallway quickly rose. Three feet.

The team crunched and clawed its way to the doors as incoming fire from the hospital staff ricocheted at random. A grenade dug into the pile, muffling its effect and absorbing its shrapnel.

The elevator doors opened, but could not close as gravel seeped in.

Crayle fired up the pickup truck as the stones rose. Five feet.

Screams from the hall indicated that hospital staff and the security squad were being sucked into the aggregate. To their deaths. The firing ceased.

Phoebe punched Street Level—*Express*. The elevator shot skyward.

At the top, the door rotated open. The pickup flailed right and left as the driver flattened the accelerator. They sped by the quarry yard's rapidly diminishing piles of gravel.

"We goin' up to the cabin, Magus?" Lenny asked.

"No. I just received a text message. Jack's jet's at the airstrip."

"I can hotwire a car, but …"

"Give me a second." Crayle smiled like Alice in Wonderland's Cheshire cat. "I'll call the president."

• • •

As Crayle slid the truck to a stop at Jack's aircraft fifteen minutes later, he heard the spooled up engines familiar whine. President Kimbel Stones clearly had reach. Crayle reminded himself not to abuse his connection to the man.

They hustled up the stairs and collapsed into their favorite seats. Crayle turned to the team. "My mind is full of plots and schemes, but something has emerged in total clarity. Jack Sommers has managed us over the past three months. He's vectored us to Hong Kong, Kaohsiung, Beijing, and France, always to face lethal threats. I'm not sure about him, but I believe his boss, Neil, is playing for the other side. It's Neil who ordered us hither and yon—Jack doesn't have that kind of authority. It appears that his boss wanted us to die on foreign soil. Actually, it's me they wanted dead, Lenny. You, and the rest of the team, were collateral."

"Not like on a home purchase, huh?"

"With me dead, Rorschach couldn't reinstall the condemning memories. The master strategies and intricacies that could thwart Chin and Lalumière would be lost to law enforcement and the Agency. The evidence of treason by Neil Wohlford would be, in effect, destroyed."

"So, you think—"

"Wohlford is our enemy."

Hekka had listened to the entire conversation with abiding interest. "How do we stop him, Magus?"

"Yeah," Micmac inserted. "I can do all the weapons on the planet, and we still can't get inside Langley."

"I'm TDA, Temporary Duty Assignment, to the CIA. Maybe I could get in and …" Phoebe's voice trailed off.

Crayle asked, "Take him out? It's not what you do. I'm not even sure Neil's at Langley." He looked at Rorschach's computer. "When we get some place where we can catch our breath, you'll need to hook me up. We can see if the Doc's files can provide the intel we need."

Aboard Jack's jet, a message flashed overhead. "Please keep seat belts loosely fastened."

Crayle, Hekka, and Lenny watched the feed on the big screen. A news anchor reported the losses in life from the bomb tragedies in China.

"Lookie, lookie, lookie. You're genius strategy worked like a charm. Even having your brain re-fed by Doctor Ink Blot and knowing Chin's next moves, your strategy won out." Lenny raised his hand for a high-five.

"Yeah." Crayle raised his hand.

Hekka reacted. "But Magus. All those people."

Suddenly, the cabin announcement system burst to life. "What's that?"

They recognized the voice of the former Top Gun pilot.

"Radar lock!" replied the copilot.

"Seat Belts Tight!" appeared on the television screen.

The pilot pushed the Falcon 7X jet into an inverted Immelmann looping dive.

Lenny, head pressed against the window, saw a flash. Having left his seat belt loose, the G-force pressed his face against the glass. "Shrowt!" he exclaimed through compressed lips.

The pilot continued, terse and excited. "Mirage fighter … mini-gun … cannon … missiles."

"Magus!" Hekka cried.

When the jet was upright once again, Micmac popped the armrest on his seat and withdrew a universal remote. Aircraft maneuvers by the crew caused him to fumble the device.

Phoebe grabbed the remote top and bottom. "Steady now."

He punched in a sequence of buttons, finishing with *Play*.

Requisite fuselage beacon lights, top and bottom, retracted. In their places emerged two high-power lasers. Micmac had modified Jack's plane with help from a man named André at Dassault, the same company that had manufactured the fighter trying to down them. He pressed *Pause*, *Auto*, then *Play* again.

The fighter pilot behind zigged and zagged to put the next missile in position. He fired.

Micmac's belly laser engaged.

Its guidance system disabled, the missile fizzled toward the ground.

The attacking pilot's courage was sufficiently challenged. He turned to run.

Now, the canary pursued the cat. The man at the Falcon's controls had a saying "You can take the fighter pilot out of the fighter, but that doesn't make him any less dangerous."

That the Mirage fighter dead ahead moved away with its superior speed didn't matter at all to the focused light of the laser beam.

"The focused light has infinite range," Micmac informed.

It caught the fleeing craft up the tail. The multi-million dollar war machine turned to brilliant yellow and red dust.

Jack's pilot peeled off the chase and checked the radars. "No other Tangos. A lone assault. Someone underestimated our gadget man."

"Mods by Micmac." The former weapons specialist popped his belt and took a bow.

Just then, the pilot wagged the plane, taking the gadget man to the floor.

"There will be no grandstanding on my flight," said the pilot. "Unless it's by me."

"Roger that," chuckled the man sprawled on the deck.

"Of the six things one wants to know about such an attack …" Crayle considered. "… we know what, when, where, and how. But not who … or why."

Hekka looked perplexed. "Who could want us all dead?"

"Chin? Lalumière? Someone else? It seems they know we're enroute to Europe to stop the Frenchman. Who would know that?"

"Jack knows," said Lenny.

"Everyone on this plane knows" added Phoebe, glancing around.

Crayle punctuated the exchange. "Jack's boss?"

CHAPTER 11

With temperatures warming into mid-December, rain drizzled onto the urban snow bed and transformed it to slush. The economic chaos had reduced the number of automobiles on the Paris streets by more than half. Still, the remaining exasperated motorists waved arms and fingers at each other as if life itself depended upon such behavior.

Neil Wohlford found the drive in a hardened Embassy vehicle from Charles de Gaulle airport not to his liking. Even the thought of noise and chaos found his last nerve. Still, he knew that, if he could focus, he would dwell on the catastrophe that had transpired in Victoria. He was lucky to be alive. Were he religious, he would count his blessings.

He observed the once proud French population as they dove into dumpsters and fought for garbage. It was clear to him that they had not done this, but rather had enabled others to do it to them. They had chosen leaders who were obviously bad, yet chose them just the same. And when the leaders did exactly what they could be expected to do, the people accepted it at first. No different than in America.

No law or other penalty against economic treason existed. The politicians became rich in the process. Many had moved to Monaco to avoid a foreseeable reckoning. He smiled his acknowledgment. The Elder had been right from the start. It was past time for change. Substantive change.

This trip was more special than others. For the first time, he had brought his wife, Chantal. Thin and elegant, she had chosen to arrive in style. Her little black dress hugged every curve of her perfect five-nine body, and leggings, ubiquitous to her native Montreal at this time of year, had given way to sheer black nylons. He felt sure, as usual, that she would present well in any formal situation.

Like any psychiatrist, practicing or not, Chantal Wohlford habitually analyzed those she met, even casually. She still used her maiden name professionally, annoyed when it was not preceded by the title, Doctor.

She had not travelled to Paris with her husband in the past, due to his employment in the American clandestine services. He'd promised to show her the town on this first visit to France. It fulfilled the requirement for a pilgrimage to her native Quebec's spiritual motherland.

Given his status at Langley, he had been able to produce sufficient identification materials for her in short order. She had complained that the lanyard and tag did not look apropos drooping onto her little black Chanel. No consequence. Neil considered Chantal a tease. She didn't like sex. His mind switched gears. Pattie came into his mind. She set him on fire.

Chantal noticed his change in demeanor. She always seemed to know when his thoughts turned a certain way.

The Embassy driver eased through a group of soggy protestors, passed the wrought iron gates into the compound, and paused. Marines closed the gates behind the vehicle, making sure no protesters had slipped inside. After they had properly displayed their credentials, an anti-terrorist barricade faced with black and yellow chevrons rotated earthwards. The car continued to a protected space—a porte-cochère where credentials, including prints and retinas, could be validated electronically. One glance at the creds and the normal confiscation of mobile phones was foregone.

"I'll be in the basement," he told the driver. "You will need to be available the rest of the day." He turned to one of the guards. "Please notify Ms. Norbrunn in the Travel Office that I require priority assistance. And see that my wife is escorted to my office. Thank you."

The driver departed. As Chantal's heels echoed down the hall, Neil glanced around before entering a nearby supply closet. It opened via the same proximity devices used at his headquarters under the Civil War battlefield park at Manassas, Virginia. Once the door latched behind him, he unzipped his fly and plucked a curly hair from his groin. He placed it in a receptacle. The receptacle turned green.

"Brace your arms against the walls," a Flori-like voice purred from a speaker in his very first covert ingress design. Still wincing from the pain, he considered revisions.

The closet's interior descended in a few seconds. Neil stepped out onto a whisper-quiet, granite floor. The absorptive walls and ceiling allowed no reverberations whatsoever. Before him, another Wohlford masterpiece.

• • •

Chantal Wohlford sat in an office prepared for her husband and basked in the sumptuous décor he had specified. Though they were inside the American Embassy, she savored its sumptuous Frenchness. A knock sounded at the door.

"Come in."

A woman more petite than her own five-foot-nine peeked around a partially opened door, and entered as if overcome by shyness. Chantal recognized the type immediately.

"Oui?"

"Excusez moi. Je m'appelle Pattie," the girl introduced herself in pedestrian French, accenting the final syllable.

"I speak English quite well, and you, my darling, could use a dose of self-confidence."

Pattie blushed a smile. She looked downward.

"Finally," Chantal observed. "I meet someone who is simple, not complex, not messed up. Finally."

The two women exited through the Embassy's defenses to the street.

"I'd like to have lunch at the Hôtel de Crillon, Ms. Norbrunn."

"Please, Pattie. And if I can call you Chantal, then we can engage in girl talk. What do you say?"

"Chantal it is, Pattie. Yes, girl talk."

"Okay, here's the bad news. The Crillon has been in business since 1758. Through revolutions, wars, the whole nine yards. It is now under renovation and will remain closed until next year. It's sad. With the economy a shambles, relics are all the French have now. Follow me. There's something you need to see."

Outside the compound, they crossed a bridge over the Seine River, passing an extensive garden and a long set of buildings.

"It's called *Invalides* … for their wounded warriors."

They circled the edifices. Fifteen minutes later, they peered down into a circular overlook at a shaped box.

"That brown container has Napoléon inside."

"He was very short. It is strange that a person so small can achieve so much."

Pattie slipped off her heels. "Like me?"

Chantal blushed. "I'm sorry. I—"

Pattie blushed back. "Come on. Enough history. It's time to eat. You want expensive, I've got just the place."

"I've changed my mind. A place with Rock and Roll."

"I like that." She led them to the right of the *Palais Garnier*, the Paris Opera House.

Chantal laughed. "The Hard Rock. I visit the one in Montreal all the time."

"Pickin' up guys?"

Neil's psychiatrist wife smiled. "We'll talk inside."

Their table was small and intimate. With the ambient music at high volume, they needed to lean in to hear each other. In minutes, they had consumed two tall island drinks and were chatting like old friends.

Chantal inspected the young woman. Innocent and pretty. She reached out and grasped her hand. "Have you ever …"

"With a woman?" Pattie blushed.

"You blush so easily. It's attractive."

The young spy turned a deeper red.

"Well? Have you ever done a woman?"

Pattie sat back. Then she leaned close. "Not yet."

For a few moments, they shared a connection.

Pattie broke the silence. "Do you know much about your husband's work?"

"More than I am supposed to." Neil's wife giggled.

"He loves France so much, he should rise in the State Department to Ambassador to France. Would you like to live in Paris?"

"I'll share a secret." She moved closer until her lips touched Pattie's ear. "He doesn't work for State."

Pattie appeared confused. "Then what?"

Just a smile in return. "I cannot say. Oh, I love that song. It's …"

"*Sympathy for the Devil.* My mother loved The Rolling Stones, rest her soul."

"Pattie, I've got to tell someone what I've been doing. I know I can trust you. It's about Neil. Okay?"

"I'm ready."

"He talks in his sleep. Now, you know that I'm a psychiatrist … I decided to perform a little off-the-books study. He mentions fantasy entities, like kings and emperors. And bombs and … what was it … an elder. Crazy stuff. And something that sounded like Grail. You know, the Holy one. That last one seems to upset him. Makes him toss and turn."

"Do you keep a journal … for scientific purposes?"

"Not necessary. I have a photographic memory. I could recite his every word."

"Does he mention names?"

"Names?" Chantal wore an inquisitive look.

"If he mentioned the Grail, did he mention Jesus? That's what I meant. I'm quite religious, that's all." Good save, thought Pattie.

Chantal finished her second drink.

So she knew, Pattie surmised, that Neil didn't work for State. Not good. And no telling what he might tell her in his sleep tonight. "I'm sure Special Envoy Wohlford will be finished with his work by now. We should return."

"Oh, let's not. This is, after all, Paris. Let's shop."

"I shop at the Carrefour. It's a department store."

Chantal fetched a credit card from her clutch.

"A Black Card!"

"Unlimited. He never notices when I swipe it."

They giggled.

"Boulevard Haussmann it is!"

"Chanel!"

CHAPTER 12

Excessive shopping finished, Pattie escorted Chantal Wohlford to husband Neil's office. A man followed on their heels, approached Pattie, and whispered a few words in her ear. His task complete, he left them alone.

"Ah, Chantal. Special Envoy Wohlford has asked me to tell you that he will be delayed. He suggested that I give you a grand tour." She giggled. "As I am the travel agent by posting, it has fallen to me to show you our wonderful Embassy."

"I suppose that, since I will be meeting all the muck-a-mucks at various cocktail parties—trying not to psychoanalyze them—touring with you would be delightful." She stood, slung her Prada over her shoulder, and followed her guide out the door. "Oh!" She stopped. "One moment." She rushed back inside and scribbled a note for her husband, returning outside with a smile.

Pattie placed her hand on Chantal's arm. "Before we begin our tour, I would like to ask a favor?"

"You have spent so much time and have provided me such a fantastic day. Just ask."

"I know your English is perfect, but if it's okay, I'd like to hear you speak with a French accent. Please?"

"But of course, my leetle frand." Chantal smiled at the young woman.

After numerous hallways and countless closed doors, Pattie assured herself that no one was watching, and opened a supply closet door. While Neil's wife misinterpreted the private enclosure and pressed closer, Pattie provided the necessary DNA sample and, in short order, they descended below ground. They exited the rather personal elevator as soon as it stopped. Pattie said nothing, letting Neil's wife survey the cold, empty room before them.

"What is thees theeng?" Chantal asked in her French-Canadian accent. "Thees cube of glass, suspended in the room. Eet touches notheeng. And why am I wayreeng my Chanel in thees, what you call, basement?"

Pattie deployed her dimpled smile and stepped to the other woman. "Here, I'll show you. The box is isolated from all outside noise. It's exceptional."

She led Chantal through the glass cube's doorway.

• • •

Several stories above, Neil smiled at his wife's note and exited his private office. In the same manner as the two women, he made his way to the basement. His first sight jumped his heart to his throat. The glass isolation cube. Painted in red. Spots. Streaks. Blobs. Barely visible at its center, the immobile form of his former wife.

"Boo!"

He jumped. His heart raced.

Pattie seized his arm. "She didn't struggle too much. That's what you wanted. Right?"

His hands slapped to his cheeks. He gasped. "It was supposed to be discreet. You were supposed to take her through the passage into the catacombs. They will find her, Pattie. You have ruined everything."

"We are close to the end. We must clean up loose ends. Your words."

"Yes, but—"

"One cleaner later, and no one will know."

"And the cleaner … no, don't tell me."

She pulled the CIA's universal remote control from her coat pocket. Three clicks. The body disappeared. Another three clicks. Streams of a classified fluid washed the interior of the cube clean. Then a rinse. Then a whooshing, drying sound.

"Cleaner done," she smiled, pocketing the remote.

He turned, grasping her shoulders. He struggled to breathe. "Do you respect nothing? Is murder so easy for you?"

"She had to go. In order to free you up. Now, we can date." She grinned up at him.

"My God! You've lost your freakin' mind!"

She stepped back, dropping her coat to the floor.

Naked.

His heart throbbing, he sank to his knees.

She moved to him. "Go ahead, Neil. Debrief me."

CHAPTER 13

"What have you done?" Neil Wohlford wailed.

"C'mon, Neil. You said she wasn't much in bed, anyway."

"She was my *wife*."

"Look. If my gig with Mitim doesn't work out, you can bring me to Langley. I'll be directly under you." She laughed at the intended ambiguity.

"If I wanted everyone at CIA headquarters dead, I would bring you," moaned Neil. "See what you've become."

"You mean since that day in Amsterdam when you wanted a threesome with my mother and me?"

"Oh!" His anguish intensified.

"Yes, Neil. I was fresh and fourteen. My mom's addiction made her a pushover for your money."

He turned to her. "And then I received your message."

"That she'd died?"

"Yes."

"That's right. She was better off. So was I."

"You—"

"Like I said, she was better off. She overdosed that same night—the one where you took my virginity."

"You—"

"So, Mister Langley boss, what do we do now?"

"Do? We?"

"You can come with me topside or you can escape from here out into the catacombs."

"I'll call Elder. He'll know what I should do."

The petite spy walked to the elevator. She turned to look at him.

"What?" asked an exasperated Wohlford.

"Fuck you, Neil." She left.

Neil stumbled into the STIF room, into physical and auditory isolation. The smell of cleaning fluid pungent to his senses, he initiated his call.

"Yes, Elder. This is an emergency." He provided a situation report to the cosmopolitan megalomaniac.

Per the norm, the Elder's voice sounded calm and measured. "You must come. We must talk. Face-to-face."

Neil Wohlford, Illuminé's mole in the CIA, caught his breath while the Elder provided directions. This was it. His heart skipped a beat. Finally, he would meet this grand and mysterious man.

"Leave immediately," brought him out of his trance. "Before anyone asks for your wife."

"Of course. It's customary to be asked to dinner and she would be expected to attend. What about Pattie?"

"She is the best, Neil, but she has become spontaneous."

"Yes. Spontaneous."

The Elder terminated the call.

• • •

Within two hours, Neil strode from the Royal Heliport into Monaco's castle. He surrendered his weapon before being led into the Elder's location of choice for clandestine conversations, the Yellow Room. He noticed the ornate surroundings, all of the trappings appropriate to royalty. He glanced at the paintings that adorned the walls.

"Please," startled him. He recognized the voice he had listened to over the years. "Please take a seat."

Neil turned to face the man connected to the voice. Behind a desk and shrouded in shadows sat the one man on the planet he had longed to meet. He noticed that the only other seating in the room resembled something akin to a Royal Bean Bag chair. He sank down into it as gracefully as possible. He realized that any guest who decided to leap from the chair and over the desk would struggle just to exit the chair.

The Elder read his mind. "A precaution, Neil."

"Yes. A precaution."

"Do you recognize my voice? Until now, we have only communicated by phone."

"Yes, of course. I just wanted—"

"It is time you listened, Neil. We are arriving at the ultimate crossroads. We are faced with the following realities. Your wife, Chantal, has been terminated."

Neil, still stunned by the fact that his wife had been assassinated—for the cause, said nothing.

"Doctor Rorschach has died in a Quarry hospital incident. With him have gone all of the research in mind insinuation and extraction we could have employed on leaders everywhere. A sad note."

"Perhaps Doctor Rikki will restart the program. May I assume she is still available?"

A figure stepped from the darker shadows behind the Elder. Her wavy red hair glowed in the diminished light. "I am in perfect shape, Mr. Wohlford."

Neil recognized the voice. He watched as she moved close behind the grand man and placed her hands on his shoulders. In that instant, he recalled a day not long ago in his office, on his desk. The woman of fire and passion was also a woman of refinement and elegance. Translation: anyone anywhere could be an Illuminé asset. And he would never know. Clearly, he was not the smartest one in the room.

"I believe you know Monika professionally and in the biblical sense, Neil."

Neil worked hard to keep his shakes under control. "Only once, Sir."

"She will see to your physical needs before you leave. You shall, henceforth, and only in private, refer to her by her true given name, Sira."

"Sira?" Neil knew he was out of his element. His natural defenses obliterated, he'd become programmable.

"Crayle's assault team took severe casualties in Victoria. Still, they persist. Kidnapped by Chin, this indelible man has survived. He is either in—or travelling to—Europe. I believe it is his personal quest to defeat our French ally, which would be catastrophic to our cause."

"I wasn't—"

"*Listen* … Neil." Clearly, the Elder did not abide interruptions. "Our colleague, Sylvain, will be working his way to the final target—with his final bomb. While you may be able to guess his destination, do not under any circumstances go there. You are a necessary component of the Illuminé future. Do you understand?"

Neil gulped. Then he blurted out, "I understand."

"We are not finished when France is ours. As we speak, Lalumière's son is in negotiations with the northern royalties. It will be for you to see that the next bomb is engaged at the specified time. Precisely. And that you are at a safe distance when it detonates. Do you understand?"

"And the spy … Pattie?"

"Forget her. She is but a tool. I repeat my previous admonition, stay away from her sexually. She has proven an extremely valuable asset, but has evolved into a psychopathic Black Widow. S-F-K.

Seduce, fuck, kill. Seduce, fuck, kill. Are you comprehending this, Neil?"

Neil grasped the full import of the Elder's comments. In his experience, the refined man always spoke in an elevated manner and avoided vulgarities. The emphasis was clear. Neil counted himself fortunate to be alive. "Yes, Sir."

"Now you must depart. As I mentioned, Sira will first put you in a mentally and physically relaxed state."

"I have one question, Sir. If I return to Paris, I will need a well-crafted story. I don't—"

"There will be no story, Neil. You have gone rogue."

"But I'm a leader at Langley. I'm the Illuminé … your mole."

"No longer. They will figure it all out, but much later. They are given to bureaucracy at the CIA these days. It will take them time."

Neil mulled it over. "Then I must ask regarding my future. I will put it on the line, Sir. I realize that Sylvain is to become king or emperor of France and that is certainly your call. But I have always believed that royalty was my destiny. It would have been a fantasy ending for me to have taken that position. But in its place, my goal is to be your number two. Without that, my best outcome is to return to Langley."

"That is no longer possible, Neil. It seems that, were you to depart Illuminé in such a fashion, it would come to public attention that you murdered your wife, and then went on to kidnap Pattie Norbrunn after murdering her husband, the American Deputy Ambassador to France. It wouldn't look good … Neil."

Neil Wohlford sank back and stared at the ceiling. He knew game, set, and match when he heard it. "You're right. I'm dedicated to my mission … to the end."

"You may be confident that I shall reward you beyond your dreams. Royalty is not out of the question. But remember, my dear Neil. I shall only reward success."

"And I'll deliver it. I must begin."

"You will not return to Paris. I have something else in mind, something you will appreciate. The logistics? With the wreckage of the previous nuclear device in the vicinity of Marseille, land transport from here to your destination is impossible. Similarly, the French government is quite sensitive about their skies. My man will take you to your transportation. It resides in the royal quadrant of our fine harbor."

Neil, happy to complete this encounter, struggled to extract himself from the Bean Bag. The Elder, beyond an enigma and out of character, rose from the desk. He stepped into the light, and offered his hand.

Neil looked up. He instantly recognized the man standing tall in a purple and gold robe. How could he not have recognized one of the most famous voices on the planet. *"Oh, my God!"*

"You may instead compare me to Machiavelli."

"The Prince!"

"Of Monaco."

CHAPTER 14

Sir. A message for you. It's been scanned externally—no traces of toxic or explosive residue."

"Thank you, Jeffrey." From his top story office, Deputy Chief of Mission Randy Norbrunn stared for a second at the *Hôpital des Invalides* across the way. And, adjacent, at the domed chapel of Saint Jérôme where Napoléon's tomb—his red porphyry sarcophagus—resided on perpetual display. He imagined early 19th Century troops aligned there, Napoléon at their head. His Paris Embassy posting was every day a wonderment.

"Sir?"

He jumped, his daydream interrupted. "Oh … yes, Jeffrey?"

"You know the drill, Sir. Please open the envelope so my phone slash monitor can test inside for ricin and such."

Randy slit the envelope with a World War II relic stiletto his wife had purchased for him as a birthday present.

"Negative for dangerous chemicals or biohazards."

"Thank you, Jeffrey." He extracted the note.

Dearest Randy,

I have just finished my destination research trip. Darling, I have some vacation time that I must either take before year's end or lose and, I'm so excited, I have a plan. Meet me in Switzerland at our special place. I promise you the reward you so justly deserve in return for what you have brought to me.

My special love,
Pattie

He placed the note into an eight-way shredder/emulsifier. A quick call for permission didn't need to get past the ambassador's assistant. "Well, I'll be damned." He glanced up. "That will be all, Jeffrey." He laughed in anticipation. "I'm taking the weekend off."

• • •

The snow had let up, leaving the streets merely wet and the sidewalks once again passable. With little traffic to negotiate, his driver transported him from the Embassy to De Gaulle Airport in less than forty-five minutes. They avoided pockets of protestors and still-smoldering vehicles, arriving intact. Even though the European Union, of which France was a seminal signatory, had no formal economic ties to his destination, there would be no security to endure at either end of his journey. As they passed up into the heavens, a man who was effectively Deputy Ambassador Norbrunn became just plain Randy, and the thought of reuniting, in all senses of the word, with his Pattie brought a wide smile to his lips.

His Embassy jet set down at the Zurich airport precisely on time, more due to Swiss requirements than to French punctuality. Once deplaned, a quick taxi ride transported him to the luxurious more-stars-than-you-can-count Bauer au Lac Hotel. At the edge of Zurich Lake, it was a treat even for the well-heeled.

In order not to appear as a wannabee whom staff would most certainly stop at the entrance, Randy had changed to his Armani suit and Bruno Magli shoes on the jet. That he had purchased them on Amazon at only $400 each was a source of pride. His religion supported success, but required frugality whenever possible. In addition, since the new President Stones had taken office, the notion that public servants could run wild with money belonging to the citizens of America had taken a severe beating.

On the short ride into town, he noted that the Swiss had once again become popular with the world's wealthy. There were more people about than anywhere else in Europe and no beggars, no panhandlers, no protestors, just the smiling Swiss. He stopped outside to admire the 170-year-old, family run hotel before he whisked himself inside. As predicted, he got a wave and a tip of the hat from the Maître d' before locating his room key in a flowerpot. Pattie loved that kind of thing. After a brief ride to the third floor, he felt her presence.

"Hello, dear," he said to the smiling face across the room as he stepped through the doorway.

"Randy!" the diminutive travel agent exclaimed. She jumped to her feet, ran to the five-foot-eight Deputy Ambassador, extended to her tiptoes, and met him with a welcome home kiss. He wanted more, but the young woman pressed away, just out of reach.

Her eyes sparkled as she spoke quickly, excited. "Come, come. I'll be busy this morning with some final tourist stuff, but I'm taking the afternoon off. I … oh, darling, welcome to Zurich!"

"How in the world did you pull this off?"

"I made everything go away. You won't believe this—I created a scheme. I met with the Ambassador before I left. He assured me that he could actually handle things without you." Conveniently, she left out that the negotiations had taken place in the Ambassador's washroom.

"I had meetings and such scheduled the whole day. I even had one of those 'Do I really have to do this?' dinners scheduled with Special Envoy Wohlford and his wife. But miracle of miracles, they had to cancel. So it all worked out."

"And how did you swing this, my darling Randy? The bellman informed me this suite costs 950 dollars. For one night. And that's on special."

"That's 950 in Swiss Francs. It's 1,026 dollars at today's exchange rate."

"On a government salary," she teased.

He grinned. "I had some budget money left over from last year. Had to use it or lose it."

"Wonderful. You'll be happy that I've planned a trip to the Reform church started by Mr. Zwingli. And we can go see the document, *Consensus Tigurinus*—the Zurich Consent that resolved the Zwingli and Calvin differences. Isn't that exciting? Please say yes."

He laughed. She was so wonderful. "Yes! Yes!"

"I'm so happy."

"This will be a trip to remember."

"Oh, it will, Randy." She beamed. "I almost forgot. There's food." She pointed to trays arrayed on a large glass and wood coffee table.

He looked her body up and down as he reached for her. "I'm starved."

• • •

"One half hour has passed since we finished our meal," Pattie announced, looking up from her cell phone. "It is time for sex."

"Darling, please don't talk like that. You know how careful we Calvinists are with our language."

Her demeanor changed. Something had clicked, or broken, inside. Her voice deepened. "How about we just fuck?"

"What? Please don't be like that. You know I don't—"

"It turns you on when I act sacrilegious. Come on, Randy, play with me."

She removed his shirt, then his pants. The always-in-authority Deputy Ambassador was now on Pattie Norbrunn's field of battle.

But it was different for her this time. Before leaving for Switzerland, she had received a call. A very secure and very special call.

An explosion has been reported at my residence in Paris, her boss Neil had explained. *A tragedy, in which both myself and my wife died. I'll meet you when all of this quiets down. Several days. I will contact you.* Then, he had provided her next assignment.

"Hello?" Randy extended his arms in a 'what's next' expression.

Pattie smiled. His starched white briefs demonstrated how much he loved to see her smooth, dimpled cheeks. She removed her business-casual outerwear, revealing blood red lace undergarments.

He moved in. He loved her sex as much as he loved her.

She turned away as he unsnapped her bra. In an instant, she whirled and clamped the cups over his mouth and nose.

He grabbed her wrists, but his arms grew weak. Too weak.

She dropped the garment, guiding him onto the bed.

"I've got some business to take care of. This one is going to have to last you, my dear. So I'll make it the very best."

CHAPTER 15

A full seven days had passed since the battle of good versus evil had disrupted the peace in Canada's beautiful seaside city, Victoria. The team entered yet another leg in their seemingly endless journey.

Jack's jet set down at the Portela International Airport in Lisbon, Portugal. Instead of heading due south to the nation's capital, the driver took them instead southwest to the seacoast resort city, Estoril.

The forty-five minute trip provided the flavor of Portugal.

As in Spain next door, they saw the common red-tiled roofs, though the Portuguese version seemed a darker red. They passed through the north side of town and were treated to a quite long strip of parkland that descended toward the sea. The driver, and part-time tour guide, pointed out an operational replica of San Francisco's Golden Gate Bridge and next to that, a statue like one in Rio de Janeiro, Christ the Redeemer. "If any of you require redemption, I cannot perform that task. Anything else, though." The driver tossed a warm smile at the glum crew in back.

They pulled up to the front of a six-story, white hotel, passing a row of parked Porsches and similar. It gave an idea of the sumptuous décor they would find inside. Their driver hopped out, yanked a bell cart from a bellman, handed him a note, paid him 500 Euros, and proceeded to load all luggage and disappear into the hotel. The team just gazed around, trying not to notice the blatant efficiency of the man.

The bellman took the rest of the day off.

A quick check-in, a short ride up the elevator, and the team entered their suite.

As usual, Lenny deduced in arrears. "We needed a big one, what with the five of us."

"Look at the view." Phoebe stepped to a panorama of windows that displayed all of Estoril plus its world-class beach in the distance. She noticed that the sun was high and heading west. Uncharacteristic, and only for a moment, Phoebe put on airs. "We simply *must* sup on the balcony."

Crayle and Micmac plopped into sumptuous, burgundy leather chairs while the P.I., true to his nature, reconnoitered.

"Hey! This place only has two bedrooms. So, which couple would like my late night assistance?"

Phoebe checked the small of her back, reassuring herself that her Glock was handy.

Crayle and Micmac stared at the women, then each other.

"Well?"

Crayle cleared his throat. "Remember what your father did, Lenny?"

"You mean stole your intel and tried to sell it to Lalumière's goons?"

"No. Not that. His job at the CIA. Security."

"Oh, yeah. That was before they upgraded him to the Inspector General's office."

"He kept the Langley offices safe. I want you to carry on that tradition for us. Here."

Crayle motioned at Micmac, who followed him to the room's seven foot long couch. They moved it against the door, pleased that the door's horizontal handle was prevented from turning by the back of the couch.

"It makes into a sleeper."

"I get it." He whipped out his Walther PPK. "If someone tries to break in, the couch stops 'em, I wake up, and take 'em out." Lenny looked excited about the potential for action, but also about providing value. He stretched out on the couch and promptly fell asleep.

"Nicely done." Phoebe applauded in silence.

"Phoebe, tonight when you two are in there …" Crayle pointed toward the south bedroom. "… think of the difference between your Glock in normal mode, and then silenced. Major difference in noise level. Please silence any outcries you might consider making." He waved his hand at the P.I.

Micmac angled his head toward Crayle. "And you know about these noises how?"

The mastermind ignored him. "I chose this room because of the large table. Please take a seat." He walked to the sofa and rousted Lenny.

Happy to avoid any furtherance of Micmac's comment, Phoebe set the precedent by sitting first. Then, one-by-one, the rest joined her.

"Here's where we are. Lalumière is alive and semi-well. He also has another mini-nuke, like the one's he used in Marseille and New York. I believe it to be the last of the breed, and here's why. Chin and Li have what they want. They don't need any more bombs, and one more going off could lead the world's intel groups to them. An extremely high risk."

Hekka wore a quizzical look. "Then why provide Lalumière with the bomb at Victoria? Why?"

"Providing the third bomb fulfilled their agreement."

"So Chin sent you, us, to stop him from using it."

"He did. He knows we will have to eliminate the threat, which keeps him out of it."

"He's a genius, too," Lenny asserted.

Crayle let that one slide. "Look. We haven't heard from Jack. Lenny, tell them what you told me on the plane."

"I helped get Jack to the hospital. They did some patch-up work. He threw a fit and demanded to be carted up to his cabin for rehab. With a cute nurse."

"That last part is new. Everyone gather around, I'm calling him." Crayle punched *Speaker*.

"Hello," Jack said.

"That's his gravelly voice," Lenny affirmed.

"Gravelly would be if I was still underground at the Quarry. How's everyone?"

"We are fine, Mr. Sommers." Hekka conveyed a not friendly mood regarding the man who continually put them all in danger.

"You kinda left without me, Magus."

"Sorry, Jack. We need to stop—"

"It's alright. I'd love to join you, but this stomach wound is a bitch. I spent a day or so at the Quarry. It drove me stir crazy. I don't like that place. I'm resting at the cabin. My doctor said at least a week."

"What'd he really say?"

"Two weeks."

"Jack?"

"Three. Magus, we don't have that much time."

"Lalumière has to get the government components convened in one place. He can't use his final bomb to force them together. Since we don't know his location, we watch the government instead. Conditions in France are the worst ever … and the holiday season started about the time we staged the Victoria raid."

"I'm not sure where you're going with this. You're the strategist, I'm a detail man. Get to the point."

"My point is this. Mass confusion abounds. The people hate the government, which is trying to keep its head on its body. The holidays can change all that. I think the government will attempt to use the occasion to bring the people back under its control."

Jack considered Crayle's conceptualization. "You may be on to something. I remember the Mexican government, years ago, in the same situation. They spotlighted religion. Told everyone to be good Catholics and have lots of kids. Kept the people busy until the extra population made things economically unbearable years later. Enter the rich neighbor, America, next door. That's why their government was handing out tour guides to the illegals."

"You're right. All politicians do these days is make unfulfillable promises and divert attention from their failures."

"It's more complicated, Magus. At the Victoria castle, when I was back a distance with the sniper rifle, I spotted a man who was the spittin' image of Neil inside, talking to Lalumière and Chin."

Crayle observed the obvious. "Jack, your boss is one of *them*. The Illuminè has had a mole in the CIA the entire time. It explains a lot."

"I'm sorry, Magus. That son-of-a-bitch used us all."

"Even before my crash. He's the one who sent me to Chin and Lalumière knowing what I could accomplish. The bombs, everything, executed like a fine orchestral piece. We'll worry about him later," said a disgusted Crayle. "When I was up close to the choppers, I caught a glimpse of the Frenchman, and he had the football with him. I had hoped he'd left it behind, but no such luck. Then, lights out."

"Okay, now it's my turn ..."

"Not yet, Jack. Listen up. There are just a few ways for us to stop this madman. One, we cause the French government to snatch victory from the jaws of defeat. That would remove the people's desire for a radical change in leadership. Lalumière's Mitim character would become unimportant. Two, find his bomb and remove it. He can't destroy the French government without it. Three," said Crayle, "find him and kill him."

Everyone seated at the table had their own intelligence and experiences working for them. None of them liked what they might need to do.

Crayle observed the moment of silence. Then, he continued. "The first option is, of course, absurdly impossible. The second and third require the same operation, find Lalumière. What do you think, Jack?"

"You're right. He's out there somewhere with just the clothes on his back. Hiding. At some not too distant point, he'll need money. A lot of money."

"And if we know the money trail …" mused Hekka.

Crayle glanced at her. She was right. "Jack, that means Switzerland."

"If they haven't already been there."

"We don't have locations on Lalumière or his son, correct?"

"Not a clue." Jack no longer received an intel feed from Central Intelligence.

"Then we go after his banker."

"His personal money man is a guy in Zurich. Name's Kobler. He'll know."

"And if he doesn't?"

"The money is couriered to Amsterdam by the son. There, it's exchanged for diamonds."

"Lenny's brother," Hekka observed.

Crayle glanced at the alerted P.I., but couldn't allow any deflection of the conversation's momentum. "At this point, they're our only two targets. Our best shot. Perhaps our only shot. I suggest a two-prong attack. One team goes for the cash. Hekka and I take Zurich. The second team goes for the diamonds. Phoebe and Micmac take Amsterdam."

"I concur. Regarding your team, it'll be a private bank in Switzerland. They don't let just anyone in, Magus."

He smiled. "They'll let me in."

"Well, if his son already has the money, he'll be on his way to Amsterdam for diamonds. What then?"

"What about me?" Lenny intervened, recognizing an opportunity to protect his brother.

"With respect to the Amsterdam team, send Lenny. See if he can get his brother to join our side. You would be able to send Phoebe and Micmac for persuasion, except—"

"Except what?"

"I received a call just before yours. Phoebe's been ordered back to Washington. It seems her boss wants a debrief on her time with us. As you may or may not know, I called in a sizeable marker to get her in the first place. I'm afraid she's gotta go."

A long pause followed. Crayle searched the ceiling, the floor, and then the team's eyes. "Great."

"It's like they say, Magus. The shit never stops."

"It's late," said Crayle. "Jack, you need rest. Phoebe and Micmac, too." He winked.

"What about me?" Lenny sat up, rubbing his eyes.

Phoebe reached for her weapon.

Micmac wrapped his arm around her, as if affecting a hug. He started her toward the bedroom.

Jack sighed, the sound hollow across the phone line. "Lenny, you did such a good job in Victoria, and on Bowen Island, I'd have kept you here with me if I could have. But you can still continue service as my lieutenant."

Lenny glanced after Phoebe, a smirk adorning his lips.

"That's all I have for now, Magus. Good luck."

"Yeah. Take care, Jack. Keep in touch."

"Ditto." Jack rang off.

"It's strange that he would say that, Magus."

"He said a lot of things."

"That son-of-a-bitch Neil used us all."

Crayle had learned to listen deeply to Hekka's thoughts. Perhaps Jack was a user as well.

She smiled into his eyes, amazed that he could read what she didn't say.

"You're security, Lenny, remember. Hekka and I will fetch some food."

They rotated the couch and exited.

• • •

Two minutes after leaving their suite, the pair stepped onto the streets of Estoril. Like many European seaside resort towns, it was quiet, even for this late in the year. Crayle stopped and nodded. "See the casino over there? It was Ian Fleming's model for Casino Royale."

"As in James Bond?"

He nodded and then pointed down the block. "There's a grocery store right there."

"No, Magus. Time for a walk. I'm sure we'll discover another store."

In ten minutes, they padded across the pillow-like surface of Estoril's famous beach.

"It's beautiful, Magus. The wet sand is perfect."

They removed their shoes and strolled, arm-in-arm, along the water's edge.

"Look!" Hekka turned to face the sea. The small waves lapped over one another as they pushed ashore. An offshore breeze made for a light chop. *"Taamit."*

He recognized the Takic word he had heard during his first visit to her ranch. "The sun."

She turned to him, surprised. "You remember my language. A very gold star, Mr. Crayle." Her attention returned to the sunscape. "We can observe its glow because of the marine haze. It's wonderful."

"Romantic."

The sun, though dimmed by the haze, produced enough light for the water to sparkle from the horizon to the spot where they stood.

"These sparkles, they are our diamonds." He turned to her. "Water diamonds."

She smiled up at him.

The beach, wide at this point, stretched perhaps 100 yards from the boardwalk to the water. Away from the moisture, the sand was soft and white. But close to the sea, it became firm, yet pliant, and reflected a deep mauve hue as it embraced the incoming tide. The area was empty due to the dire economic circumstances in the region.

Hekka unbuttoned Crayle's black shirt. Slowly. The sun showed less of them as it sank into the sea. For the first time since their initial meeting, they became naked at the water's edge.

"Taqt, nuht, pat," Crayle whispered.

"Man, woman, water," Hekka translated.

They knelt and then stretched out on the beach, entwined. The largest waves of a set splashed them with chilled water, generating a hypersensitivity.

Hekka's head began to throb from her wound.

Crayle took her hand, concerned.

"It's okay. The salty water will help it to heal."

They kissed. Other parts began to throb. They achieved fruition just as the sun set, a bright orange flare in the distance.

CHAPTER 16

Before an hour had elapsed, the satiated lovers returned to the room with food, as promised.

"It's about time," Lenny complained.

Micmac saw it in their eyes. He knew the feeling, because of Phoebe. "Okay, we've got some work to do here. We have to get Rorschach's computer set up, memory stick and all, and take our best shot at plugging those French memories back in."

Hekka shook her head. "But we don't have Rorschach's expertise, or his experience with this device. What if—"

Lenny stepped in, flipped on the computer, and inserted the stick. "Ready for the cap, boss."

Hekka pushed Lenny aside. She affixed the skull cap to Crayle's head. Micmac connected the computer and cap with a special USB cable.

The room tension peaked. They could lose him.

Hekka broke first. She yanked the cable from the cap.

Phoebe grabbed her. She stared into the eyes of Crayle's Indian lover. "We must do this."

Hekka returned her stare. "You're right. He's not just my lover. He's our leader, and he's the only one who can receive the remaining memories. What'll we do if something happens?"

"Nothing's going to happen," the FBI agent reassured her. "We have to do this."

The newest spy recognized the absence of choice. She replaced the cable. "I will begin the process. If we are … not fortunate, I will tend to him. My heart is committed." Her eyes welled.

"Jeesus Christ! Cue the violins," Lenny said, covering his own deep feelings. The others ignored him.

Hekka pressed her lips hard against Crayle's. "Are you ready, Magus?"

He nodded.

She pressed *Play*.

Phoebe and Micmac grabbed for Crayle's arms as he began to fling them wildly about. His eyes snapped shut. Then, re-opened. Then, shut. His head shook left and right, and back again.

"Hekka, Lenny, help!" Phoebe cried out as Crayle's strength came into play.

The battle lasted no more than five minutes. Then calm. Crayle slept. They eased him back onto the bed and left the room. All except for Hekka.

Outside the bedroom, the three caught their collective breaths.

"Wow," said Lenny. "God, I'm sorry for what I said. Magus and me, we're like brothers."

"We've become family," Micmac asserted, embracing them both.

• • •

Six hours. The three paced and sat, paced and sat the entire time. No sounds emerged from the bedroom. None.

The door finally opened.

An unsteady Hekka emerged. Tears streamed down her face.

"He remembers!"

• • •

The team sat around the table while Crayle recited the entirety of his strategic plan-building year with Lalumière. Then, he ventured into a dose of reality.

"Phoebe and Micmac, you're going to D.C. Don't say a word about what's going on with the bombs and all. And the battles. New York …"

"It'll be a brief debrief," Phoebe assured.

"I'll go ahead," Lenny inserted.

Crayle frowned. "What?"

"We can't wait. I'll find Wolfie and persuade him to help us."

Phoebe grasped his arm. "He hates you. Did you forget?"

"At first, it might be a little difficult, him blaming me for his mom taking her life and all. But I bet he'll come around when I explain about the tens of thousands of people his pal Jean-Marc's dad has helped kill, and the possible destruction of his entire way of life … he'll listen."

"Then off, the three of you, to the airport. Hekka and I will need access to Jack's plane on a moment's notice if we get a Lalumière or Mitim sighting, so you'll have to use regularly scheduled airlines." Crayle added a rhetorical, "Okay?"

"Am I going with them?"

"Lenny, get your stuff and get out of here."

"In Jack's absence," cried the P.I. *"Rock and roll!"*

• • •

Nine hours later and eleven hundred and fifty-eight miles to the northeast, Lenny walked in on his brother, Wolfram.

"You bastard!" cried the diamond broker, jumping up from his seat.

"And the horse you rode in on!" Lenny countered.

"And your mama!"

Lenny swallowed a reply that would have referred to Wolfie's mother. One long-awaited hug later, the half-brothers cut to business.

"Wolfie, I need you to get me a value on a diamond." He tried to keep a poker face. But the fact that this request had come directly from Neil Wohlford, bypassing Jack, made him quite nervous.

"Diamonds are us. Color? Carat? Clarity? Cut?"

"One hundred carats."

The brother laughed from his belly. "That's funny."

"Not funny."

"You're serious? Look, I even ask about such a rock, the mob's all over me."

"Estimate, then."

"Anything over five carats and the prices go asymptotic."

"You're speaking Dutch."

"I'm speaking math. It means prices go straight up, but I think I can give you a minimum." He pecked at his computer. "The Amsterdam Diamond, 33.74 carats, auctioned for $352,000. And that was over ten years ago. So, you're talking one heck of a to-die-for diamond."

"Yeah." Having run out of things to say, Lenny turned to leave, forgetting to bid his half-brother farewell.

"Lenny? Let's get a bite."

Lenny stopped. He and his brother had never been close. Perhaps it was time to resolve that. "Yeah. A bite. And a beer."

"Terrific. Just give me a second … of privacy … I'll meet you downstairs."

Lenny nodded and departed the room. He was so turned around by their mutual civility, beyond his wildest expectation, he didn't concern himself with Wolfie's call. He closed the door, paused part way down the stairway, and peered through an open door to observe the window girl. Beautiful, blonde, and smart. Two out of three.

Back in his bedroom-turned-office, Wolfie took a deep breath. It had been years since he had seen his half-brother. He still had deep feelings about what had happened in the family, but that was overridden by what he had to do next. He dialed a special number.

"Yes, Sir, he's here." He waited. "Yes, I will keep him in Amsterdam."

CHAPTER 17

The flight from Estoril to Zurich had been routed around the Marseille airspace over the French Central Massif. The plateau area, carved by rivers in all directions, caused disruptions in any weather systems that pushed that direction from the Atlantic. For Crayle and Hekka this meant a thunderstorm and consequent turbulence, making both wonder if they would survive to see Switzerland. The weather calmed as they passed over the Rhone Valley, but picked up with another heavy storm as they approached the Alps.

If there was a calming influence, it was that the pilot was a friend of Micmac's and a former Navy fighter pilot. As they were buffeted from side to side on approach, their pilot displayed his experience at landing on aircraft carriers, the equivalent of hitting a moving target with a wobbly dart. He got them down safely. Before the plane came to full rest, Hekka unbuckled, entered the flight deck, and kissed him on the forehead. "Thank you, ma'am," muttered the surprised aviator.

"We will go to our hotel room, and I will drink," Hekka announced with folded arms.

"Good," Crayle surmised. "It'll keep your mind occupied." As she turned toward the exit ramp, the smile slid from his lips. Soon enough, he feared, the real danger would return. Full force.

Partially due to Rorschach's final memory restore, Crayle recognized Zurich's Kloten Airport as if it had only been a week. The Nikon D7100 DSLR hanging from his neck produced the impression of a serious photographer. Hekka, an encased 400mm lens strapped crosswise, appeared to be his assistant, although her butterscotch skin, black tresses, and exceptional beauty turned the heads of the otherwise stalwart Swiss.

"Last time I was here, it was July. There were rock and roll stages everywhere. Groups from all over Europe came to play. Music all night. It's a celebration of the city's founding. They call the festival *Zürifäscht.*"

"Tsoori fesht?"

"Well done. You sound like a native."

Hekka reasoned that, if she could handle the difficult language of her tribe, surely the Swiss language was within her reach. She smiled. "Some day, when all of this spying is over, *we* will play."

Their taxi bore them to the luxurious hillside Dolder Grand. Within minutes of entering the lobby, the Maître d' stepped up to the couple with a glittering smile. "Ah, Herr Griffing. So nice to see you again. We have for you your favorite room." As he turned to signal a bellman, the smile vanished. "*Entschuldigen Sie. Bitte.*" He rotated back to them. The burnished smile returned.

"Oh, this room," Hekka exclaimed as they entered a sumptuous suite. "And the view. Look down there at the huge lake, and the beautiful city. Magus, it's so far from home, yet …"

He tipped the bellman and secured the door. He walked up behind her and wrapped her with his arms. "Yes, someday, we will play."

His thoughts turned to the business at hand, as well as to the destruction and mayhem sure to follow.

True to her word, she parked her suitcase on the king-size bed, walked straight to the honor bar, and began to chug the contents of a bottle of the local liquor.

Crayle, late to intervene, tugged the bottle away. He held it up to the light. One-third gone. "You'll be asleep in twenty minutes." He would use the time to create a tactical plan. He had learned from his Chin memory restoration that time allowed his mind to reconnect memories so he could digest and correlate them.

He was almost right. It only took Hekka fifteen minutes to fall asleep. From the window, he watched the wind blow the lake water eastward. The only craft operating was the lake ferry. He had a vague remembrance of a long ago trip to the lake's other end, not far from Liechtenstein. Rapperswil. As had been the case too often, he didn't remember why.

He glanced across the town, recalling target practice in its southern area at the gun club. He remembered a girl, a redhead, but nothing more. He started. The memory connected. Lalumière's daughter. He'd pronounced her name, Alice, in the American fashion. She had corrected him with a smile. "Ah-*leese*."

"I remember now, Doctor. I was an operative on a mission. The girl had been an object of convenience as the manual terms them. Spies encounter them from time-to-time. Relieve your tensions dispassionately and move on. With death always at your door, morality gets muddled."

He took the short walk and studied himself in the bathroom mirror. "Who is this man who stares back at me?"

Then, it struck him. He had been delivering an internal dialog to Doctor Rorschach, a man who lay crushed under a mountain of rock in the foothills of a Southern California valley. Thousands of miles away. There would be no more analysis of his observations and meanderings. But then, with all of his memories restored, there would be no need.

Feeling complete and knowing from experience that Hekka would be out for several hours, he ordered a Town Car. He headed into central Zurich to its go-to clothing smorgasbord for spies, Jelmoli.

Perhaps the oldest and best-known department store in the world, one could find all manner of cover garments. With Jack's special credit card and an hour of his own time, he returned with European-style garb for the two of them. He hoped he'd gotten her sizes right.

Almost four hours to the hour, Hekka began to come around. "Oh. Why did you let me do that, Magus? Oh." She rubbed her head with one hand and her eyes with the other.

"If I'm supposed to confess to letting you quaff the better part of a bottle of liquor, then you have it. Personally, I think you should go back to whatever you drank before you met me."

"Did you take advantage of me?"

"Taking advantage of drunken women is not what I do."

"Women? Plural?"

"Here. Look at what I bought for us. We'll look more European and only sound American when we talk."

"We could speak Takic, like my father and I."

"Except for one minor problem. I don't understand a word."

She stood at the honor bar again, this time seeking mountain water. "You understand three words."

"We can't go around talking about man, woman, water all the time."

She examined the garments lying on the bed. "I love my new clothes." Hekka modeled her charcoal wool slacks, her red flounce top, and topped it with a black, vertically stitched jacket. "This is so warm." She cuddled into the fabric. "Remember the night? On the mountain?"

He closed the distance. They helped each other disrobe. In seconds, they reprised the night on the mountain, although in a more civilized fashion.

CHAPTER 18

A quick in-room lunch and transport by hotel limo down the hill and across the city's primary bridge delivered them to the world famous Bahnhofstrasse. It was the ides of December, the fifteenth, and the air chilly, yet comfortable.

"You must walk from here," the driver intoned. "This street is pedestrian only. If you have been to Rome or Paris, you will appreciate this."

The driver waved off a tip and departed.

"They seem to be secretive about dropping passengers at a Swiss private bank. This way."

Crayle led the way to the street number he had memorized and pulled open the gold door. Hekka stepped inside. She glanced at the subdued, gold-embellished walls and then up at the 30-foot domed ceiling. Their footsteps echoed, not just due to the marble floor, but also due to the paucity of furnishings. A sole item, a podium, stood to their right.

A woman, her blonde hair pulled back, clad in a beige Armani, and Hermés silk adorning her neck, stood behind the podium. *"Guten Tag, Herr Griffing. Wie geht es mit Ihnen?"*

"Geht's guet. 'S Watter eesh hoota shlaacht." The guttural final word would have sounded strange had it not come from a man with half-Scottish heritage. Returning the high-German initiation of the hostess with a Schwyzerduutsch response completed their verbal handshake.

Hekka looked up at Crayle, suppressing a smile.

The woman motioned.

The pair surrendered their gear to a military-looking man who'd appeared from nowhere.

"The elevator is to your left and behind." She gestured.

The elevator, tiny by Lilliputian standards, denied an assault team this means of ingress. The two pressed together. Crayle exhaled. Aroused. Hekka wanted a kiss, but assumed they were being watched.

The door opened onto a large room. At its center stood a man clad in casual wear. "*Tag, Herr Crayle.*" He noticed the reaction to his wardrobe. "Oh, the Swiss banker dress code … it's a myth." He smiled a banker's smile.

"*Wie gehts, Kobler.* We continue in English?" He nodded at Hekka. "She can hear everything we have to say."

"Please, step into the library. It is warm and cozy, as you say. We shall have tea."

They entered the dark-paneled room, feeling the warmth exuded by an immense 19th Century fireplace. Kobler closed the door. "Excuse me. I should introduce my daughter. She assists me from time to time. You should call her Angel."

Crayle's head spun toward the young blonde woman, who peeked around from a burgundy leather wing chair. He mouthed, "Pattie."

"*Tag*, Herr Griffing. So nice to meet you."

Crayle met her extended hand. She dragged her middle finger along his palm as they released. Kobler led them to a period sofa and took a chair next to Neil's spy.

"Your lens," Kobler handed the confiscated tube to Crayle, who entered a code. The cap released and he extracted the lens, then unscrewed the sunshade and tilted the lens onto a table. Out slid a black, ballistic nylon bag.

"Ah, yes." The banker fondled the bag. "The China diamonds."

"Precisely one pound of perfect, one-carat diamonds, Herr Kobler. Twelve-and-a-quarter million dollars."

The banker glanced at the ceiling. "Those U.S. dollars are precisely 11.39495 million Swiss Francs, at this moment's rate."

Hekka checked out the ceiling.

"Would you prefer safe deposit, currency of your choice, or both?"

"Ten thousand in Swiss Francs, ten thousand in Euros, ten thousand in Norwegian Kroner. Store my diamonds, net of currency, in my safe deposit box."

"Very well. Angel will see to the details."

"But—"

Pattie was gone.

"Tut, tut, Herr Crayle. As you Americans like to say, I would trust her with my life."

• • •

Financial transactions complete, they passed a trolley station as Crayle led Hekka along Zurich's famous Bahnhofstrasse promenade. While its name identified it as Railway Station Street, vehicular traffic was prohibited and all the upscale shops of New York, London, Paris, and Rome had a presence.

"This is the one." He opened a heavy, glass-paneled door. Inside, a number of display cases greeted them.

"The Belgians and Swiss fight over who's number one in chocolates. No matter. This place—Sprüngli—is my choice for world-class truffles."

They picked a half dozen from an array of chocolate spheres. Crayle ordered Swiss coffee, black, to be served outside. No sooner were they seated, than the goods arrived.

Hekka took a bite. She moaned. "Magus, these are …"

"Sexual?"

"Mmmm."

"I knew you'd like them."

She stopped after the first one. "I have something serious to say. I don't care that you've been here before or that you have a safe deposit box in a private bank. I don't care what you did before. I love you."

He clasped her hand. "But there's something weighing on your mind."

She glanced down at her coffee, then back. "I have only two things. The first: now that you have all of your memories, did you know this Angel before?"

He sat back, staring past her. Unfocused.

Hekka let a few moments pass before commenting. "My brothers discussed the thousand-yard stare. I understand."

"I have the memories restored from Rorschach's archives, and those I've acquired since my crash."

"I see. So you have no prior knowledge of this Angel woman."

"What else?"

"The second has to do with me. With my father gone, it is the most important thing for me to do. To achieve my own closure. Someday, you must take me to Finland."

Happy for the subject change, he relaxed. "It's about your mother, isn't it? Please tell me what happened."

Hekka moved uncomfortably in her seat. She had never had someone outside her family with whom to discuss such matters of the heart. "Years ago, she was summoned home. Her parents were quite ill, we were told. Father and I had never been without her."

"Something happened to her?"

"For the duration of my entire life, she and my father were a single entity. Inseparable."

"Didn't they communicate while she was away?"

"No. Once she was gone, nothing. Ever. It's why my father just sits there … sat there … in his chair each day, as if he had been emptied. He still expressed his love for me and my brothers, but it was like his fire had been reduced to embers."

"When we're finished here, I'll take you. I promise."

"Thank you, Magus."

Just then, the sounds of a distant crash interrupted their thoughts. It was beyond their view, but not far. And quite loud.

Fifteen minutes passed as they played with the remaining truffles, eating a few. Pensive. On impulse, Crayle pulled a tablet computer from his bag. Activated by the heat of his hands, it switched on automatically and selected a local news station.

An English-language version followed an initial exposition in the local Germanic dialect.

"*Breaking news.* A major accident has occurred. A black Mercedes has just been struck … by a trolley. A man has been pronounced dead at the scene … wait … we have identification … Karl Kobler, a banker, was killed instantly. There is little of the car remaining. According to eyewitnesses, a young woman jumped from the vehicle just prior … oh, she was taken in an ambulance … wait! … oh, there has been a second tragedy … the ambulance has plunged over an embankment … into the Limmat River on the north side of Zurich. I am hearing that the strong Winter currents are dragging the vehicle westward, toward confluence with the Aare River, and then in the direction of the Rhine. It will be some time before we learn the woman's condition, name, or of her relationship, if any, to Herr Kobler. The only item found at the scene, a black bag. Just an empty black bag."

"Shit!" yelled Crayle. He jumped from the chair. He grabbed Hekka's hand. "It's Pattie! She's got the diamonds!"

CHAPTER 19

Pattie Norbrunn crawled from the River Limmat thirteen miles downstream from Zurich at the spa town, Baden. She shivered from her sopped clothing and wished she could partake of the town's Roman-era hot springs. As she distanced herself from any search pattern, she sought a compact from her waterproof purse, which made a hiss as she unzipped what doubled as a flotation device.

Compact in hand, she took a look. She winced. Her makeup had run, and her hair drizzled river water. Within the first block, she entered a clothing boutique, claiming a weaving bicyclist had bumped her into the river. Could they help this frightened and shivering young victim?

The clerks looked at the distraught figure. In unison, they provided the typical Swiss answer, *"Ja, ja."*

In minutes, she'd undressed, been dried, clothed, and sent on her way. Her darling smile and a sincere *danke schön* satisfied the clerks. In Switzerland, helping someone in need represented an honor. The 500 Euro note she passed to them for their trouble—merely a bonus.

Pattie, no stranger to the Germanic northeast quarter of the small nation, used a sequence of public transportation busses and trolleys. She arrived back at her staging location, the grand hotel Bauer au Lac, in just over an hour.

"Where have you been, my sweet? I've been worried." In attempting to rub his eyes awake, Randy Norbrunn did not notice her complete change of attire. "The economic malaise of Europe is spreading here, as extremists seek to blame capitalists … and their bankers."

"I'll be more careful, darling Randy."

"So, where've you been?"

Pattie stood at a crossroads in her life. This she realized full well. "I just took a walk to appreciate this beautiful city. That's all." She excluded mention of her undercover meet with Kobler, Crayle, and the lovely Hekka Poppi. And the subsequent dispatch of the banker. And the ambulance crew. "But you're right, as usual. I feel much safer with you. I think I'll change out of these clothes. After a brisk walk, they're a bit ripe. I'll take a shower. Teddy?" she teased, flushing a bright red.

"Ooh. I can't wait. You are so sexy in a Teddy."

"Sexy? Must I remind you, Mr. Norbrunn, that you are a Calvinist?"

"You make me forget—it's not your fault, I mean—just for a moment."

Pattie was relieved. Inside the bedroom, she closed the door and stripped naked. Placing her new clothes in a CIA travelling burn bag, she pulled a new outfit from the dresser and closet. Next, she took a satisfying, burning hot shower, where she relieved the day's tensions, and donned her traveling attire.

When she finished, she found Randy seated at the kitchen table, reading the *Neue Zürcher Zeitung* and munching on nuts from a bowl. A kettle steamed on a cook top.

His refreshed wife extracted her compact from her purse. "Would you like some tea … or me?" She smiled coyly as she moved to the kitchen counter.

Her diplomat husband relished the 234-year-old newspaper's accurate depiction of the stock market and its neutrality in assessing international affairs. Attempting to follow the in-depth intellectual banter for which the paper was famous, he didn't look up. "Don't forget that I take honey as a sweetener."

As he chuckled, she held her compact over the teacup and pumped the lid with her thumbs. Opaque drops, with honey flavoring, plunged into the steaming liquid. "Here, darling, just as you like it."

In just seconds, the additive took effect. She removed the cup as Randy rested his head on the table.

She sat next to him and glanced into his eyes. "You've been a wonderful husband, my darling. It is with great sorrow that I must leave you. I know you love me with all your heart, and that makes this exceptionally difficult. Well, not really. You see, my dearest, it was actually a simple decision. Stay in this life with you and someday become an ambassador's wife … or travel an alternate path and become queen of France. You do understand?"

Randy could not answer. He could only listen. A solitary tear ran down his cheek.

"But I will provide you my full ritual."

She twisted the compact's lid, then reached over with the bladed compact and sliced a small line across his neck. Blood oozed onto the table as she walked to the refrigerator, retrieving a carton of ice cream. Removing a cone from her purse, she pressed one scoop on top. She turned to the immobile man a few feet away. "I know that you'll understand that I never waste this sort of situation, Randy."

Cone in hand, she returned to her seat and began to seek her own pleasure with her fingers. As she saw the light failing in her husband's eyes, she proceeded to her climax. At the precious instant of his expiration, she raised the cone to her lips, and bit hard into the frozen substance. "Ahhh!" she cried. "Oh! Ahhh!"

And then, it was over. Still gasping for breath, she applied her lipstick to the walls to indicate that some anti-capitalist extremists had penetrated the sacred boundaries of Swiss capitalism and had targeted the American Deputy Chief of Mission. And had kidnapped his wife.

Pattie Norbrunn had now murdered, among countless others, her CIA handler's wife, a Swiss banker, and her diplomat husband. She stepped one last time into the bathroom, removing her makeup and washing out the hair color with special creams to reveal another persona, a redhead with freckles.

A thought intruded. She'd enjoyed her role with the diamond seller in Amsterdam. In truth, she'd liked the taste of him. He had been a little skittish, but she'd liked that, too. She'd believed, in error, that she could convince him to help her fence her newly-acquired pound of diamonds. Too bad.

She also liked his friend, the young Frenchman, although he was often too business-like to make love to her. She considered the prospect of killing him if she bedded him again.

She leaned close to the mirror, producing a fog with her enhanced breathing.

Then, with her little finger on the fogged mirror, she wrote RLP.

She stepped back, her psychosis complete.

• • •

The next day, the Swiss Police received a call from a hysterical maid at the Bauer au Lac. Performing her normal duties, she had walked in on a grisly murder scene. She erroneously reported the mirror visual as the letters RIP. From the maid's sparse report, the authorities initially categorized the gruesome event as a mercy killing by a native English speaker.

Later, two detectives on scene examined the evidence Pattie had planted.

"Clearly, this was an act of anti-capitalist radicals, who had indeed kidnapped the poor wife of the dead American."

"*Klar*," responded the second man. "It is clear."

The detectives were sure of something else. Whatever the perpetrators' identities or motives, they'd messed with the Swiss national meal ticket. There would be hell to pay.

CHAPTER 20

Given near-perfect weather, the flight from Hong Kong covered the 300 mile distance in one hour. The team of Chin's daughters—Black, Red, Gold, Green, Blue, Purple, and new Beige—descended on the large, southern Chinese island of Hainan.

The girls sat along the sides of a remodeled flatbed truck as it trundled away from the capitol, replete with skyscrapers, of Haikou. The city of just over two million at the *mouth of the sea*, as its name translated, quickly transformed into farms. As the team of young women entered a dense forest, Black daughter read them in.

"We shall use this island as it has been traditionally used, to harbor political prisoners. Some of us will be stationed here for a brief time—then leave—never to return. You will train. You will monitor and correct the prisoners. Above all, you must keep them imprisoned. To do so, you must understand this island."

"It sounds simple. Simply keep them imprisoned." Red daughter's understudy had been killed in Victoria. Her replacement, new to the clan of Chin's acquired progeny, had just turned thirteen.

"This island is separated from the southern mainland of our country by a narrow and shallow straight called Qiongzhou. If you allow these once-powerful prisoners to get to the north end of the island, they can easily cross and become a threat to Father. There are several ethnicities in this place, and even more dialects. You will receive training in them and be expected to practice with one another. As you know, Father always places an emphasis on education."

"With all the education, at some point, we will be smarter than Father," said new Beige. She turned to be appreciated by the others, but they all averted their glances.

Black took note and continued. "Other escape routes are the many rivers originating in the center and flowing radially to the coast. As you can tell by the warm temperature in mid-December, we are in the tropics and escaped prisoners can hide indefinitely. What does this mean?"

"They must not escape," Green reinforced.

"How much force can we apply … to ensure they do not escape?" It seemed Red increasingly expressed a desire to commit violence. Something to watch out for.

"All force necessary." Black threw three quick moves that defined a two-second execution. The others stared awestruck at her finality and grace. "Any questions relating to this critical matter?"

They all knew the rules of Chin. They waited in silence for additional instruction. As they did, the truck became enveloped in White Pines, plum-yews, and coconut palms. Because of the dense forestation, visibility was cut to less than fifty yards.

"You are lucky. The monsoons and typhoons drop over sixty inches of rain in the Summer season. If you should irritate Father," she glanced at new Beige, "you may find yourself back here. Oh, I almost forgot. In the next few months, the island will be shrouded in fog. Better to cover an escape, but not good for us."

The truck finally bounced its way into a compound. There were a few large buildings and an area of hard-packed dirt for parking. There were no other vehicles.

"Li's forces have brought the remainder of the People's Republic leadership to this old factory complex. It remains from the Mao Tse-tung era," Black informed. "As on the mainland, the island was governed by party and functionary elements. The party elements, for obvious purposes, have been added to the other political prisoners."

"They fabricated washing machines … and dryers here," said new Beige.

Black smiled, eyeing her with care. The girl's Beige predecessor had spoken up during a Chin soliloquy in the Dragon Building training room. She had finished out the day in a burial plot. "I'll continue. The facility has been reconfigured as a barracks and production facility for the re-issue Terra Cotta Warriors in demand worldwide. Their popularity is such that a billionaire, a Mr. Soros, has his butler and staff dress in their manner."

Because their world had been necessarily small, none knew of the referenced individual. Still, they understood the high level of arrogance that would require such a charade. They entered the old factory, taking seats in the final row of the auditorium.

"Good afternoon, my countrymen," boomed a voice from the front wall.

Looming over the entire room was the portrait countenance of Father, Chin Yao-wu. Black glanced at the ceiling, the hundreds of dangling steel shafts a familiar sight. The daughters gathered a collective breath as Chin continued.

"General Li's men have brought you here for your retirement. I regret that I can't be with you in person, but this huge screen will serve a similar purpose. As you have demanded of the common people, you will be required to earn your keep. Your choices are necessarily limited. Now that I own this entire island, there is no longer a tourist trade, only a terra cotta mine. Here, you will create an army like never before. For the new emperor. Me."

The comment drew gasps, but no dialog from the prisoners save one. The former Communist Party Secretary jumped up from his seat in the second row. "Chin Yao-wu," he spat. "There will be no warriors. There will be no emperor. You must return us to Beijing. I demand it!"

There was absolute silence as the gathered watched Chin's reaction. He lifted a remote control, and pressed a button.

Whoosh came a rush of air from above. As it was in the Dragon Building training room, a silver bolt fired down into the skull of the Secretary.

Crack!

His lifeless body flopped over the front row.

"Should you choose not to participate, you shall be relegated to the island's new sport. It is here that I will train my assassins. Do I make myself clear?"

A hush fell over the captives. Chests heaved. Careful glances, left and right.

"That may sound cruel, but it was your governmental predecessor, an official in my home province, who raped my mother. I am the product of that horrendous event. I saw to justice over that horrible man. Your kind ceded the absolute power, which he used for evil. I now have commandeered such power, but for the good of our people. Because of my own disbeliefs, I see morality through non-religious eyes. You, by your actions, have created what I shall call a debt in the cosmos. You will repay that cosmic debt here, and beyond."

Heads spun side-to-side and from the row in front to the row behind. Whispers, harsh whispers. This man had dismantled their world. Who knew what to do?

"My daughters and Li's guards will see you to your quarters. Perhaps the following irony will not escape you. All clothing, toiletries, and nourishment have been defined for you by my people. And there will be no sex. Sensors have been installed in all showers to detect motion more rapid than deemed necessary. In my mother's memory, of course."

The captives stood, preparing to be marched to their barracks. Each understood. Everything they now possessed or could utilize would be provided by Chin. One committee member, the one who had always come up with bad ideas in the past, seized the opportunity.

"He can't kill us all. If he did, there would be no one to build his warriors. We must stand together—"

Whoosh!

CHAPTER 21

The Hong Kong dawn gave way to a partly cloudy canopy with a light breeze. On days such as this, the clouds morphed from shape to shape like a Disney cartoon. However, this day was serious.

Chin Yao-wu and General Li lounged in extreme comfort. The top floor room of the Dragon Building faced the island's most prominent feature, Victoria Peak. They clinked glasses for the fifth time.

"Do you see the activity, Li? Do you know what it means?"

"It would be difficult to miss the bulldozers and earthmovers, the scurrying workers, and the transformation as the central keep takes shape. Soon the walls of your new compound will be in place. You have proven that the right resources, mustered under authority, can accomplish miracles."

"Yes, Li. My reign—my legacy—will chronicle one success after another. We shall become a model for the world."

"The world, as you have termed it, is crumbling under its own political obesity. Radical change was required and, in a way, we have accomplished in our country a second revolution."

"Might I correct you, my friend and ally? Revolutions are of and by the people. We have simply replaced a governance." Chin smiled while his mind processed the status change he had indicated. Perhaps a vertical friendship was in order, preserving the chain-of-command.

"Simply?" The general shook his head. "We have detonated two nuclear weapons in our homeland. Beijing is a model of devastation. Tens of thousands died."

"We achieved our goal. Beijing is no longer the seat of power, and the bomb in our western province destroyed the internal Islamic threat."

"We must drink to that."

"Blue! Where is she?"

"With the others in Hainan. You dispatched Black, Red, Blue, Green, Purple, Gold, and new Beige to that purpose, I believe."

"Yellow!" Chin cried out. "A fine single malt! The oldest!"

"You knew that the youngest would not have travelled. Your mind never ceases to amaze me."

"It is a fine gift from my sainted mother."

"Sainted. That raises the question of religion in the new China. It is an entity that would compete with your authority."

"An issue we must resolve. Other regimes have attempted to suppress it, but in so doing, repressed the human spirit. The spirit must live for us to prosper and thrive. It is a conundrum, Li. One we must solve."

"Perhaps the master problem solver, Magus Crayle, could assist."

"Hmmm." Chin's intellectual light switched to bright. "Write this down, Li. Find Crayle. Track him. When he has finished with Monsieur Lalumière, and I'm confident he will, bring him back. Engage him. Send Black … and Red." He smiled.

"But the ceremony. It is just days hence."

"Write it. Black. Red. And an assistant. New Beige. Remember that Crayle is a danger magnet—his luck will not last forever. Send the message. At once. Use our knock-off of the American NSA's internal encryption technique."

"There is a problem. We don't know where he is."

"We must access the Rorschach computer. Crayle's strategies would exist there, would they not?"

Li sat back. He had, of necessity, not informed Chin that his technical wizard, Gao, had cloned the Rorschach system. Problem two: memories were to be restored in the subject from which they were taken. Gao was the only one who knew about the system. And the only candidate for restoration. Of course, if the process destroyed Gao's mind, that would eliminate a threat. "I will set about determining Crayle's whereabouts."

"Move quickly."

Li stood, bowed, and departed the room. He returned in twenty minutes.

• • •

Li glanced at the construction. "Already you provide jobs."

"And for all to see." Chin waved his glass across the panorama.

"When will the palace, your palace, be complete?"

"By Spring, Li. You will have sumptuous apartments worthy of a warrior." He stopped the train of thought. "I have reached a momentous decision."

Li appeared shocked. It was the realization that big, unilateral decisions would be the purview of the new emperor. He would have to remain careful and vigilant. Co-opting a daughter or two might be a necessary ploy.

"I am taking you deep into my trust. I have told no one else what I am about to tell you. My decision is in reference to my twelve daughters. As you are aware, they were conscripted at age 13 to be trained and educated to my purpose. I have kept them close at hand and have shared my world views. For my own protection, and you will appreciate this, I formulated a policy."

"You are a man of such high intellect, Chin, I am sure your decisions are sound."

"My daughters were given the incentive to leave me at age 20. They were informed that they would receive full support—school, whatever they chose."

"But their knowledge of your plans would make them serious potential threats?"

"Precisely. Their maturation and matriculation were rewarded with a premature exodus from the world of the living."

"Death?"

"Death."

"I am not a heartless man, but I must ask … no, it is too personal."

"Black daughter?"

The general hesitated to enter further discussion. The addition of a bond of friendship on top of their professional linkage bode potential disaster.

"I have seen your reaction to her …" Chin smiled. "… and it is understandable. And I have detected a possible romantic future for you."

Li couldn't believe his ears. "If I may interrupt, you refer to the ideal match between myself and …"

"You bait me, General, but yes. Red daughter."

"But …" Li wanted to announce his outright lust for Black, but swallowed his protest. The minefield of friendship loomed large. "They are no longer to be executed?"

"No." Chin walked to the window, unaware that Li had previously discovered the future emperor's intercourse-free homage to a raped, dead mother. The general knew he must keep that playing card to himself.

Yellow refilled their glasses. Chin used the occasion to change the subject. "We must discuss Mr. Crayle."

"Ah, yes. The American spy lives on—harder to kill than a Brazilian mosquito."

"You've travelled to Brazil?"

"Once. A beautiful Brazilian soothed my pain, in many ways. But I'm afraid the alcohol, Caipirinhas, caused me to speak more than I should have."

"Were you forced to ..." Chin drew his forefinger across his throat.

"An unfortunate lapse. When I awoke, she was gone. A check of my wallet revealed that all of my money was missing. She was just a whore, masquerading as a flight attendant."

Chin shook his head in affirmation, but considered the general's loose life a potential liability. He noted the coincidence with respect to Flori, the flight attendant who doubled as Neil Wohlford's CIA operative. "Is your drink up to your expectations?"

General Li smiled.

"I'm afraid I was too abrupt earlier. I apologize, but Crayle is of major import. At this point, we are all but owners of our country. He has received memory restorations that would be extremely dangerous to us if revealed. On first examination, he should be eliminated."

"First examination?"

"Governance is a monumental task. History has demonstrated that no known ideology produces even modest success. Crayle proved to me, with mathematics, that ideologies—those labels ending in *ism*—are capable of benefitting no more than 13% of a population."

"That can't be correct."

"A mathematical certainty. The rest of the population, 87% or more, is damaged. Every time. He showed me, Li. He used the Soviet Union as an example. Seventy years of absolute rule under Commun*ism* harmed all but the privileged few. In our country, the far left of Communism had to be balanced by the far right of Capitalism. Still not enough, since they are both radical ideologies."

"I see. So prior to our coup, only 26% could benefit."

"Something like that." Chin remembered Crayle mentioning the combinatorics of ideologies—whatever that meant.

"Then what would he counsel us to do?" For the first time, the general became nervous about what they had accomplished.

"I couldn't disagree with him. History supports his numbers and formulas. Greece, Spain, Portugal, Italy, France, Sweden, and on it goes. The ideologies have failed and failed predictably. I will not let that happen to us. Mr. Crayle proposed a failure-proof solution grounded in his mathematical methodology. Like our Blackstone Strategy, it can't fail." Chin had just accomplished the ultimate tease. "I'll show it to you, in broad strokes, another time. Never forget that the man, the genius, enabled us to pull off the greatest *coup d'état* in history. He could help us in the governance arena like no other."

"We would have to co-opt him to that purpose. My men could kidnap someone he loves."

"Too heavy handed, I'm afraid. And too late. The only one he had, the Indian woman, is gone. Still, a willing Crayle would provide us an immense advantage. An un-willing Crayle … could plan us into oblivion."

"A tough decision. Given that we couldn't even destroy him with our mini-nuke explosions in Marseille and Beijing."

"Yes, Li. We seem to have a quite difficult puzzle to solve. We'll call it our Crayle Conundrum."

Chin saw to it that suitable erotics were delivered to Li in their conference aftermath. A lure away from Black.

CHAPTER 22

Even with the lateness of the season, sunshine was in abundance. It caused the tall, light-brown sandstone formations to appear as cigar-shaped clusters, pointing at the heavens. Its appearance of serrated ridges had earned it the name, Montserrat. At 4,017 feet above sea level, the air was only moderately thin. Although peaceful in appearance, the activity in its large monastery, with its numerous eclectically sized and shaped structures that clung high on the mountain's side, spoke otherwise.

"Have you seen her, Mother Superior?"

"Who, my dear?"

"The new one. Sister Magdalena. The one who replaces Sister Catherine."

"Please don't mention that … that woman's name in my presence. I have relegated her to the Monastery of Santa Cecília. I am quite pleased that it would take her at least an hour's walk to return here to annoy me."

"I believe she had some good qualities." Sister Laura teased. "She was inquisitive."

"I will not tolerate such nonsense. Things are what they are."

"You mean, they are what the old white guys say they are."

Realizing that the younger woman was trying to find her last nerve, she changed the subject. "Bring her in."

Sister Laura found the young one waiting in the vestibule and fetched her into the nave.

The nun, small in stature, looked at the floor in deference and curtseyed.

"It's okay, Sister Magdalena. This is Montserrat. We are less formal. Less hierarchical."

The newbie looked up, pleased at her acceptance. Her rounded face produced a dimpled smile.

"That will be all, Sister Laura. I will send for you should the need arise." She turned to her new charge. "Come take a seat. I will inform you of your chores and other responsibilities here at Montserrat."

Once Sister Laura closed the door behind her, the new nun spoke for the first time. "I have a secret, Mother Superior. You see, I'm here to collect one of your hermits from up on the rocks."

"You can't do that. They are called hermits for a reason. Only food and supplies may be delivered, and that without visually engaging the man."

"This particular man has places to go and people to see. I need your permission for the ride up the funicular to the top."

"Insolence will not serve you well, Sister."

"There won't be any insolence removal," Magdalena informed the older woman. She raised her cross as if to defend herself against the devil. "Do you see the size of my cross? Some say that the cross must be proportional to one's need for salvation." She turned it upside down, grasping the short vertical member as a handle. With her other hand, she whipped off the longer piece to reveal a four-inch blade.

"You seem to be in my way, Mother Superior."

• • •

The pathway veered close to a precipitous drop. The trek would have been difficult enough without the multitude of white stones that slowed her progress. Nevertheless, the fearless little nun forged ahead, stopping only once to peer down into the valley below.

Her journey from the upper—Catalan-named—*Sant Joan* funicular station should take twenty minutes, Mother Superior had informed her before she was required to die. The inclement weather added another twenty-five minutes before she applied a gentle tap to the oaken portal of the stone hermitage cottage.

"Oui?" came from within.

"C'est moi, Mitim."

The door creaked open to reveal a weary-looking man.

"Good," said the nun. "The full beard causes you to look like a proper recluse. No one would recognize you."

The man appeared dysfunctional. "I've been isolated here for more than a week. Here," he said, indicating a tray of food. "Have some of my cold Brussels Sprouts and broccoli."

"I'll pass." Without further ado, she removed her habit, revealing a black, red-trimmed bra with matching panties. "Feast on this."

The violent sex completed and France's number one fugitive fully relaxed, the nun continued her mission. She replaced her holy garments, speaking in brief. "Good news. We're outta here, Sylvain. Headed north."

Weakened by his most recent confinement and the sex, he spoke softly. "Not another prison. There have been two … no, more. I will remain in this place until I die." He pressed open a window.

"Do you hear those sirens? They're coming here. It seems there's been a violent death down below."

The hermit turned to face her.

"It was you! You can't stop!"

"What I must do is complete my mission."

Lalumière stumbled to the window. "You must promise me … no more prisons … no more isolation … no more captivity. Or I'll jump." He leaned out.

"Look down."

He did. He leapt back.

"You don't like heights. Look, come with me now. We're leaving for the low ground. You'll be safe. You must trust me." In nun garb and with a sincere look, she recaptured him.

They clasped hands and headed for the funicular, careful not to topple over the precipice that capped Montserrat.

• • •

The Spanish *policía* serpentined up the two-lane switchbacks of Montserrat. There were no high spirits regarding a new case to solve. The tone was dour. The two vehicles' occupants hated violence at the monastic compound. In transit alone, the trip added two hours to their day. Each way. They didn't even notice the maroon Spanish-made SEAT Léon sports coupé edging its way past, nor the nun and heart attack candidate dressed as a hermit. They sought a murderer. And from accounts of the crime scene, a psychopath.

CHAPTER 23

After a long drive, and a special stop, a tired and frustrated Lalumière vented. "Picking that obscure automobile was clever, but asking it to pull a trailer with an animal up into the Pyrenees was too much." Though he loved his country dearly, he wasn't really sure whether a French auto would fare better.

"Who would question a nun and a pilgrim—and you look the part—on the road of the great Saint James pilgrimage to Santiago de Compostela in the northwest of Spain? Remember the old man a few miles back who told his son and daughter that our donkey—Otie—would be used for the actual trek, just as they were in olden days."

"We are not on a trek and our transportation … *c'est finis.*"

"My darling, CIA plans don't always pan out, but we agents are resourceful. The car died. Otie becomes our backup."

Before they could release the donkey from the trailer, a car slowed, then pulled off the road. The driver popped out of his car and approached them. Short and squat, he conveyed attitude.

"We have trouble with the car," Pattie pleaded. "Please help."

He laughed. "A nun and her hermit friend certainly can't present a danger to me. So I stopped, but only to change cars with you."

She placed his accent as east Texas. "You will give us your wonderful car. Bless you."

"That was the good news. The bad news? The expensive car you see ahead … is stolen." He jumped into their vehicle and began to manipulate under the dash.

"Help me," the nun whispered to the hermit. They removed Otie and pulled him uphill to the BMW. "One second."

She returned to the car and hopped into the back seat.

"If you're abandoning your hermit for me, you'll have to forget the celibacy."

She couldn't see the smirk on his face. No need.

Quickly, she removed her special beads and twisted the string around the man's neck. He struggled, but her positioning and the headrest thwarted him. He slumped across the console.

"Don't kill him. Please." The hermit pressed his palms together.

"He's only unconscious."

"What will we do? We can't take his car, because it is stolen. We can't take this one, because it is broken."

"Watch." She maneuvered around the slumped body and into the driver's seat. After yanking the gearshift into neutral and pulling her habit tight around her, she dove free of the car just as it started to roll backwards. The tandem of car and trailer twisted and screeched until it reached the first turn. It sailed over the cliff into a chasm below. The terrain amplified all of the horrific sounds.

"You *did* kill him!" Lalumière shrieked.

"I didn't kill him. I was polishing my beads." She displayed them for inspection.

"You killed him!"

"Did not."

"Yes. You killed him!"

"No, no, no, no. It was the fall."

• • •

"Must I continue to ride? This inferior animal moves like a snail with a hip displacement. I feel my kingdom slipping away."

"Have faith, Mitim. That's what this is about."

"There is much more to this than having faith. I have a bad feeling that Mr. Crayle will not allow me to escape this time. If he finds me, he will end my life and with it, my hope."

"He will never look for a Spanish pilgrim or a nun leading said pilgrim to the promised land."

"We are travelling north in the Pyrenees mountains. That man is brilliant … he will find us. There is no kingdom in this place. And we have no weapons."

"Whoa there, Otie." Pattie pulled heavily on the donkey reins.

The donkey, sensing danger, stopped.

"We travel at the pace of my diminutive legs attached to my diminutive body. If you want faster, Brother Mitim, you will have to walk while *I* ride."

They switched places. The bearded Mitim picked up the pace. Sister Magdalena felt the rhythm of the saddle astride Otie. She moved forward, angled herself against the horn, and worked herself to the limit.

Passersby gaped at the orgasming nun.

"Mother! Father! Look!" shouted a child in Catalan.

The Frenchman took five more steps and stopped. He gave a quizzical look. "What manner of Spanish name is Otie?" asked the man who would be king.

"Do you remember Cervantes?"

He stopped abruptly. "I see." He grinned for the first time in a long time. "He is Donkey Otie."

The nun sighed.

"And what did you pay for this grand and historical animal?"

"Sex. Always sex."

Mitim's smile faded. "And death."

The terrain morphed into a valley road. It ran alongside a hill. Below, a large city loomed. A strange out-of-character structure punctuated its far side.

"We've reached Andorra la Vella, this tiny nation's capitol. It is respite from the Catalonians to the east, who hate the Spanish, and the Basques to the west. They, too, hate the Spanish."

"I know of them from my studies. The Catalonians, with their trading heritage, are excellent negotiators. The Basques, on the other hand, blow things up to get their way."

"Bingo! The exact pair of qualities required to take power … and keep it. Put them together and you have the next king of France."

He peered into a shop window and did not see king of anything. Then, something caught his attention. "What is that bizarre set of buildings in the distance?"

"A world-renowned spa. I plan to hide you there until I find us a motorized ride north."

"Into France?"

She nodded.

"Thank God."

"Sylvain." Eyes closed, she inhaled and then breathed out. "You are Illuminé. There is no god."

"Then, how can I become king? Kings are ordained by God. I must have a god!"

"Calm down. I believe you have a choice. Let me run it down for you. If you choose to become king, fine. And I, your queen consort."

"But—."

"Shhh! Should you, however, break with the Elder, he does not tolerate defiance. He would play me thus. 'Pattie, Sylvain has gone rogue, as they say. How would *you* like to be queen of the realm?' "

"But a queen is still ordained royalty."

"I become queen and marry Elder. Then, as king of France, he denounces the church. We become emperor and empress. I'm telling you, he targets a person's motivation."

"You would have to …"

"Oh, you're quick. So Plan B, becoming an emperor might be your best bet."

"But my son, Jean-Marc. There is no right-of-succession in empires."

"I'll personally see to Jean-Marc. You have my word."

Lalumière nodded, missing the subtlety of the world's deadliest female.

He did notice, however, that something seemed amiss with Sister Magdalena. He stepped close.

"Donkey Otie, Mitim. I have to be clever to be a … oh!" She grabbed her head with both hands. "Oh! My head! It hurts."

He pulled her to him.

"The pains are more frequent … and more painful. A pharmacy will have what I need. They are symbolized by a bright green cross. Do you see one nearby?"

He pointed. "Just two blocks away."

"You stay here. Mind Otie." With that, she wandered down the street.

Sylvain Lalumière suddenly realized that he stood alone in a strange land, looking like a hermit, and in the company of a donkey.

CHAPTER 24

Magus, we've been in this place for two days now."

"Today is December 17. I gather from the newspapers that there's still no plan to pull the French government together in the wake of the Marseille explosion. Lalumière can't force it with another bomb. He needs the one he has, and if we believe Chin, the only one he will ever have, to wipe them out and create a political vacuum."

"I understand, but where are our allies? We need them." Hekka scanned the scene as if seeking obscured answers.

"I haven't heard from Jack in a while. Phoebe and Micmac are still in Washington, D.C."

"What about the private investigator? He could help."

"Lenny was headed for Amsterdam last I remember. I believe he's gone dark, trying to behave like an operative."

She looked up at him, her face plaintive. "We can't do this alone, can we?"

He looked at her. He had learned long ago not to even suggest that she leave for a much safer place. Without her head scarf, he could see the groove on the left side of her head. From Vancouver. Just millimeters had spared her life.

"I'll call Phoebe. What time is it in D.C.?"

• • •

"It's afternoon over there, Mick. I wonder what Magus and Hekka are doing."

"You're worried."

"Yeah. I wanted to tell my boss the whole story today. Everything that's happened. And about the bomb that's either headed for, or already in, France."

"But you realized they'd either lock you up … or debrief you for days, maybe weeks."

They studied each other for several seconds.

"I'll call."

Phoebe reached for the special cell-sat phone she'd left with Micmac for safekeeping while reporting in at the office.

"Hello?"

"Hello?"

"It didn't even ring," Crayle and the Agent said in unison.

They laughed hard. It indicated the degree of tension that remained.

"Phoebe, what's up? Are you still in D.C.?"

"Affirmative. I did the obligatory sit down. I pulled the 'it's classified' crap on my boss. Pissed him off." She dragged out the last sentence. "FYI on the FBI. It always ticks us off when spook-types pull that shit."

"And now you *are* one."

"Yeah. He said he needed me back in service, but I pulled the *I have to take vacation or lose it* routine. I nearly had to perform CPR."

"What then?"

"I don't particularly like the guy, so I might've had to pull the manual on the CPR stuff. So I'd get it right. Could've taken a while."

Crayle could tell. She was smiling now. "How much time do you have?"

"A month. Don't have to be back 'til … mmmm … January 16. Of course, I may not have to go back at all with all those diamonds you liberated in Kaohsiung."

"Uh, yeah. Well, they've changed hands."

"Uh, oh."

"I need you both in Amsterdam."

"*I* may need the CPR," she huffed. "Really? You're serious? You don't have the diamonds?"

"Remember the little spy you first met as Anne-Isabel?"

"Yes, I do. That lying little twerp turned out to be Pattie something from the American Embassy in Paris."

"Pattie Norbrunn is Neil Wohlford's CIA asset working out of the Embassy. Long story short, she grabbed the diamonds and has gone rogue over to Lalumière's side. No more CIA handlers or controls."

"I knew she was no good."

"The odds are that she'll use the Frenchman's fence in Amsterdam to exchange the diamonds for some cash."

"I thought Lalumière had cash in Switzerland. Wasn't that why you went there?"

"She killed the banker. They need the cash to complete the job."

"You want us in Amsterdam and you want us to relieve her of the stones … with extreme prejudice. Right?" Under her breath she whispered, *please say yes*.

"We need the rocks, so you need to intercept her." He provided the office address of Lenny's brother.

"On the card?"

"Jack's black. Next plane, Dulles to Schiphol. Oh, and be sure to make it First Class."

"Stick it to Jack. I like that."

"The money comes from *We the People*, Phoebe."

"We get screwed again!"

"To be clear: your mission is to intercept Pattie in Amsterdam, take her out, and grab the stones."

"Speaking of Stones, did you catch what the president just did?"

"Kimbel? No."

"He gave Iran a deadline regarding their nuclear program. It passed. He took out Tehran."

"Son … of … a … bitch!"

"Yeah. America is *back!*"

"An American president with backbone. That'll change the political landscape. Alright, back on point. Given the time, you'll be doing an overnight. Text me when you arrive. Code it. Say something about being seduced. Maybe Micmac will take the hint."

"Forget Micmac. Seduced by those beautiful little crystals they have there in Amsterdam, one of which is destined for my ring finger."

Crayle heard an indecipherable grunt in the background.

"Get yourselves on a plane ASAP. Dress warm."

"Roger that," Micmac tossed in the phone's direction.

Crayle disconnected. He turned to Hekka. "They're still in D.C., but Phoebe played the use-it-or-lose-it vacation card. They'll be in Europe tomorrow!"

Hekka smiled. Then, she laughed. She watched the energy reappear in the man before her. With that spark and his intelligence, they would have a fresh start. They would find, and they would take down, the monster who would do so much damage and kill so many people for his own selfish gain. She felt her love resurge and reassert itself once again. They would triumph.

CHAPTER 25

The Falcon 7X belonging to Jack Sommers Airlines entered Dutch airspace in the early afternoon. A flurry of snow had blown through the region overnight, but the last vestiges of white had disappeared as the plane touched the tarmac. The pair deplaned and, with luggage that would have alerted submachinegun-toting security in an instant, passed through a special incarnation of customs without so much as a passport check.

Phoebe stopped first, setting her boogie-bag on an empty wheelchair. Realizing he was walking alone, Micmac turned and retraced to where she stood. Hands on hips.

"Why is it again that you followed me back to Washington for the impromptu required meeting with my FBI boss?"

"Phoebe, my dear, I would love to take credit for being ever by your side. So, I will. I prevailed on Magus to send us both. That way, when we deployed back to Europe, we could move as a team."

"Nice try. He put us together because he didn't want you to be taken from me while I was away. Magus is a romantic."

Micmac took a second. "Yeah, but who loves you?"

Her traditional demeanor disappeared. Eyes glistening, smiling broadly, she leaped into his arms and whispered her answer in his ear.

He groaned, the pain from two bullet wounds still in evidence.

The forecasted temperature—a typical 39 degrees Fahrenheit—had prompted Agent Bransfield to don a charcoal, rolled-collar wool coat over three layers. Given his arm and shoulder wounds, the former UDT man carefully lowered his bundle of woman. "The blonde hair fits right in."

"When our time comes, and it will, we won't live in a place that is cold. Ever. I'm thinking San Diego."

He nodded his agreement. "Okay, super-spook Bransfield. I'm in need of some operational intel. What do you know about this place?"

She withdrew a book from her bag and waved it before him. "I know what I picked up while reading this wonderful tour guide on the plane. There are 800,000 folks of whom half are Dutch and the rest, Other. There are canals everywhere. The government allows sex-for-money and collects taxes. Apparently, the Dutch were slow to understand that their elected leaders were screwing them for money, so the politicians made it official. Lastly, I know that everyone here smokes pot and, therefore, that no one cares about the damn government."

"Lucky Lalumière is French. If he were here, he couldn't get the time of day from these people let alone their support."

"If we're gonna be spooks, we have to talk like them. Would you like some *actionable intel*? I heard Magus use that phrase."

"Okay. Okay. I'm not used to this spy shit. What do I use for cover? Navy SEAL, or does Underwater Demolitions sound more sneaky?"

Phoebe shook her head. "You're an American rock star. That, you can sell. We'll get you fake tattoos. Mess with your hair. Unbutton your shirt." She started with the top button.

"And you can be lead groupie." He smiled.

Phoebe stopped. Her hands went to her hips. "The crazed one. The stalker. Furious at being classified as one of those …"

"Did I say something wrong?" he teased.

"*Deadly* furious."

"My manager?"

"Perfect." The term manager trumped the term groupie, and put her in charge.

"Let's see. We'll need a cover story." Micmac screwed up his face for a few seconds. "Ah! I believe we need a diamond broker to turn our rock star piles of cash into something more portable."

"Yes." She smiled broadly. "Diamonds."

"Something special about a diamond?" He grinned.

Just in time, his inside forearm block deflected her right cross. It glanced off his healing shoulder.

"Ow!"

"I'm sensitive … about certain things."

He pulled her tight. "We're getting past this gig. There's a long, long life waiting. Together."

• • •

Leaving Amsterdam's Schiphol Airport, they passed two young men, one tall with long, dark, wavy hair and the other not so tall with a balding, well-tanned head. *Puff, the Magic Dragon* they played on their guitars. It seemed that it would have been right for another time. A short cab ride got the spies to downtown.

"Why is it you Navy guys always carry a duffel?"

"Sometimes we Navy men must move fast."

Phoebe patted her Glock through her coat pocket. "When I encourage you to pop the question, you'd better be movin' fast for my diamond."

"Yes, ma'am."

Satisfied, she asked the operative questions. "39?"

"It's up here on the right."

"And you know that how?"

"There it is!" Micmac pointed to a four-story row house.

Phoebe stowed her question—for the moment. A young-appearing, Playboy-esque redhead with braids was positioned behind the front window.

"Oh, look. Pippi Longstockings." No matter that her Army brat upbringing had educated her about service men and their proclivities, she bristled that *her* Navy man might ever have frequented such a place.

"That's not Pippi. It's her sister."

The FBI agent's lips pursed.

"Focus, Phoebe."

A petite blonde led them upstairs to an office labeled W. Silberweiss, Gemological Specialist.

"If you'll wait here ..." She motioned to a red velvet loveseat. "... he'll be with you shortly." She exited down the stairs.

"Did you see that? She had a bulge under her top."

"Two, actually."

The pair sat quietly on an eighteenth century loveseat for what seemed like fifteen minutes.

"The son-of-a-bitch has the Lenny Lipschitz *inconsiderate* gene. I'm going in." Phoebe cracked the door. "Holy shit!"

Micmac reached into his pocket, embracing his automatic. He followed her into the room, closing the door behind him.

On the desk ahead sat a black velvet tray. On its edge, a head rested. A pool of blood encroached on the surface, encircling the several diamonds in its path.

"Quick!" Phoebe grabbed a cloth and pressed hard on Wolfram Silberweiss' neck. "C'mon, man!" she hushed. "We need your ass!"

Micmac stepped forward and grasped her arm. "If you press hard enough to stop the bleeding, you close off blood to his brain. A cut across the throat is a one-way deal."

The door opened. Phoebe and Micmac spun, their weapons ready to engage. The man who entered dropped both of their jaws.

"*Wolfie!*" Lenny cried. Supported by the CIA-issue crutches he used for a cover, he stumbled forward. He glanced from his brother to the two. "You did this! Magus sent you!"

He stumbled as he lifted a crutch at Micmac. A shotgun blast blew a hole in the wall over the Navy man's head. Lenny, regaining his footing—his eyes wet—dropped the depleted crutch and raised the other.

Phoebe closed on him. "I'm sorry." She threw her signature right cross, knocking him cold.

Micmac yanked her away from the unconscious P.I. "Quick. The blonde. It was Anne-Isabel, uh, Pattie. We've got to catch her! The bulge you saw under her top … the diamonds!"

She grabbed his arm. "What about Lenny?"

"He can stay behind and bury his brother on his own time."

"Then, we're outta here."

Down the stairs, they ran past the door to the exhibition room. Inside, the spy-turned-psychopath sat in place of the usual redhead. She watched them run out of the brothel and down the street. In her lap, she fondled her razor-sharp sentry knife. The fresh blood stained her fingers.

CHAPTER 26

With success times three in his recent memory, Jean-Marc Lalumière was walking on air. He would meet the other royals, the ones who refused to co-locate with the Russian czarina due to fear for their lives and the future independence of their countries.

The Polish Baltic focal point, Gdansk, was murky, but a little less cold than Tallinn, the Estonian capital, had been. A fine rain wafted now and then. Jean-Marc settled for a British MacIntosh over a bulky sweater, cotton slacks, and silk thermal under-garments.

As he crossed the cobblestone and sand courtyard, he noticed the nearby jail and prison. After his father's incarceration in the Paris Bastille, he wanted to conclude the meeting and leave.

He'd visited the Malbork Palace long ago on a summer tour from graduate school. Restoration had produced a notable prewar likeness. He was certain that the famous red brick castle, ravaged by the Germans and Russians during the Second World War could, with luck, return to prominence.

His guests on this visit, the provisional royals, had arrived the prior day and had been housed in the Upper Castle dormitories. The

Middle and Lower Castles were devoid of anyone save armed guards. Today's gathering would take place in the "proposal" room, where visitors of an age gone by met with representatives of the monarch. Perfect for today's session.

The future controlling monarchs of Sweden, Denmark, and Norway had insisted on meeting together. Jean-Marc could feel their alliance even though the three sat far apart. A different approach, a less selfish one, would be required. In this case, he sought to impress the majority of the trio.

Spaced at an angle to each side of him, the future Polish king glared intensely at the German. He and the others had been forced to choose between a meeting that included the Russians, or this one. History considered, a difficult choice. "You know how we feel. So we will move forward. I would like to mention, however, that our countries are performing the best, and yours, Germany, is at the top of the list. We must work together to complete the overthrow of *all* democratically elected governments."

The German wore medals and adornments he couldn't possibly have earned, but so did the rest. "Candor is critical." His steel blue eyes bore into those of the Nordic royals. "We have observed the mother of all disruptive technologies. The mini-nuclear bombs, with their high-density radiation absorption, have initiated the change of history. In grand fashion, they have put Western democracies to the test. These systems of governance are approaching the breaking point. We must push them over the cliff."

The Norwegian spoke. "I suppose, had your predecessors achieved the nuclear bomb, we would be conducting this meeting in your native language, rather than English."

"English was proposed by the young Frenchman to remove such conflict. This is your meeting, Prince Lalumière. Please."

In his father's stead, Jean-Marc took the stage. "Your goals will coalesce with what is occurring in my country. Prior to World War II, Kaiser, your country blamed Jews for the catastrophic economic problems. With the pain of a loaf of bread costing a billion Deutsch

Marks, the masses were ready for a scapegoat. Hitler gave that to them."

The prospective Swedish queen had been silent. An avid chess player, she brought her skills to bear. "Your Iranian move created the potential. The Marseille move took it to the Muslim enclave in that city. France, already in economic chaos, was ripe. It appears that a diversionary move against the Americans was deemed necessary, to prepare for the final one. Checkmate."

Jean-Marc liked this woman. Intelligent, attractive, and adept in politics. He considered a special alliance. "Using your chess analogy, we have our government in check. We have also assured that they have no moves left. They will not move against the Muslims and have no money or credit left for anything. Soon, they will be a matter of historical insignificance."

"You can't just blow them up," said the Dane.

Jean-Marc glanced his way. He smiled. "As was the case in Beijing?"

"Why should we be sitting here, planning to rely on the Germans. They invaded Norway and Denmark."

"And forced we Swedes into neutrality," came the coy interjection from the queen.

Jean-Marc became frustrated. "Can't you all see? You are hamstrung by your pasts."

"Perhaps the young man is a burgeoning Metternich," mused the Dane.

"Was he not the diplomat who finally got Napoléon laid?" asked the German.

They all laughed.

"This is most serious business," Jean-Marc reminded. "Prince Metternich bedded many fine women, some of them royal, and in your very own homelands. Why, you could be his offspring."

Silence.

Then the German broke the long silence with a burst of laughter. The rest joined.

The German settled into a smile. "I believe I have some royal blood left. Gentlemen, and Lady, I believe we have our conduit, our catalyst. I propose a toast. A royal toast. Royalty *über alles*!"

"Royalty above all," the others mimicked.

They quaffed the fine champagne provided by their host. Northern Europe would, as the dominoes fell, return to monarchy. And not the hideous constitutional kind invented by the Scots.

CHAPTER 27

I know you said this may come in handy, Magus," Hekka Poppi sighed as she examined the trio of hair dyes. "I understand the hair and eyebrow requirement. What do they mean by privates?"

"The CIA wants to cover all circumstances. And before you ask, I love the color of your hair, eyebrows, and …"

"Privates?" She teased.

"… the way they are."

She replaced the items on the vanity and turned to him. "We've been hiding here for four days. I am becoming claustrophobic in this place."

"I have some good news in that department. I dropped by Kobler's bank this morning while you slept. The police are gone."

"That you can come and go while I sleep is not comforting."

"Do you realize what else I just said?"

"Then we can leave? Go home?" Her eyes wanted to sparkle.

"We are here with a little money and Jack's credit card. We've lost contact with Jack, Phoebe, Micmac, and Lenny. We have no clue where to find Lalumière and his nuclear bomb, and our best bet for intel, Kobler, is dead." He couldn't control his frustration.

"Oh." Her head dropped.

"If I say I could get you home on Jack's jet, you'll be even more upset."

"Yes, Mr. Crayle. You are correct." A smile replaced the gloom. "We are a team. We will see that whatever needs doing is done."

He sat next to her. "We're back to the same realization. Lalumière has to catch the French government in one place at one time to kill them all." His phone rang. "Yes?"

"Hi, Mag, it's Phoebe."

"My God! Where—"

"Listen."

"Go."

"We're in Amsterdam. We don't know where Lenny got to, but we found his brother. Dead."

"How?"

"It was that little shit from before. Anne-Isabel, or whoever the hell she is these days. We saw her leave."

"But why?"

"She likes to kill?" Phoebe posed her reply as a question.

"No. She took out Lalumière's moneyman here in Zurich. Now, it's his diamond guy. She's removing links. Let's see, who else? The people still living who know what she's done seem to be Jack, Neil, her husband—no, he wouldn't know. He's a diplomat."

"Would that be the Deputy Chief of Mission in Paris, one Stephen Randolph Norbrunn?"

Silence.

"Micmac just picked up an International Herald Tribune. It's in English." She sounded elated. "Anyway, her diplomat husband is on page one. Victim of a grisly murder. Zurich police have reason to believe she's been kidnapped."

"No, Phoebe. She's in extreme disposal mode."

A moment passed.

"Magus, you have your French memories back. I find this tough to ask, but when you were over here building the Frenchman's strategy, did you have a relationship with her?"

His silence lasted too long,.

"I see." She trailed off.

"Phoebe, I saw her here four days ago. At Kobler's bank. Something in her eyes. I believe she's lost her mind."

"Swell."

"The two of you grab a flight—Schiphol to Kloten. We're at the Dolder Grand." He provided their room number so they wouldn't need to ask. "We'll all work from here."

"Will do. Keep the faith, Mag."

"Yeah."

• • •

Crayle and Hekka ordered in. They attempted to find news of Pattie's latest murder, but were unsuccessful. They ventured out onto their balcony and took up residence in a twin lounge chair. Catching them almost at rest, two jets from the Swiss Air Force screamed over the lake. Hekka jumped.

"Relax. That was the entire Air Force. We're okay."

They snuggled close and watched the lake. Crayle glanced up for a weather check. "We're in a high-pressure situation."

"You have taken up understatement, Magus?"

"No. It means the weather on this day, December 19, is nice because of the excess air pressure downward. And, as long as it's here, it will keep the nastier low pressure systems elsewhere."

"Ummm. Let's sleep."

They slept for several hours until a harsh knock at the door sent them into a scramble for weapons. Crayle stood to the side of the door, leaned toward its center, and checked the peep hole. A moment later, he opened the door and drew the new arrivals inside.

"I hope, Phoebe, that you enjoyed your stay at Amsterdam's top hotel."

"Jack's a real mensch." She fought to keep the sarcasm from her voice. "We made up for it in room service." She glanced around. "This can be stick-it-to-Jack week."

"It's the taxpayers, remember?"

"Oh, man. Screwed again."

"I said *enjoyed*, past tense, for a reason."

"Uh, oh. Back in the barrel," Micmac declared.

"Perhaps we should try to locate Lalumière's daughters. We're afraid Pattie may have taken them out, too. If not, they may have been contacted or know if he has associates near the French capitol."

"Sounds like we don't know squat."

"Just a second. Something on the TV. Now the politicians are blaming Catholicism for the economic train wreck that won't go away. And the old pope, on his death bed with dementia, is threatening to excommunicate France."

"Christ, Magus. I remember when some guy with a history of screwing up said, *Can't we all just get along?* Time for the governments and religions to knock off the crap."

CHAPTER 28

He was home. After he removed the dust covers from the furniture, he was truly home. In the absence of his lovely late wife, Chantal, he would enjoy the full flavor of family life by himself. Like all residents and guests who didn't wish to move their vehicles at 5 A.M., he had parked outside the 50-foot castle walls to be shuttled in by Philippe. The vehicle, a Renault Kangoo panel wagon, barely negotiated narrow ancient streets intended for horses and carriages. With the five Louis Vuitton suitcases supplied to him upon his reentry into France at Cerbère, he had all that he required.

A knock. Had he forgotten to tip Philippe? Perhaps a neighbor wishing to greet him? He hefted open the door.

"Surprise!" said the two.

Shock overtook him. He stumbled backwards, glancing back and forth in disbelief.

"We're pilgrims, Neil," said the petite nun as she ushered in her charge.

"Who is this scruffy ..."

"*C'est Mitim.* It's Sylvain. It's Lalumière," she sang.

"You can't—"

"Of course, I can. And I must. We've got places to go, and a city to fry."

Neil's plaintive manner professed exasperation. "You sound different. I gave orders that you guard him to Level 5 secrecy … atop Montserrat."

"Alas, an event brought the police," she explained. "For a Mother Superior. Suicide."

Neil knew Pattie Norbrunn as did no one else. In less than two seconds he felt certain he knew what—no, who—had killed Mother Superior. He also knew his primary spy to be a conqueror of men at a time and place of her choosing. Were it not for the other man, she would already have him in bed.

While Neil Wohlford caught his breath, Lalumière wandered to the window. He gazed across the rooftops and the ramparts of the ancient city into the distance. To the fields where the peasants surely must reside. "I feel like a king in this place. I feel like Mitim in the final throes of destiny."

Neil Wohlford leaned closer to the nun. "He is nearing the edge as *he* approaches *our* goal. You must keep him intact … six more days." He nodded affirmation as a question.

She nodded back her resolve to see her mission to completion. And she noticed the lust, regardless of the bulky habit, in his eyes. "Would you like to go to confession before … or after?"

CHAPTER 29

On a normal day, Neil Wohlford would just travel to the nearest fine restaurant and dine by himself, or with someone worthy. Today, he found such indulgences to be impossible. For in his home, his houseguests summed up as the man most wanted in all of France, in fact, on the planet, and the woman most likely to resolve problems, or her personal needs, with murder. He utilized a Jack Sommers tactic, much to his chagrin, and reduced the insurmountable problem to its basics. Food and a private conference with the man known as Mitim covered the necessary universe. He would take great care, lest the conversation be repeated later to the woman.

Still, with all that was at hand, he had not misplaced his misogynistic arrogance. "Pattie. Please, fetch some food for us. Sylvain and I need to catch up."

At first, she wanted to take issue. Fresh air, and the potential to grill Lalumière at a convenient moment, won out.

As she huffed out the door, Neil said a silent prayer for the people of Carcassonne. He smiled at the *other* Frenchman and poured them both a thimble-sized glass of Napoléon Brandy. "We are in this together, Sylvain. We've competed in the past, but now that I've met the Elder, that's at an end. I was not born in the State of Maine as my documents say. I was born in the south of France."

The hermit quaffed his drink and sat back.

Neil continued. "I was taken to a place not far—near Rodez—to learn American English and to speak it without an accent."

"The same thing the Soviets did in their special villages?"

"Yes. Since France is friendly to the U.S., our people are not suspect. A name change, new identification, a cover story, and I was acquired by the CIA. Mostly as liaison with France's DGSE."

"So, deep cover to mole."

"Yes."

"But at some point you lost your religion—necessary for membership in the Illuminé. How did you make the journey from this place, as a child, to our organization?"

"There is deep history in this part of France. I wondered early about the regional Cathars. They viewed God as good and as the creator of spirituality. All physical matter, they said, was created by the Devil, and was evil."

"That must've gone over well with the Catholic Church."

"The Roman Church took exception to this contrary religion and took up arms. It attacked what is now the region of Languedoc and this fine castle. In 1321, Guillaume Bélibaste was not merely murdered by the Roman Church, he was burned alive. Catharism, and its opposition to Catholicism, was destroyed."

"When you learned all of this history, it turned you off to religion?"

"They attacked … and murdered."

"They murdered? Surely—"

"Exactly, Sylvain. No one in the U.S. had heard of the Cathars. I wrote some articles of the tragedy for my college paper. They were noticed. Shortly thereafter, I was recruited by the Illuminé."

"Interesting. You know where *I* have been, Neil. Tell me about *your* recent travels."

The two men took seats at a substantial, dark-stained wooden table. The chairs were of similar materials, scraped when moved, and were padded both seat and back with a red velvet.

"Sylvain, I have sailed on an odyssey. For the past six days, like Odysseus, I have journeyed a path from Monaco onward."

Lalumière sensed that the former CIA man might have also lost his bearings. Odysseus?

"First to Tunis, then to a small village in the northeast coast of Menorca. Ciutadella. I was hidden in—you will like this, Sylvain—a palace."

The word hit the fugitive like a lightning bolt. "I am the next king of France. I deserve palaces, but I get prisons. I get monastic retreats."

"Easy, my liege." Neil chuckled. "Though my overnight residence was once the palace of Arab conquerors, it is now the city hall."

"Then?"

"A trip to the Spanish border with France. A place called Portbou. It's where they change trains from the Spanish gauge to the French gauge. I was easily spirited into France and alighted in a coastal village. Cerbère. Have you heard of it?"

"No. I have spent my years in the northeast of France and in the Middle East. My travels to the Paris Bastille, south to the D'If prison, Monaco, Canada, and that ice-cold hilltop in Spain are both new and unpleasant."

Lalumière's discourse stung Neil. Monaco was where he had intended this man to die. Later, he would speak with Sister Magdalena in private.

"Please continue."

"In Cerbère, I was provided clothing, this resplendent luggage, and transport to Carcassonne. There. You have my Odyssey."

"The Odyssey of Greek literature lasted ten years. I doubt that yours will be so recorded, Neil."

"Not so fast, my dear Sylvain. I was taught as a child that I was born to greatness. After all, I grew up in this, the greatest of all remaining walled cities."

"I see why you became disgusted with religion." Lalumière was himself disgusted with Neil's interminable arrogance.

"Mmm. Things just are. They exist, that's all."

"Therefore, no more thought on the subject is necessary."

Neil looked long and hard at Lalumière. "There is something I want you to hear. I was able to check my encrypted cell-sat dropbox."

"You spies always have a drop this and that."

"The voice is that of Doctor Rorschach. In his final moments. Ignore the delays and human sounds he makes. It is what he said that is critical."

The hermit was exhausted from his trip. As best he could, he focused his eyes and his mind on the phone.

"Mr. Wohlford, I was knocked unconscious. When I awoke, I heard the rumble of the stones. In my panic, I yanked open my door. The gravel poured in. I pushed a button on my phone and your name came up as it dialed. I don't have much time. I am only barely able to climb between the rocks and the top of my doorway. The emergency lighting flickers and is of little help. I know there is just one chance. I am crawling over the rising pile to the vehicular elevator. My mind is blank except for a horrific visual of a bloody man. The people who did this to me have gone."

Neil paused the recording. "What you hear in the background is rocks from a quarry above the hospital."

"It is caving in?"

Neil skipped over the hospital's unique security feature. "Listen."

"Mr. Wohlford, they took my computer." More crunching and moaning. *"Ahhhhh!"*

Like Neil Wohlford, Sylvain Lalumière was unaccustomed to being anywhere near lethal action. He looked and sounded horrified. "He's dead?"

"Yes. But more important is that I participated in his early mind experiments. All he was trying to accomplish at that time was to take memories from my brain and transfer them onto a hard disk."

"Let me jump ahead, Neil. With Mr. Crayle, he was able to save the memories, and then restore them."

"What it means is that, if Magus Crayle has the computer, it is possible he can restore the memories of all the planning he did for you. It also means, and I'm taking you into my trust, he may learn things about me that can doom us both."

"Why are you telling me? I can't do anything about this Crayle. I must carry on to my destiny."

"I've kept my man, Jack Sommers, in the dark about Illuminé all this time. Now, he is wounded and recovering. Of little use. We're desperate. You must help."

Before the two men could escalate their confab into a full-blown pissing contest, Lalumière rose and walked into the bedroom. "I am sleepy now." With that, he stretched out upon the bed and fell into a slumber.

CHAPTER 30

With Pattie fetching groceries and Lalumière fast asleep, Neil considered his options. He concluded that it was time for the call he'd hoped he would never have to make. He knew he couldn't do the deed himself. Not having field skills caused him to rely on operatives with lesser brain wattage than himself. It made him vulnerable, a condition that drove him to drink beyond his limits. Still, he smiled at his ability always to be many steps from any noticeable culpability. He exceeded plausible deniability to the point that no one ever asked an accusatory question in the first place. And to attain that separation, he had to assure that his minions bore the entirety of any backlash. Now, having returned to his calm, patrician state, he punched in the numbers on his cell-sat phone. He caught Jack on the second ring.

"Crayle's gone rogue."

"He left Hong Kong and went off the map, Sir."

"Spies only leave the fold, Jack, for one of three reasons. Do you remember?"

"Money, ideology, or ego—most often for revenge."

"Money is not what drives him. He's a patriot. He has no ideology other than America. That leaves revenge."

"Why on Earth? We got him his memories back, he should be grateful."

"Jack, we removed them."

"What?"

"As you are aware, I have been working closely with Dr. Rikki for some time …"

"On top of your desk, if I remember right."

Neil bit his lip. "She was in the loop. When she heard of Crayle's car crash, she suggested we set up a, uh, situation."

"So, both of your … desires … compounded into the mindfuck program as it applied to Crayle. That pisses me off, Sir. I was in the middle of this. Why wasn't I read in?"

Neil considered reading Jack out—permanently. But once again, the former operations man was necessary. "He knows Rorschach restored too much. And he's got the computer."

"How do you know he has the computer?"

"Remember the Vestige tracking chip? It has one."

There was a silence, which Neil interpreted to be Jack surmising that he, too, could have a tracking chip.

"How is old Doc Ink Blot?"

"Not well. He's had a breakdown. He has fits of anguish, throughout the day. No words. Just copious amounts of tears. He seems to have lost his mind." He left out the fact that the Quarry had collapsed on itself, with Rorschach inside.

"Too bad."

"Jack, we have a situation with Crayle. Here's what I need you to do."

At that instant, Neil Wohlford's second line rang. He answered, nodded three times, and hung up.

"It seems a man in uniform with nametag Crayle was manifested to Zurich. I need you in Europe ASAP. Take my Falcon."

"Yes, Sir. I'll find Crayle and bring him back."

"No, Jack."

"What, then?"

"Terminate."

CHAPTER 31

Twenty minutes had passed since Pattie Norbrunn, dressed as Sister Magdalena, had departed. The door swung open and the nun-cover spy entered with two fabric bags of groceries, which she placed on the hardwood dining table. She turned, leaning back and catching her breath. "Where's Mitim?"

"In the bedroom. He found the exposition of my journey fascinating and, I'm sure, memorable, but he desperately required sleep. It is just as well. You and I need to talk. Don't you agree?"

She plopped into a chair. "So tell *me* about your trip." Playing to his ego worked every time. As had happened many times before, his natural wariness and suspicion departed. She cherished the vulnerability—in other people.

He picked up his half-full glass of whisky and walked to the window. His view west allowed him to observe the distant fog encroaching on the beautiful early winter day.

Pattie cleared her throat to get his attention. She motioned at the whisky bottle, then watched the most inconsiderate man she had ever met pour her a two-finger drink. He did hand it to her before returning to his visual panorama. And his dreams. He began softly, as if talking to a biographer.

"I was fearful at first. The boat was not big, perhaps forty feet. As we progressed away from shore, I looked back. I saw the castle and Monte Carlo in its glory. I began to think about *my* glory. But I related this already to Lalumière."

"Had I not been deemed expendable and dispatched on an errand, I would have heard. The short version, Neil."

He didn't want to argue. As he reconsidered, it provided for another moment to reflect in his characteristic success. "We sailed around Sardinia. It seemed forever until we sighted land again. We made landfall on the Spanish island, Menorca. It was then I made my discovery. I had purpose. I was on an odyssey, like the Greek."

"That trip took ten years, Neil. I'm not making the connection."

"Six days, ten years, don't you see? It doesn't matter. By the time we had transited to the Spanish-French border, I realized that the quest was not for some port or some land, it was for oneself."

Pattie eyed the man. She had never seen him this serious. But the self-focus was pure Neil Wohlford.

He laughed. "We had to wait while the Spanish modified the train from their gauge to the French. In moments, I had returned to France. Like Napoléon, coming home."

"And all this time, did you think of your wife?"

He paused, and took a deep breath. "How unusual. Not once did I think of her."

Funny thing, narcissism, she thought. "I understand. It's been a whole week." Pattie Norbrunn tilted her chin. "Chantal needed to go."

"You've gotten to the point that you create your own orders. Not good. I could rely on you before, and your perfect record. Now …"

"Now, I'm just as good, even better."

Neil nodded toward the bedroom, and the sleeping Lalumière. "In Monaco, it was *he* who needed to go."

"So I heard. You picked the Arab for the wet work."

"How did you know?"

"I overheard Elder—at the castle. He caught me. He ordered me to remove the Arab turned Iranian general. I did." She smiled at her partial fabrication.

"He would have eliminated Lalumière. Then I thought you and I …"

"And Chantal?"

He shook his head. "As far as the world knows, she was the victim of an explosion, and is officially buried at Père Lachaise Cemetery in Paris."

"Next to Jim Morrison?"

"That is not funny. She was a fan of his music." He refocused. "Look, I need you to go into the bedroom and terminate my competitor. It will be easy for you. Sex is not even necessary."

"Sex and terminate go hand-in-hand, Neil. Inseparable."

He could see it in her eyes. She had found her own power. "I'll do it." He moved toward the bedroom.

She stepped in front of him. "I need him. He will ascend the new throne of France. He believes that, and so do I. You need to hop on board."

"And what, become the court jester?"

"How about Head of Security?"

Neil Wohlford, in control most of the time, considered losing it. But, like the aristocrat he felt himself to be, he calmed.

The faux nun swished about the room, taking a position behind him. She listened.

"As you say, then. It will take us days to move him and his device north without being noticed. I have decided that we will cross the Central Massif to the Loire, then on to our final leg to Paris."

"Neil, you know nothing of field work. I think, for once, you need to listen to me."

Her comment assaulted his inborn arrogance. "I—"

"I'm changing the op, Neil."

He turned to find her nun's habit in a pile, and her—stark naked. She stepped close enough to touch. "Sylvain is going to ascend the throne, and I shall be his queen."

"From time to time, Pattie, you say such silly things." He faced her.

She worked at his belt. "It's decided. I'm going to be queen. *Off with their fucking heads*, I shall say."

"You're insane." His pants fell to the floor. "The place of power in France will reside in the south …" She removed his shirt. "… and you *shall* do as I order."

"I've been at the Embassy long enough to have visited Versailles. The king and I shall reign there."

Anger spiked in Neil. "You will follow orders. And I'll tell you what. As soon as Mitim, or Lalumière, or whoever he thinks he is that day, finishes up for us in Paris, he's history. He's a pawn. That's all."

She picked up a pair of candlestick holders from the table. "Do you remember these, my love? They were my present to you and your lovely wife, Chantal, when you married. In your underground cathedral."

She activated buttons inside the hollow bases. The spikes receded, allowing the candles to fall to the floor. She turned back to him and positioned the concave bases toward her, pressing them against her breasts. "Did you like Madonna?" She rotated side-to-side, stepping toward him. He backed to the wall, his respiration a series of gasps and wheezes.

She pressed the candle ends against his chest.

"Here." She took his hands, placing them at the base of her breasts. "Squeeze." She squeezed his hands. The pressure forced her nipples inside the base against levers, which expelled the five-inch candle spikes into the CIA manager's chest. His eyes went wide.

She stepped away, extracting the holders and their spikes.

Neil had known she was deadly from long ago. His lungs deflated by the punctures, he staggered forward two steps and collapsed to his knees. He clasped his hands over the holes, attempting to think his way out. But the diminishing oxygen caused his brain to fade.

"The Elder. He said … not to sleep … with you. No matter what …"

"While I worked for you—while I was under you—it wasn't a problem. But now, Neil, I've gone rogue. I need Mitim. You, it tortures me to say, have become expendable."

She straddled his back and pulled her cross from around her neck. She thought about the blade, but decided against it. She wrapped the heavy gold chain around his neck, aware that he couldn't withdraw his hands from his chest. She twisted the chain four times, cutting off any possible air. Together they tumbled to the floor.

In twenty-two seconds, Neil expired. Pattie remained sprawled atop him for several minutes.

"Versailles," she whispered in his ear.

• • •

Outside the walls of the ancient fortress city of Carcassonne, the expression on driver Philippe's face conveyed ecstasy. Taken there by a nun, no less. His cell phone rang, ostensibly another transit request. He didn't answer. He, too, was dead.

CHAPTER 32

Fifteen minutes after Jack Sommers' Falcon jet landed at Kloten Airport, he stepped out of the terminal. He could move fast without luggage. He hailed a cab.

"*Geht's?*" asked the driver.

"*Guet,*" Jack replied. "*Hauptbahnhof, bitte.*"

At his request, the transport from Kloten dropped Jack Sommers at Zurich's main train station. It served at the center of the city's downtown expanse. Although the streets had been plowed, they remained wet. The former CIA operative turned NGO project manager lit one of the Dunhill cigarettes he carried around for this purpose. Jack hated smoking, but the process allowed inconspicuous surveillance of the immediate area. He turned up his collar and bought a *Neue Zürcher Zeitung* at a street kiosk. The New Zurich News carried international affairs as well as financial and intellectual fare. He didn't plan to read it, but toting it around provided excellent credentials for entering classy hotels.

Memories struck him. It had been some time since he'd been to banker's town. He had never had two dimes to rub together, let alone the $50,000,000 plus it took to interest the Swiss private banks.

He imagined saying, "Hi, I'm here to open an account with ten million dollars."

"Security!" the terrified banker would cry.

He stepped into a store to purchase a wool scarf. He had no need in the U.S., and those sold in colder climes such as the foothills of the Alps were superior, anyway.

He was supremely aware that, with Crayle's health of mind and body intact, his mission could end poorly. The spy-mathematician could see and analyze every situation, estimate potential occurrences, and act with objective precision to a frightening degree of accuracy.

Jack Sommers shook his head and walked to the lake's edge. He paused between the trees that bordered the shore and looked across the wide expanse. This could be his final day of life. He took a moment to ponder that potential reality.

His last time in this place had been a vacation of sorts. A little known fact—spies did take vacations. He and his female colleague had travelled from their operation in Monte Carlo, ostensibly to visit their money. The summer day was beautiful and warm. He remembered challenging Marli—his pet name for Marilyn—to a pedal-boat race from the north shore to the south shore, and winding up at the chocolate factory that had been the model for Willie Wonka. She'd seemed disinterested until he mentioned chocolate.

Then, her competitive nature kicked in. "Loser pays."

"Look to the south, over the mountains. A storm is coming our way."

"You're chickening out," she accused.

At that point, both succumbed to the wager and the challenge.

She tripped him as he approached his boat. Quick as a rabbit, she jumped in the metal craft and pedaled mightily out onto the expansive lake.

"Hey!" he yelled before taking off in pursuit.

The winds picked up, holding them mid-lake. The harder they pedaled, the harder the winds blew. Then, the clouds turned angry, spewing lightning, and flooding first the mountains, then the foothills.

"Turn around," he had yelled. "The metal boats will attract the lightning!"

"You're trying to cheat!" she'd shouted back.

At that moment, a crack sounded unlike the sounds of thunder. Red exploded from her chest. She sank to the bottom of the boat.

Decision time.

She was clearly dead. He bent over in grief.

Another crack.

The bullet skimmed the metal structure, missing Jack by an inch.

Bent in half, he pedaled with the wind at his back toward the north shore marina.

As the storm crossed the lake, rain descended in torrents. The sniper fire ceased, but lightning strikes on the water surface caused his heart to pound.

He reached the shore and ducked behind cover. Through the downpour, he saw nothing. Marli was gone.

Some time later, he learned the rest. The winds had drifted her craft to shore. Her protective vest contained Hollywood-style blood bags so a shooter would see a red spray and believe her dead. Several Swiss transported her to a hospital.

Their covers had been blown. A devastated Jack was ordered back to Langley.

Women were funny, he surmised. If you abandon them, no reason matters.

He transited the bridge over the Limmat River to Zurich's Old Town. The more he walked, the more he resigned himself to a fatalistic outcome. Climbing to the hillside location of the Dolder tired him. His lower back screamed for a couple of shots of Schnapps. Physical effort was, certainly, below his pay grade.

• • •

Hekka sat on a desk chair playing with a TV remote. It seemed no combination of buttons would activate the device. She glanced at Crayle, who sat on the edge of the bed and stared out the window.

"Magus, the banker is dead. And the diamonds, they're gone. We must leave this place."

"And go where?"

"Home."

"Lalumière has a nuclear bomb and I must stop him, even if it means I die."

"You cannot die. You are part of me."

He fell back on the bed. "We were right to go to Paris before. My memories confirm that. He discarded the original plan in order to attack New York. My efforts to destroy his financial empire … to end this without more deaths, more destruction, have failed. When I next see him, he will have the bomb. You should return to your home."

"Magus, he's had twelve days since he left Victoria with the bomb. Why hasn't he exploded it?" she asked with the patience one would employ with a toddler.

"I know that, too."

"From what Rorschach restored?"

"Yes. Lalumière belongs to Illuminé, Hekka. They don't believe in a supreme being—only in the supreme intellect of an elite group of men."

"Only men?"

"Only men. He will pick Christmas. I am 98% certain."

"98?"

"It represents a probability of point-nine-eight—"

"Stop! I'm not a mathematician. I'm the woman who loves you!" Tears streamed down her cheeks.

"Mathematician. Spy. Lover. Killer. Not what you signed up for."

A sharp knock interrupted her reply.

"I'll get it." She wiped her face as she approached the door. Her mind elsewhere, she removed the security devices.

Jack burst in, bouncing her off a wall and knocking her to the floor.

Crayle's eyes went to the silenced automatic in the other man's hand.

Jack shut the door. He didn't bother to reinstate security—he'd be leaving soon. "Sorry, Magus."

"And you'll kill her, too." He motioned at the unconscious Hekka.

"That's the drill."

"It's not you. Who?"

"Neil said you'd gone rogue …"

"Rogue?" Crayle smirked. "I'm going to stop a crazy Frenchman with a nuclear bomb. That's not rogue. It's human." His voice elevated. "It's honor. It's the only way I can get myself back."

"That won't matter now."

Jack ambled forward, inadvertently stepping on the remote that had dropped from Hekka's hand.

The TV blared on, causing Jack to whip around. Crayle jumped up from the bed and slammed into his lower back.

"Ahhhhh!" Jack cried at the pain.

The pair of extended family spies crashed into a mirror, its shards cascading onto them both. In a clump, they pounded onto the floor. They struggled to their feet, grabbing and grappling until they once again slammed to the floor.

Taking on Crayle hand-to-hand amounted to a death wish. Jack glanced around for his weapon. The television interceded.

"In our Sign of the Times segment, we have *Breaking News*," said a sculpted blonde with an Australian accent. "This just in from southwest France. The body of American businessman, Neil Wohlford, has been discovered in the walled city of Carcassonne, France. Mr. Wohlford was discovered under his bed with two holes in his chest. A pair of candlesticks, each with a five-inch spike protruding, were found next to the body." She gave the address.

"That's Neil's place!" cried Jack. "I just talked to him …"

As a black body bag was being zipped, a shot of the victim's face confirmed Jack's observation.

"Operation aborted?"

"Shit!" Jack sat for a long time. "Shit, shit, shit!" He glanced at Hekka's still form. "Put her on the bed."

Keeping his eyes on Neil's former project manager, Crayle complied. "It's a new game. For you …"

"But he's—"

"Your boss? He was. Help me, Jack. I'm begging you. Help me save Paris."

Time passed. Heartbeats. Jack repositioned, his back to the wall. He dropped his head to his chest. His next statement embodied the tone of capitulation. "If it makes you feel better, check by the door. I think that's where my weapon went. Feel free to shoot me." He looked tired, not just for what had happened this day, but for all the days, months, and years past.

"The Japanese would call you a ronin, Mr. Jack Sommers. A samurai with no master. What do you say? What if the rogue and the ronin give it a shot? We'll get some sleep. We'll take that plane, which you now own free and clear, and we're going to save Paris. What do you say?"

• • •

The Dolder Grand's Maître d'Hôtel had been born and raised in the western segment of Switzerland. The region's French ancestry and his own parentage had gained him entry into the ultra-secret Illuminé. It was he who had called in the sighting of Magus Crayle and Hekka Poppi at his Zurich hotel. It was he who had supplied the room number for Neil Wohlford, and Jack Sommers.

He listened outside the Crayle party's door and heard nothing. He knocked three times. "Room service."

Hekka, awakened, noticed that the two men had moved out onto the balcony. She moved off the bed and turned, back to the wall beside the door casement. She reached with her free hand and turned the handle.

The Maître d' burst into the room, silenced pistol at the ready.

Her induction into the spontaneity of the spy world long since completed, Hekka spun. Her quick draw practice played out. With both hands securely on the handle, she drove her 10-inch Bowie knife through the man's chest.

His eyes went wide. He staggered inside. Dropping his gun, he grabbed the knife, as if to undo the damage. He fell forward, bouncing off the bedside and dumping onto the floor.

Crayle witnessed the event from the balcony. He seemed to cross the room in an instant. He bent over the man as soon as he came to rest, feeling his pulse wind down. Jack ran to the bathroom, returning with a shower curtain. The men quickly wrapped the corpse to prevent a difficult-to-explain pool of blood.

Silently, Hekka closed the door.

CHAPTER 33

With the Maitre d' threat past, the trio of spies just stared. At walls, at the window, at each other. Freeze frame. Jack broke the silence.

"Don't worry, I've dealt with surplus bodies before. Reminds me of my last op with Marilyn."

Hekka's voice came from the bathroom as she cleaned her blade. "What happened? Not with the operation. With you and your wife."

"That's an easy one. I chose mission over Missus. I chose our country. She didn't support that decision."

"Perhaps she wanted you to save her, and then worry about our country afterwards."

"It's old business, Hekka." He turned to Crayle. "Next topic. What, Mr. Strategist, do we do now?"

"We need to look at the broader scope of this mess. This whole affair, at least from the Frenchman's and Elder's perspective, is about governance without God. Without a religion. It makes the Catholic Church the enemy of the Elder's Illuminé, doesn't it?"

"I'm not sure about religion, Magus. A famous physicist, English I believe, seems to have proven that the universe, in all its glory, does not require the existence of a supreme being."

"I am familiar with the notion, but it's a false proof. For a big bang to create a universe, it must have something to bang with. We call it matter."

"Uh, oh. Whenever my college math professor took that tone, there was an implied 'you dumb shit' that went along for the ride."

"You're not dumb. Your renowned physicist couldn't explain the status of things before his big bang, so he changed the rules. He proclaimed that time didn't exist prior to the explosion, so we couldn't even discuss what might've gone on before. Whether there needed to be a god to create all that is out there is still up for grabs. Like Lalumière and this mysterious Elder, the Illuminé don't believe in a supreme being."

"Yeah. In case they're wrong, I suppose I'd better be ready to explain my life when the time comes."

Crayle rubbed his fingers back and forth on his forehead. His demeanor turned serious. "We seem to have gone out into the weeds with our thinking. We have to get back on point." Feeling he could finally relax his defenses and desiring to maintain eye-level contact with Jack, he took a position on the floor opposite his former project manager.

Hekka returned, her sparkling Bowie reinserted into its scabbard. She sat down next to her man.

"Jack, my restored memories have Lalumière and his petite handler arriving in Paris with the bomb he obtained in Victoria. That's all I have."

"Why did he need a new bomb? Wait … I've got it. The attack on New York via the Queen Mary 2. That wasn't in your original plan, was it? So, after that little diversion, he was out of bombs and still needed to attack Paris. Sound about right?"

"Precisely. He was to have three bombs. The first detonation, in Iran, set the stage. Then, Marseille to insinuate the problem close to home and precipitate a congress of politicians. The third and final one was intended for Paris to topple the government. But the potential intervention of America—coming to France's aid—caused him to modify the plan. Now, he's obtained a replacement bomb for Paris." He glanced at the pair of intent listeners. "What you need to understand is that the whole point of my strategy was to accomplish in France what Chin and Li did in China. The current situation is that Lalumière has to get the entire French government in one place once again … and then blow it up."

Crayle, Hekka, and Jack stared. Not at each other. Just stared. The calm that had overtaken them ended abruptly. With a knock.

Then a voice. "Room service."

Jack glanced at Crayle. "Backup?"

Crayle tossed Jack his weapon as Hekka drew her Bowie. She resumed her former position next to the doorway. Back to the wall.

Crayle made no sound as he moved to the hinged side of the door. He placed his fingers over the eyepiece to attract interest. No bullets through the door.

Holding his breath, he leaned in to peek. He exhaled. He pushed his free hand toward the floor, causing Jack and Hekka to holster their weapons. Crayle arced open the door.

"Hey, guys!" FBI Agent Phoebe Bransfield strode in. "Bet you liked the room service bit."

Micmac followed her inside. "Sorry we're late. The Amsterdam airport was shut for three days due to protests and a strike. The gig sucked. We found Lenny's brother in his office. Murdered."

"I'm sorry for Lenny." Crayle felt the pain.

A wide-eyed Hekka pointed to the TV. "Magus, look."

CNN World displayed a view of Paris with the Eiffel Tower center stage. The subtitles scrolling right-to-left told all.

> *All components of the French government have agreed to meet in Paris to resolve differences. France suffers problems of the heart and soul, a spokesman said, the parties will gather in*

public on Christmas Eve. They will demonstrate solidarity at midnight by proclaiming La Belle France and its grand citizenry rescued by them from the economic and moral abyss. The president, the National Assembly, and several major religious leaders are expected to attend. —CNN World

"We have a conundrum. Neil was killed in Carcassonne. I'm thinking Pattie for this. I'd put money that she took out her ambassador husband after killing Lalumière's money man, Kobler."

"She's probably gone to ground," Phoebe reasoned.

Crayle nodded. "Evidence at the scene of her husband's murder indicates she was kidnapped. I don't believe it for a second. She used that feint to disappear. Change her look."

"It fits," Phoebe said. "But what now? Given her skill set, she could be anywhere."

"If she's still working the Frenchman, they'll have to make Paris before the big confab."

Jack held up his hands, drawing everyone's attention. "I know where to get the actionable intel we need. Let me make a call. Then we'll head to the airport."

CHAPTER 34

The diminutive nun broke the silence. "It's SOP, Mitim. In this case, it's the destruction of evidence of our transport and arrival to this place."

The small, open boat they watched drift from the shore was identical to the one the spy had used to spirit fugitive Lalumière away from the Bastille nearly two months before. He observed it, comparing his seemingly adrift life to its meandering, and ultimate submersion. He knew that the waters of the Rhone River, like the rest of his beloved France, would continue unaffected into eternity.

"Moping isn't allowed. Come. We have destiny to achieve." She led him by the hand in the moonlit night up a street with large sycamores adorning its edges. As the sidewalk canted upward, as if anticipating the foothills ahead, they entered an ancient walled town.

Using her finger to indicate silence, she led him through an archway of large, brown stones. A sign to the left proclaimed the street ahead of them to be *Rue de Château*—Castle Street. Even the notion of the proximity of royalty and power didn't cheer the Frenchman.

His euphemistic road, thus far, had been long and hard—it had worn him down.

"This pathway between the buildings is narrow. I am tired, Sister Magdalena. The structures seem to press in on me as if I will be crushed. Do you feel it?"

Prepared to admonish him for breaking the silence, Sandrine thought better. She moved closer. "What I feel is you pressing against me. Let's be clear about something. I understand your phobias. The closeness, the heights, the water. I will hold your hand, but I need you to loosen up."

He stopped. "Look. I reach to the left and touch the building. If you reach, you touch your side. They are too close."

"This is the way it was done in those days. Just wide enough for a horseman or a few foot soldiers. Tactical. And strategic."

"You mentioned the water. I have conquered that phobia. My trip from the Château D'If to Monaco." He smiled. "I developed a love for the fluid essence. Can you imagine?"

"So that's why you were so calm and quiet coming here in the boat. For the first time in your life, you enjoyed it. Stick with me. I'll get you past the closeness now, and I have plans to address your fear of heights another time."

"You used the word strategic. It brought Magus Crayle to mind. What a magnificent intellect. Is he still out there?"

She shook her head. "Before his exit, Neil informed me that he'd dispatched Jack Sommers to deal with your nemesis. Jack's good. Really good. I've known him for a long time."

Lalumière glanced at her nun's habit, and then into her eyes. "In the biblical sense?"

She ignored him, although her answer would have been in the affirmative. In fact, it was she who had come—in all senses of the word—between Jack and his spy wife. Neither had realized it. It was at that juncture that she, as Pattie Norbrunn the spy, knew she possessed a talent for her work.

They continued a hundred yards up the pathway, sometimes stumbling on the stones, to a building likewise made of stones. She led him up a stairway to the door.

The residents of Vivier's old town grew flowers in planters or hung them outside their doorways in iron hangers. Watching his step on the narrow staircase, Lalumière banged his head against one.

"Ooh. Take care. We'll need that head intact. Remember what happened to your ancestors."

He looked up. "That's not funny. They were of my blood."

"Sorry." She withdrew an old iron key, pronounced it a master, and opened the heavy, studded, wooden door. She stepped inside ahead of the Frenchman. "We're home!" echoed inside the sparsely decorated residence. "Have a seat."

The Frenchman sank into a chair at an oak dining table for four.

"I'll shut us in, and we'll be safe." After securing the portal, she peered down at the top of her cross, and read the display. "We have an intel update. Looks like you've moved down the trending list. We can't stay here too long. It's the Hollywood circumstance. Out of sight, out of mind."

Pattie stepped behind the slumping man and felt his shoulders. "Tense, even through the exhaustion." She massaged for ten minutes until the tissue softened. Satisfied, she approached a fireplace fabricated like the entire town—walls, streets, and towers—of stones of various shades of pale brown and gray. An absence of vibrancy and of a visible population suggested lonely isolation.

Reaching up, she pulled a long, flat stone and a small oil can from the hearth. Seating herself across from her charge, she removed her cross and its lower sheath. A little oil, and she began to stroke the blade across the wet stone.

"It doesn't affect you? The Holy Cross. The blood you have taken with it. You are numb to these killings?"

Without looking up, she answered his questions. "I don't enjoy killing, Sylvain. It just happens that, in cases like ours, people are like stones in the road that must be removed to permit progress. It doesn't matter the color of the stone, or what it's wearing, its gender, or sexual orientation. If it's in the way, it has to go."

"And if I am in the way? What then?"

"Sylvain, you are to become the next leader of France. Period."

"What if I am tired? What if I can't continue?"

She added pressure to the blade. "Then there would have to be a new game in town. I can't return to Langley and sell the notion that I offed one of their middle managers because his ambitions superseded those of the mission. You see, the higher-ups don't know about this Illuminé scheme. It's off-the-books. The inconvenient truth is that Neil insinuated himself in the CIA as the Elder's mole, and I can't change that."

It was now quite clear to Lalumière that the operation would no longer be supported by the American CIA. The young woman continued.

"The CIA is not a ship of fools. Those people learned with Fidel Castro that you can't replace a government with someone you believe to be friendly and expect it to remain that way. Dictators, like governments, have interests. They don't have friends."

"Sandrine …" Lalumière sounded pensive. "… do you believe in your heart that our situation is hopeless?"

"The Americans don't know of what we do. That's all."

He nodded acceptance of the reality of her words. He changed the subject. "Without Neil, your linkage to his mission disappeared. Sandrine, you need not kill again. I am certain."

For the first time, her single-minded focus dissolved. She glanced down at the table surface, and ran her finger across the grain. "I …"

The most significant man in her life pondered a moment. "I have decided. I shall abandon my quest. You can leave to do whatever you wish." He sat back in his chair, not resolved with the momentous statement he had just made.

The tragedies that still lay buried in her mind caused it to take a different tack. If Lalumière, as Mitim or otherwise, could not go on, then she would have to escape. In that instant, she realized she cared for this man. She had not had such a feeling of closeness before. Least of all with her deceased husband. But she would need to escape. It was in her nature.

The operative known within Central Intelligence as Pattie Norbrunn stared at the desolate, beaten-looking man. In the next instant, her vision blurred. When it regained focus, a line of red began at his left ear and continued around his throat. Expressionless, her Mitim gazed into her eyes while the blood poured down his neck onto the table. Her head bobbed. Her voices began. *"He must complete. He must become king. You, as his woman, must become queen."* Her head began to throb. She grabbed it with both hands, then banged it on the table. And again.

Lalumière jumped up from his chair. He ran to her, grabbing her hands and pulling her up to him.

"Please! Do not hurt yourself!" He drew her closer still. His resolve returned. "Forget what I said!"

"But—"

"We shall be one, my darling!" He calmed his pounding heart. "No one can stop us. You shall be my queen."

He carried her to the day bed situated in the room for a passing traveler. Slowly and with a great deal of effort, he pulled the habit from her, piece by piece. He straightened and removed his clothes. Neither expressed emotion or desire. The lovers made the slowest, most passionate, most sincere love ever.

In the aftermath, Lalumière peered into the darkness of the room. Relieved. There would be no more killing. Until Paris.

• • •

The silence was broken by curtains hitting hard against their stops.

"Get up, Mitim. We fly to Paris today. The City of Light, my love."

Lalumière, who hadn't slept well, struggled out of bed. "I need a shower. I need clothes. I need to eat."

"Get dressed, my love. Car's waiting. And so's your crown."

After twenty minutes of preparation, they ambled over the stones and back to the sycamore-lined street. Pattie pointed to a long, black car.

"No. This must be a joke." He approached the hearse.

"No joke. Fully prepared and endorsed by the Science and Technology Directorate of Uncle Sam's CIA."

His mood was much improved this new day. "This uncle has an STD?"

"Not funny."

"You are a spy. Can't you steal something else?"

She gestured at the long side window. "This is what's provided. If you complain, I will have to lock you in back."

He peered inside at a mahogany coffin, long enough for his tall body. In two minutes, they were buckled in up front and heading northeast, to the banks of the Rhone River.

"Listen to me, my dearest Mitim. It may be December 23, but the weather in Paris is near perfect. A storm system is being held west in the Loire region by a high pressure area over our target."

"That's good news."

"The weather there is expected to break at any time."

"How bad is the storm to the west?"

"Bad. Perhaps evil. Do you believe in the Devil?"

"Let's pray that things remain to our advantage until our mission is complete."

"We are Illuminé, my dear. We cannot pray."

"Hope, then."

"Of course. Timing is everything. Once again …" She leaned toward him, testing his rote memory. He recited to perfection her operational dictums. Then continued.

"We must arrive at the park at the time I calculated. I will complete the wet work with an hour to spare. We'll be on our way out at twenty minutes to midnight."

"At midnight, it is Christmas."

"That's the plan."

"Brilliant. The crowd should be enormous and ravenous. The gendarmes will hold them at bay while the government attempts to speak as one."

"I wonder why they all just didn't flee the country."

"The politicians' egos have them believing that they can still control the masses with words."

"But why the high clergy presence?"

"It is simple, little one. They are politicians, too."

"You are so wise, Sylvain. You simply must become king."

"And with your notable assistance, I shall."

The hearse, enhanced to all-wheel drive by CIA affiliate Mick MacKay, navigated all manner of road surfaces with little difficulty. But it was strangely silent.

"Where did you acquire this machine?"

"The S and T folks sent it over. The entire body is solar, so it runs on electricity. A huge supply of batteries under the coffin gives it a 300-mile range. And, if someone doesn't hear us coming, *boom!* We toss them in the back."

"Did this item come with a special mortuary?" Lalumière half-kidded, although nothing would surprise him.

"You are so smart. It does. It's located near Paris—just outside the kill and destruction radius of your final bomb."

Lalumière mulled over the nearness of the catastrophic event, and the nearness of his dream. "I understand. We will exit Paris to this mortuary, and then we will head south, as if transporting a body."

"Yes. The logic is perfect. Bodies would have to be moved to make room for those from Paris. After our bomb."

"This is our exit plan?"

"It's the Butterfly Tactic."

"What?" His brow furrowed.

"You flit this way and that, seemingly at random, but ending up where you wanted to go."

The man went from furrowed brow to totally puzzled.

"You've seen a bird fly. But you've never seen one snag a butterfly out of the air. Right?"

"No."

"The bird can't discern where the bug will be a second from now, in order to get there at the same time. The more the bird observes, the more certain it is of the hopelessness of attempting an intercept."

"And you can create his maneuver … for us?"

Before she could answer, Lalumière grimaced. He gasped and threw his arms around his abdomen. "Oh! It's my nerves!"

She pulled to the roadside. "Honey, you need to relax." She unzipped his pants and went to work. Neither she nor her subject noticed the police unit that had just parked behind them. Nor the officer who strolled to the driver's side and, shading his eyes, peered into the window. They didn't see him walk back to his vehicle, muttering something about morticians and their lack of respect for the dead.

CHAPTER 35

Phoebe returned from the head and plopped down opposite the project leader. "Where are we going, Jack? We don't have any idea where Lalumière is. He could be in Paris already, for all we know."

"Yeah, Jack," Micmac added. "You're not telling us anything, and we *do* have the need to know."

The situation aboard the aircraft simmered on the verge of a roiling boil. As Phoebe massaged her Glock, her pulse increased.

"Really, guys! It's classified!" Jack was on the edge of his nerves, as well.

The entire team made for the only person on the plane who knew where they were headed and why. They would make him talk.

The jet dropped. Team members hit the deck, the bulkheads, and each other as the plane jogged left, then right. The pilot worked to regain control.

Masks fell from the ceiling.

"Grab a mask!" Flori yelled from the flight deck doorway. "Pull down! Put it on! Breathe deep!"

For a moment, the plane leveled. Every one of the team performed the operations as instructed. Except Jack. And Flori.

"Breathe!" she pleaded.

They did. Within twenty seconds, all slept soundly. The jet resumed normal flight. The pilot moved a lever from *Dose Initiate* to *Dose Maintain.*

"Nice, Flori. Thanks. They'll understand when we're on site."

"Always glad to help. This plane of yours has more gadgets than—"

Jack smiled at his flight attendant. "C'mon. Step inside the bedroom. I have something I want to show you."

"I've seen it."

The intercom clicked on, interrupting the repartee. "This is the captain. Touch down … twelve minutes."

"Buckle up, Mr. Sommers."

• • •

The Jack Sommers Falcon jet vectored onto approach. Not to any of the Parisian airports as one would expect. They had departed Switzerland and headed in the other direction. Southeast. The co-pilot grasped a lever marked *Terminate* in order to conclude the induced sleep. The wrong one. Realizing his mistake, he moved his hand to *Terminate Dose*, making a mental note to relabel the other, more drastic, selection. He then replaced the slumber gas canister with a freshener, and the team came around quickly.

"What the hell's going on, Jack?" a wide-awake and unnerved Crayle demanded.

"I can't say just yet. There's a credible source just east of here. He says he knows exactly what Lalumière intends to do."

"Credible?"

"Beyond question."

A landing strip appeared at the edge of a plateau. The pilot brought them in low over landing lights set on tall lattice-works embedded on the hillside below. Any plane coming up short would meet a fiery demise.

The team deplaned at the end of the runway into a dark green, extended SUV. The area surrounding the airport, also green, appeared barren. No structures, no people, no traffic. Nothing.

"We're headed east, team. I know this place. It's beautiful now, but a few years back …"

Hekka peered between the seats. "There are mountains ahead, Jack."

"Bosnia. Off to the right about eight clicks is Montenegro. When sides were chosen, it was Bosnia and Croatia versus Serbia and Montenegro. I tend not to mention the latter two when I'm here. There's still beaucoup animosity."

Phoebe spoke. "I love it when you butcher French words."

Jack considered introducing her as a Montenegran, but let it slide. The Dalmatians of lower Croatia tried their best to forget the Balkan War. Bringing up their archenemy constituted a bad idea.

The vehicle pulled onto a drive way and, 100 feet later, braked to a stop. The team piled out in seconds. Jack led them past a mill house built of stone. It appeared to be hundreds of years old. The River Ljuta had been diverted into two tunnels to turn the two grinding wheels inside. The rush of the water provided a pleasant, peaceful sound. Crayle hesitated.

"Jack. I look past the buildings and see hundreds of thin trees that appear like a thicket. I imagine combatants during the war. With no place to hide and no viable field of fire."

Hekka scanned the forest. "This is a place where peace belongs."

"Amen." Crayle considered their own situation. "Peace has the hardest time finding a permanent home."

Ahead, a matronly woman clad in ethnic costume held open a door. No more than 5'2", her blue eyes sparkled a welcome.

The team, minus Lenny, entered the matching stone house and found a long, heavy table not unlike the drinking tables in Munich's Hofbräuhaus.

"Forgive me, ladies and gentlemen. I am in preparation," said a man across the room. "It is the time of year when new things are born."

His tailor continued with the measurements. "Please remain still. I cannot measure, Bishop Zoran, if you wave your arms. It moves the fabric."

The man beamed. "While my father was of this country, my mother is Italian. I must move my arms, or I cannot speak."

"We will require privacy," the bishop announced.

The man spoke a few words of Croatian. The woman stood to leave, waving her Italian arms as she vented her displeasure at being dismissed in front of her new guests. The Milanese tailor followed, gesturing in kind.

"Mother," shrugged the man. "Please sit. This won't take long and will be well worth your while." He pushed a tray of shot glasses across the table. "It is our very own. A brandy. The colored liquids are fruit flavored. You probably want to work your way up to the clear ones."

Jack reached for the tray and spun it around so the clear shots were nearest. Members of the team took one, Jack mumbled *na zdoroviya*, and they tossed them down. What happened next appeared to be a nuclear reaction taking human form.

The four, less Jack, jumped from the table, howled incoherently, and stomped around the room. They coughed, wheezed, shook, stammered, and wept involuntary tears.

The Vulgarity Vase, as Lenny had named it, would have overflowed in five-dollar bills with what ensued. A full ten minutes later, the team settled down and reclaimed their chairs. Jack was already on number four.

Crayle, throat still on fire, spoke. "Thanks for the warning." He leaned onto the table. His eyes transfixed on those of the special man across the room. "Now, please tell everyone who you are, and your allegiances. Tell us what we need to know to stop Lalumière."

The man considered the questions, then brought two full carafes of water to the table. Then five glasses. "I suppose I should have done this first."

While the team flew into firefighting mode, the man began his story.

"It was many years ago. The war was over. I had to make choices. My mind was at odds. At first, I blamed God for letting the destruction and carnage take place. I'd lost many friends and relatives. Good people. Innocent people. I didn't know whether to grasp God by the hand or by the throat."

The carafes were now empty, the faces beet red. He supplied two more.

"I chose His hand. I went to a seminary and became ordained. A natural leader, as I was told. Just last year, I was named Bishop. Of Dubrovnik. Then, with all the turmoil in the world, and my own steady hand, Archbishop of the coastal dioceses. I will accept the title tomorrow. But more relevant to your needs, during the earlier times, I became familiar with an organization called Illuminé. I know you've heard of these people. They have forsaken God for intellect. They intend to use the economic devastation to ascend to dominance in many countries. France is just one."

"How do you know of them and their intentions?" Crayle did not yet believe the prelate's story.

"Long ago, I moved to France. Avignon. I sought answers there. I met a man. He convinced me that God was irrelevant. That if He had created the world and all living things, that He had clearly abandoned them. He asserted that no one, no matter how well-intentioned, could govern a people with the nebulous entity called religion standing ready to countermand every order. And with the authority of a supreme being."

"That's the reason Hitler, Stalin, and other despots renounced religion, isn't it?" Crayle asked in an accusatory fashion.

"But those people have come and gone, haven't they? God is forever."

"Time is running out. Tell us, who was this man? And what's all this got to do with us? With our mission," said Jack.

"Then again," the man said, "perhaps our God had, despite his previous successes, created a species that defied his guidance. Bibles, Torahs, and Korans were no help. I forgot to mention. This young individual was of royal blood. He showed me proof." The archbishop gave each member of the team an engaging look. "He seemed honest and genuinely wanted to help me in my quest. Before we parted, he suggested that I assist this overwhelmed superior being. That I return home. That I become a man of the cloth, which is what I did."

"But what about the Illuminé thing?" Phoebe said, sounding perturbed.

"And Paris?" Micmac chimed.

"I am Archbishop Zoran. I have achieved the highest religious post in all of Dalmatia. You can trust what I am about to tell you." Again, he peered directly into each pair of eyes. "Illuminé intends to rule utilizing only the intellect, knowledge, and experience of each country's brightest stars. For their grand beginning, they have chosen France. Paris will be their target."

Crayle's jaw tensed. "We know that Paris is the target. My memory restoration confirms that."

"Restoration?"

"It's not important. What is important is that Paris is a huge city. Forty square miles. More than two million people before the economic crisis. With the Illuminé's reach, we can't trust any more than the people right here. With this small force, we have to know exactly where to look. Help us, please," he entreated.

"I have been invited for The Convergence, as it's called. The one that will take place on Christmas Eve. I will be among the religious contingent to meet with the French government. It would be simple to find us all in one spot and to detonate a powerful bomb. With us gone, I believe power will pass on to this man, Mitim, that the French public seems to worship. Even here, the people wear the T-shirts."

"That's the one we're after." Crayle paused, sizing up the man before him. "He's Illuminé."

"Oh, my God!"

Crayle knew he was close. "Where? Where will you meet? At the National Assembly? Where?"

"No. Not the Assembly. You, of course, know the Tower. The Eiffel Tower." They all nodded. "We will all be given candles of hope. We meet in the plaza below, just prior to midnight."

Crayle inspected the man's eyes. They didn't evade. "Security?"

"Security will be everywhere. On the ground, on the water, in the sky. Everywhere."

"We're done. Jack, we have to leave. Now! We'll plan on the plane. We'll need … we'll need … I don't know." Crayle dropped his head into his hands.

"Mr. Crayle. I must travel to Rome first. Something special. Something I can't talk about at this time."

"Still, *we* need to fly to Paris. We—"

"No, Mr. Crayle. You must travel to this place." He held up a note on folded parchment. "You will find your man, and his bomb, here." He placed the paper into a book.

The archbishop walked around the table and settled his right hand upon Crayle's head. "For you and your grand team, Magus Crayle, I will pray." He handed the exasperated team leader the Holy Bible. "You shall find guidance within."

CHAPTER 36

The team arrived in the early evening. The terminal building told them what they needed to know. *Aeroport de Carcassonne en Pays Cathare*. Of the memories that Rorschach had not removed, Crayle recalled that Pope Innocent III ordered a crusade against the un-Catholic Cathars of this region and what he deemed their Church of Satan. Allowing women as spiritual leaders was one of their crimes.

Before deplaning, Crayle snapped shut his bible going-away present and placed it in a cabinet. He retained a velum the archbishop had placed inside. It had directed them to this fortified city in southwest France. More than that, it provided them a hand-drawn map to their target destination—the kill zone within.

A hardened SUV shuttle from the airport dropped them off in a hard-packed dirt parking lot that skirted the city's 50-foot walls. "It is okay." Their driver, new to the job, pointed to a small door at the base of a tower. "It is open. Go inside, ask anyone for the address you seek. It is simple."

Simple it wasn't. The double-walled city of Carcassonne was laid out like a maze.

Well-meaning Carcassonneans ended each set of directions with something like "When you find yourselves lost again, ask someone. We are all friendly."

Finally, they located the man who looked after Neil Wohlford's property. He took some monetary convincing, but soon they had the keys and he was gone.

Inside, Jack took the lead. He pointed at Phoebe and then to closed doors, as if dragging her image across a computer screen.

Phoebe cleared the few rooms in her usual fashion and followed her final "Clear" with "I'm starved. I'm sure everyone else is. I'll step across the street and pick up some food."

"I'll help," Hekka said.

The two women left, leaving the door closed, but unbolted.

Crayle, Jack, and the former UDT sailor surveyed the adjacent rooms for no more than thirty seconds before Micmac's voice came from under a bed. "Magus, did you hear the front door creak?"

"No."

"That'd be a little quick for the ladies," Micmac chuckled.

"I'll assist with the food."

"Altruism lives," Jack followed.

Crayle stepped into the living room and stopped dead. His jaw dropped. There, in the doorway, stood a battered-appearing man sporting a three-day beard. Crayle recognized him immediately. "Lenny …"

Dropping his satchel, the man staggered toward him. "You son-of-a-bitch!" he screamed. "You son-of-a-bitch! … I asked you not to … you killed Wolfie!"

The smaller man plowed into Crayle, forcing him backwards. They slammed onto the oak dining table.

In seconds, Micmac arrived and clutched the P.I. by the scruff of the neck, disengaging him from his target. He jammed the small man into the wall, pulling his arms behind. "Stop it! Now!" He took a deep breath, and calmed his voice. "We didn't do it. That's why we didn't take you out. It's why Phoebe decked you."

"Did I hear my name?" As with Hekka, Phoebe's arms were encumbered with to-go boxes of food that neither one could see over.

Micmac whispered into Lenny's ear, "We good on this?"

Feeling the fool, the P.I. nodded.

When they had set their items down, the women saw Crayle pull himself off the table and Lenny face-planted against the wall. Hekka spoke first. "Did we miss something?"

"You could say that," Crayle answered.

"You might've bolted the door when you left." Jack twisted his head toward Lenny.

"I figured we'd have our arms full. Elbowing and kicking the foot-thick door," she exaggerated, "wouldn't grab your attention. And with Lalumière and his side-kick gone, I felt it wouldn't hurt to leave the door unlocked."

Micmac waxed philosophical. "I had an instructor who told us to watch out for the word ASSUME. He said it makes an ASS out of U and ME."

"He probably didn't have a girlfriend," Phoebe guessed.

Micmac released Lenny and Crayle took the stage. "Everyone. Time to catch our breath … grab some food … and catch each other up to the present. The stakes haven't changed. Please, take a seat." His energy depleted, he plopped down in the nearest chair. The rest followed suit.

Lenny didn't wait. "Magus, I need to go first. To get this off my chest."

Crayle knew the little man was right. It was best for the rest of the team as well. He waved his arm. "Go."

Lenny placed his elbows on the table, cradling his forehead in his hands. "Even though Wolfie and I never got along, I had to come for you. His throat was slit." He stopped a moment to wipe a tear from his cheek. "In the few seconds he had left, he dipped his finger in his blood … and scrawled this." He tossed a black velvet diamond tray onto the floor. Even upside down, the red stain was unmistakable. CRAYLE.

"How did you find us?"

"He wrote something else—the word Carcas. I thought it was about a body, and he couldn't finish the word. But in his sorry state, he'd taken care to capitalize the first letter. Later, in my hotel room with a bottle of Jack Daniels, I checked it out on my computer. Short version, Carcassonne."

Phoebe placed her Glock on the table. Everyone drew a breath. "Lenny, we came out of Wolfie's office chasing Pattie. We knew right away that she had killed your brother. We also thought she was getting away with the diamonds. We couldn't stop to explain." Her fingers stroked the receiver of her weapon.

Lenny peered down at the table. "I suppose I did jump to conclusions."

"The shotgun blast from that fake crutch did come a little close," Micmac said.

Crayle sat back. "And close is what we are not … to stopping Lalumière."

• • •

The hungry team dispatched the meal in short order and with no dialog. When he finished, Lenny laid his head on the table.

Crayle reached over and touched his arm. "You're a wreck. Go in and get some sleep."

The diminutive Lenny took the hint. Within seconds, snores advised the team he was asleep.

Everyone sat in silence. Some enjoyed a moment of quiet. Of mindlessness. Others thought about the hopelessness of their mission and yet another victim, Lenny's brother. It didn't take much.

A substantial groan sounded from the bedroom. Hekka rose to check. Two seconds later, she stepped quietly out of the bedroom, closing the door behind her. "He was restless. He shifted around a lot. A lot of torment."

Ten seconds later, the door opened. Lenny's head poked out. "You'll wanna come in here, Magus. Look what I found." He lifted a sheet and pointed to a cell-phone. "It woke me up."

Jack rubbed his chin. "It could have belonged to Lalumière. Maybe Lenny can penetrate its security."

Crayle shook his head. "It's probably the girl's. She may have left a trail for us to follow. Knowing what we know, this could help, or hurt, or merely be a function of her insanity."

Micmac pursed his lips in frustration. "I think this Lalumière guy thinks he's in charge, but I don't think so."

Phoebe nodded, "It's the Old White Guy Syndrome—what can I say?"

"Trouble is," Lenny said as he screwed up his brow, "this could be misdirection or a trap."

Crayle concluded, "We have to see this through. We're going to bet that they are travelling the back roads."

"Micmac, why don't you take a first pass with the phone."

"But—"

"Gimme a second." Lenny opened his computer. "Hey, Wi-Fi is on. I'll check the news." Seconds ticked by. "Wow! Look at this! They found a body floating down the Seine. North of Paris. Giverny. Where Monet lived. Body was messed up—they estimate ten days dead. Looked like a cross between a Renoir and a Picasso."

"Times are rough everywhere in this country." Crayle stepped to the window. There was unique beauty of the rooftops and ramparts. If he survived, he would return.

"Oh, shit!" Lenny squealed. "It's been ID'd." Holy Christ! Chantal Wohlford! Neil's wife. Wow, wow, wow!"

All eyes transfixed on the P.I. After what seemed like forever, Magus Crayle drew the conclusion.

"It's Pattie. She's gone rogue and every connection must go. It means she believes she'll succeed, and she's leaving no voices of dissent for afterward."

Hekka pointed out what no one else wanted to say. "That would include us."

Crayle turned to the gadget man. "Micmac, how are you doing with that phone?"

"I can't figure this out. I'll keep after it, but time is running out."

"Do we know whose phone it is?"

"Background picture. Wohlford's picture of himself."

"What's the sticking point?"

"Getting in, for starters. There doesn't seem to be a PIN at all. It goes to the keyboard entry message screen."

"Try *Pattie*."

"No."

"*Illuminé* with no accent mark."

"No."

"Backwards."

"Bingo! And this guy was CIA?"

"Bureaucrat level," Jack informed the team. "Not a doer."

"I'm afraid Pattie made it easy."

"Oh! Check this out. Right on his calendar. An itinerary."

Crayle looked over Micmac's shoulder and reviewed December. The names of the places, towns and villages, were cryptic. "The letters could be transposed. Or it could be a simple substitution code."

"I can help," Lenny said from the kitchen table. "My dad showed me his work using security apps. *Sapps* he called 'em. They're still on my computer."

Micmac glanced at Crayle, then handed over the phone.

The private investigator poked the keyboard several times, then grinned. "How much would you pay—"

"Lenny!"

"Jeez-Louise! It's a bi-level. It decrypts to a crypto in a foreign language. Any guess of a second language?"

"Probably like you," Phoebe assessed. "English was his first and second language."

"Cut it out. French?"

"Nope."

"Italian?"

"Nope."

"Lenny, she counted on you being with us. You're Jewish. And your father?"

"Yes, but—"

"Try Hebrew—transliterated."

Lenny shot Crayle a questioning glance.

"Transliterated. Hebrew characters spelled with English letters."

"Ah." Lenny pecked. "Ah, ah, ah!"

"He sounds like Oddjob."

"Phoebe …"

"Sorry."

"Alright, ye of little faith, I have, thanks to my father, Samuel Silberweiss, the itinerary."

Hekka posed a question. "If they still intend to blow up Paris and the entire French government, they will need money. Magus, you worked for the CIA. Jack, you worked for the CIA. Didn't she cut herself off by killing Mr. Wohlford and her husband?"

Not to be left out, Lenny opined. "And Lalumière can't get any money unless his son mules it."

"Maybe from this Elder," Micmac suggested.

"Wait!" Crayle had something. "Remember the slaying of Lenny's brother in Amsterdam. Phoebe, you mentioned a black velvet tray, and a few diamonds like the ones we liberated in Kaohsiung."

"Yeah. Covered in the guy's blood."

"Was there any kind of container? Even an empty one?"

Before Phoebe could answer, Lenny spoke up. "Uh, I wasn't going to tell you. I was going to be selfish for once. But too many people have died and, if this helps, maybe I can assist in stopping further mass murder." He reached into his satchel and withdrew a black ballistic nylon bag.

"That's it, Magus," Hekka cried out. "That's the bag Pattie took from Kobler's bank. Our diamonds were inside."

"They're still inside," said Lenny. "All of them."

"Then, even that is making sense. Pattie killed Wolfie, but did she manage to exchange our diamonds for cash? Perhaps Wolfie smelled a rat and refused. She killed him, heard the buzz-up from below, and left without them."

"She didn't fail completely, guys. She removed one more link in the chain."

"You're right, Magus." It was Hekka's turn at deduction. "The only ones left in Europe are Lalumière and his son."

"That's not all."

"What?" Hekka looked at Crayle.

"Remember what you said earlier. Us."

CHAPTER 37

Have you seen the news?" Lalumière was over-the-top upset. "The politicians. They meet tomorrow night. In Paris. Under the Eiffel Tower!"

"I was afraid of that."

"We must go to Paris now. But no more water, no more heights. By train!"

"That won't work."

"Then call Neil Wohlford. He will help!"

"That would take a séance. Let me think …"

"We have no time!"

A broad smile and dimples made him even more furious.

"Butterfly Tactic. We have to fly. I'll call my operative friend at the mortuary. Here, let's get you fixed up."

The fixed up version of Sylvain Lalumière exited the hearse at the Lyon airport and Pattie rolled him inside in a wheelchair—a standard component of French hearses in case the passenger in back needed fresh air.

The air terminal at Lyon appeared deserted. A lone clerk stood behind a counter.

"You're it? *Oh la la*." Pattie checked the surveillance cameras. The red operating lights were off. "What about security?"

The young man, dressed in black, shrugged. "Gone, Madame. How may I help?"

"We require a flight near to Paris. Orleans, for example."

"*Désolé*. There is no airport in Orleans. Perhaps Tours, Paris-Orly?"

Lalumière's eyes lit up.

"Oh, he likes that," the clerk observed with a warm smile.

"How about Toussus-le-Noble. Between Orleans and …"

"Versailles?"

"Yes, young man. Near Versailles. Is there a plane, a charter, available?"

"*Oui*. But he's very …" Having observed their appearance, he rubbed his thumb and forefinger together.

"Write it up."

"Oh! *Oui, Madame*." He scribbled on some multiple copy tickets and called to the gate. "Fifteen minutes. *Voilà!*" He lifted his head and peered into the business end of Pattie's silenced Manurhin.

Pfft.

Pattie, still in nun's attire, stepped behind the counter, opened two cabinet doors, and hefted the short, thin man inside.

The phone rang.

"Shit!" cried the nun.

Lalumière's face flushed red.

She lifted the receiver and coughed into the mouthpiece. "*Oui*." She coughed again, then hung up. "They are ready for us to board."

• • •

Inside Neil Wohlford's home in Carcassonne, Crayle gathered the team around the dining table. They improvised an additional chair for Lenny.

"Lalumière's not calling the shots. It's the girl. I believe she's lost it, which makes her even more dangerous."

"For example?"

"The letters, RLP, on the mirror in Zurich. Neil's wife. Leaving the diamonds behind after she killed Wolfie. *Crap!* The phone … quick … give me the phone."

Lenny complied.

"Contacts. There. RLP." He pressed *Call.* The second hand on his G-shock Stussy Bape Frogman, a present from Micmac, moved like an hour hand. Then …

"Hello, Magus."

He could feel the warmth of the dimpled smile. How to deal with a psychopath became his next problem. He tried it straight up. "I need you to come in. With Lalumière."

"And the football?" She laughed. "It's a game, Magus. Like the time we played *Find The Submarine.*"

He knew she'd used the fact that he couldn't remember his pre-crash operational days—they still resided only on the Rorschach computer.

"This isn't about submarines. It's about life. And death." Keeping her engaged provided his best chance at intel. *Death* was the magic word.

Her insanity pressed to the forefront. "I love playing cat and mouse—or is it, pussy and mouse. Did we play that?"

"You're breaking up," Crayle managed.

"Oh! My battery is low. I must hurry and tell you where we are." Her next laugh sounded off the charts unbalanced. "Here's the clue: Mitim is going to save France. Long ago, someone else saved France. Someone just like … me. We are at—"

Crayle heard a click.

"Hello!"

Silence.

"Pattie!"

• • •

Lalumière snatched the phone from her hand. "What are you doing! We are so close. Are you crazy?"

"We'll leave this single-use phone here. They'll track it."

"They'll find us!" He drew back the phone, taking aim at the hearth.

"No!" She kneed him, snatching it back. She plugged the phone into an outlet. "We'll be gone, my Mitim. Just west of Paris."

"Versailles?"

"*Oui.*"

She fabricated a circle with her fingers. The man, much taller, knelt before her. She placed the imaginary crown on his head. As he straightened to his full height, she stepped back. She knelt, recreated the circle, and then placed it on her head.

• • •

Lenny was too frustrated to peck on his keyboard. Now, he pounded. He searched everything. "No, no, no."

Phoebe brought her hand to her mouth. "It was the girl."

Micmac gripped her shoulders. "You need to set aside your hatred for this Pattie."

"No. Not her. The one who saved France."

"Joan?"

Crayle picked it up. "She's leading us to Orleans. It's north of here. South of Paris." He stopped. "She's luring us."

Hekka broke her silence. "She's luring a dangerous animal away from her destination. Serrano lore has such stories."

Crayle agreed. "Once in Orleans, we would likely be prevented from a direct entry to Paris. She has a clever plan. We only know the final destination. We need a way into Paris."

Lenny looked up. "The president?"

• • •

"You said we would land in Orleans. A large city. We are in the middle of nowhere. *Toussus-le-Noble* it says on the terminal. Even I know this is not the birth place of the maid, Joan."

"The Orleans bit was for Magus and crew. We need to see the palace one last time."

"You believe it will be destroyed, don't you?"

"Doesn't matter. When you're king, we're taking the French capitol south."

"If we explode underground, this place will be spared."

"We want the world to see, Mitim."

"There will be no more Paris."

"And no more Parisian waiters."

"Hmmm."

"January will be your first month in charge. Repeat after me. Off with their frikkin' heads."

"That's what they said about my ancestors."

"Off with their balls, then."

"That would just leave women."

"Works for me."

"Ah! I have a crazy one leading me to a disaster!"

"Crazy is relative. Speaking of which, where's Jean-Marc?"

"You have the only phone."

"Yes, with a multitude of virtual throwaway phones."

"Virtual?"

"Most spies get a phone, use it once, and throw it away. So they can't be tracked. It gets to be a pain … and expensive. On my S and T phone, I can employ a virtual phone, then delete it. *Voilà*."

"Then call him."

• • •

The young man—tall, lean, and exhausted—peered out from the Great Room at the family château garden. His Louis XVI chair, riddled with bullet holes from the Crayle team's assault in the early Fall, still held together to support his tall frame. He plucked his phone from his pocket. His ring tone, the initial bars of *Argent Tros Cher* by the French rock group *Téléphone* never grew old. It reminded him of his crucial meeting with his father in Luxembourg City so long ago.

"Jean-Marc."

"This is codename Angel."

"Codename?"

"It's Pattie. I'm with your dad."

He scanned left and right as if the voice was in the room. "Where do you have him?"

"Need to know. You must meet us in Paris. Tomorrow night. You must land at the Orly airport at five minutes past twelve."

"That would be Christmas Day."

"Just barely. Well?"

"I will charter a flight. It will be wonderful to see Paris from the sky at the stroke of midnight."

Pattie smiled. She had barely missed the Crayle team on its approach to Marseille with such a ploy.

"I heard," remarked Lalumière. "Thank you for including my son. He will be part of the new France." He kissed her forehead as she peered up at him.

Her smile was genuine. She was doubly happy. She had been with Jean-Marc on several occasions and liked him. She liked the taste of him. But for the royal line of succession to work for her, there could be no male heir in her way. Not even a legitimate heir. His midnight arrival would be his last.

CHAPTER 38

The drone of the Falcon's three jet engines didn't compare to the droning in Crayle's head. It seemed that, no matter the degree to which he pursued a resolution of all the data items, he remained in a fog. And, with him, the entire team. To make matters worse, their pilot seemed to be purposefully bouncing the aircraft around while skirting a major electrical storm.

Crayle hit his special direct dial key.

"Stones."

"Crayle here. Do you—"

The president chuckled. "Magus Crayle, I've been informed that you are out and about."

Crayle plowed ahead. "Mister President, it's going to be Paris. It's going to be tonight."

"Going to be what?"

"Lalumière, the man who tried to blow up New York. Didn't I tell you? He's alive."

"Impossible! The explosion off New York was nuclear. Five megatons. It lifted the Queen Mary 2 completely out of the water. He was in that water."

"He's alive, and he's procured another nuclear bomb—he's taking it to Paris." Crayle breathed harder now. He could tell from the sounds at the other end of the line that the president was shuffling papers and checking monitors.

"I have no NSA or CIA intel on this. That means they have nothing from the British Fivers and Sixers nor from the French DGSE."

"Not surprised. The people behind him are called Illuminé. It's a secret society offshoot of the German Illuminati. They've had a mole in the CIA this whole time. His name is Neil Wohlford. Head of the Strategic Situations Office. He kept their operations contained. He's dead. You'll want to check into his stuff."

"How can I not know this shit?"

Crayle heard the president typing. "I believe it's under Other Specialized Staffs."

"As in OSS? At the NSA, we learned that the spooks have an unusual sense of humor." The typing continued. "I'm finding nothing."

"Sorry, Mr. President … Kimbel. Hiding a huge covert op like this was easy. What's important is that I and my team are enroute to Paris as we speak. We need a way in … to the handshake-and-smile event the French president concocted."

"Oh, yes. I received an invitation, but chose not to get any of *their* shit on *my* shoes. Still, I can speak to him."

"Not today. They're in lock-down until tonight."

Silence.

"And all of their internal law enforcement is out of reach."

"You have something in mind, don't you?" Kimbel Stones pressed.

"Code name Charleroi."

"How—"

"Never mind, Kimbel. The man's a legend in the French spy agency, and we need their help ASAP."

"I'll get back to you in fifteen." The president hung up.

Crayle glanced at the team and observed the obvious. "Time is running out. And before anything else runs out ..." He jumped up, making for the plane's head, just as Lenny spun in his seat.

Crayle tripped over the P.I.'s foot. He tried to break the fall, but still had a death grip on his special phone.

Whack! The sound reverberated as his skull struck a table edge. Crayle crashed to the floor.

Lenny, the guilty party, was first to his side. "Magus, I'm sorry. My dad always said I had big feet." He lifted his leader to a sitting position. Surprising to all, Crayle's eyes popped open. Alert.

"One of my new old memories just connected. You won't believe this. Kimbel Stones was my NSA counterpart."

Phoebe interjected, "I thought he left the NSA to become mayor of that little California town ... what was it ... San Ernestino."

"Yeah," Lenny affirmed. "This goes back to before the accident, doesn't it, Magus?"

"Yes. His backstory goes far beyond his ascent into the political realm."

"So, with every lost old-memory restored, you know more about what you did in the CIA. We're no longer talking mathematics here, are we?"

Crayle shut his eyes. He grimaced. "Hero. Lover. Killer. Spy."

Twelve minutes later, Crayle heard the president's voice once again. "You're cleared to land at Paris-Orly. Transportation arranged."

"I'm happy your name Magus indicates that you're a Magic Man. This one'll take all the magic you can muster."

"I just need Lalumière's bomb, and the means to prevent it from going off. Piece o'cake."

"Since I now own the Central Intelligence Agency, or so I'm told, I've got someone pulling Neil Wohlford's files as we speak."

An attractive woman approached his desk with a box. She placed it gently, winked, and turned to go.

"Thanks, Dot."

As she reached the door, she turned for a longer-than-necessary glance. She followed it with a smile.

The president returned her smile. The door closed. "Okay, we're alone again. Let's see." He extracted the box's sole item, a tourist souvenir version of the Eiffel Tower. He flipped it upside down, and smiled once more.

"A memory stick." He popped it into his standalone computer. "Encrypted. No problem." He pulled the stick and pushed it into a recessed port marked NSA USB on the back edge of his desk. When a red LED turned green, he plucked it and re-inserted it into his computer.

"I've checked back at my old alma mater. Unofficial. An old colleague found a cell-sat dropbox that Wohlford used. Mine is a transcription."

"Actionable intel?"

The president related Rorschach's final communication.

"What put you on to that one piece?"

"That number was Rorschach's only speed dial number."

"You should've called it NSU—No Stone Unturned."

"Yeah."

"Kimbel, we don't have Neil, but I'm betting the computer we took from Rorschach has his memories. We can't perform a restore without the man himself, but we can look at the pictures. Might be a clue there. I'll have Lenny check it out."

"By the way, give him my condolences for his brother."

Crayle's tone was accusatory. "How'd you know about that?"

"Take it easy. I'm new at this job—I just got an update from Central Intelligence. I've flagged all matters relating to your team, Lalumière and his son, and the periphery."

"Sorry, Kimbel. We're on edge over here."

"Understandable."

"Anything else?"

"Just one thing. There's a brasserie in Paris called Les Deux Magots. Hemingway and his pals hung out there long ago. The name translates to two rich guys. There's no detail, but Chin and Lalumière fit the description."

"Maybe the Frenchman and his son. Or someone else."

"That's it, Magus."

Crayle was unsure whether to hang up on the president of the Unites States.

"Wait! I wish you could see this. I'm seeing architect's drawings of the Eiffel Tower and all the structural and other modifications since it was built. And schematics for the crawlers that travel up and down the legs."

"Send them to my phone. That might be something we'll need. Thanks, Kimbel."

"Good luck."

"The City of Light is at hand. Prepare for landing," came Flori's sultry voice over the intercom.

• • •

To preserve its iconic appearance, the Eiffel Tower required painting from time to time. With the economy in a shambles and his party clamoring for respite from the increasingly riotous citizenry, the French president had authorized the make-work development of something inexpensive in government terms, but highly visible. Necessary in order to boost public morale, he insisted.

Small L-shaped crawlers had been designed to attach to the top of each of the Tower's four legs. Paint was applied as two painters guided them down the structure. Upon reaching the plaza, the units were then removed and stored. On this Christmas Eve, workers would utilize them to adorn the Tower with holiday lights.

The impromptu gathering in the plaza, and the entirety of France wishing him to burn in hell, caused the French president to order the installation of lighting he had curtailed as an austerity measure. The party leader, noticing the potential danger to life and limb, changed his party's name from Socialist to Liberal-Conservative. It helped little.

Two members of the lighting installation crew for the Tower's northwest leg arrived late. They pushed through the screaming crowd and a security cordon. At a table designed for that purpose, an officer inspected their one piece of luggage. A vertically-striped blue, white, and red backpack.

"Two bottles Evian and a … *oh la la* … a football?"

Dressed in work clothes, Lalumière laughed and shrugged. "It was left in there. My son favors the American game."

Similarly clad, Pattie also shrugged.

The inspector shook her head. "At this moment, you and your colleagues are the most important people. Please hurry with the lights. All of France awaits." She scanned beyond the cordon. "And beware. This crowd can easily become a mob."

They skirted the Tower base to the leg assigned to their two Pattie-deceased predecessors. Lalumière glanced up. He froze.

"One thousand sixty-three feet to the top, my darling. If a smaller number will help, it's like an 81-storey building." Pattie examined his face. "Turning gray is not an option. You conquered your fear of the sea, of *water*, during your journey from the Château D'If. We're going for *height* this time. Here." She reached out. "Hold my hand, Mitim."

• • •

Magus Crayle and his team made ground fall on the approach of dusk, the sun a mere fifteen minutes above the horizon. A bent over man clad in a dark coat and a matching fedora met them. He pulled a children's wagon, which contained a cardboard box. He opened the box, doffed his hat, turned, and departed.

Crayle took charge. "Quick. Jackets and ID's."

The team members dove into the box and grabbed jackets, swapping for size in some cases. Hekka struggled with a zipper as she turned away from the group. Bright yellow letters on the jacket's back proclaimed DGSE.

Micmac peered into the box. "Hey! There's one more."

"A spare?" Phoebe guessed.

"In case of bullet holes," Lenny added.

"Am I late?" asked Jack's flight attendant.

Crayle realized he had been right. Flori's talents extended far beyond her sultry voice and what occurred aboard Jack's aircraft.

Jack smiled.

While Micmac distributed the remaining jacket, Crayle assessed. "Everyone … listen up. We'll be in close proximity up there. Watch your crossfire. No one is expendable." He turned to the P.I. "Can you do this, Lenny … after what happened to your brother?"

"I've resolved that, Magus. Wolfie picked the wrong crowd. Karma bit him in the ass. That's all. The girl did it. And she's up there!" He pointed at the Tower's peak.

"Mission, Lenny?"

"Mission."

The team donned lanyards purporting to contain identification. Crayle led the way to the Tower.

None of the three hundred law enforcement officers at the scene had ever observed a DGSE jacket. In point of fact, it made no sense. The *Direction Générale de Sécurité Extérieure* was France's spy agency. They didn't advertize. Neither did they operate on their home turf.

And because the French president's closest ally, the former American president, had committed suicide after the Queen Mary 2 catastrophe, no one challenged the team, fearing the wrath of their increasingly volatile and despotic national leader.

• • •

"Hekka, we go on that one," said Crayle, pointing to the southwest leg. "Phoebe and Micmac, southeast. Flori, Jack requested a partner for you—she didn't show. You take the northeast car alone. Jack and Lenny, take the elevator. All of you. Understand the following: Lalumière won't enable the bomb until he's ready to leave. When you spot them, don't negotiate. Take them down. Hard."

CHAPTER 39

The spy, Pattie Norbrunn, grabbed the Frenchman's hand. "Look up. Always up. And remember, my Mitim. Chin has *his* black stone. This one last act will earn you yours."

At the apogee of the northwest car, Sylvain Lalumière leaned in to affix a cradle for the football beneath the aircraft warning light. Pattie stretched, but in sport shoes instead of spiked heels, she lacked sufficient height to help.

"What's that?" she exclaimed. "I feel a rumble!"

Fearful, the Frenchman glanced down. "The other crawlers must be climbing."

Pattie leaned over the car rail for a better view. "The lights are already strung! This can't be good!"

• • •

Crayle and Hekka felt as if they travelled in slow motion. But, in just a few minutes, they arrived atop the southwest leg, their eyes fixed on the Lalumière car the entire trip.

"I go first, Magus. My legs are strong from the riding at my ranch. I can shinny." Gingerly, she left the car, wrapping her legs about the wet cross-beam. Crayle, taking her style lead, quickly fell behind.

Pattie's head spun. She worked her way onto the beam, ready to protect her Mitim and his bomb. Seconds later, they clashed. Atop the Eiffel Tower, the battle to dismantle or engage the bomb escalated. The women's battle blocked Crayle from the Frenchman.

• • •

As soon as Flori jumped inside the northeast car, another woman joined her. She remembered that Jack had sought a partner for her. No ID or description. No code phrase. She made a spy's usually fatal mistake. She assumed.

As they neared the top, the other woman yanked something from her pocket. Flori defended, utilizing her Brazilian grappling technique. Wrong choice. The other woman sported a high-power taser and jammed it into her midsection. The wetness of her clothing magnified the electrical discharge. Flori collapsed.

At the top, her attacker left her for dead. The woman sprang onto the cross-beam with the skill of a tightrope walker.

• • •

Fifteen feet from the bomb, Crayle pulled up behind the struggling Hekka. "Stop the insanity, Lalumière!" he yelled. "I created the Blackstone Strategy. I'm calling it off!"

"Over my dead body, Crayle!"

Not far away, and with his football securely mounted, Lalumière pulled at the radiation sponge. "No one must come here again. Paris must die!" he screamed.

Pattie turned. She started after the deranged Frenchman. "Leave the sponge intact. I'm going to live in Versailles!"

"You're both insane," Crayle yelled. "Hekka, pull her off!"

Hekka wrapped both arms around the diminutive spy, tugging and pulling until they broke free.

The women plummeted twenty-five feet, slamming into the top of the elevator. Rotted wood had been replaced with budget-sensitive clear plastic. Before they could re-engage, they and the plastic crashed to the floor. Only the clear layer separated the women from Jack and Lenny, who'd been flattened by the impact.

The elevator reached the top platform. Pattie crawled toward the opening door, her mind focused on Lalumière. "He's not going to destroy my dream!"

As the shaken Pattie rose to her feet, Hekka slammed into the spy. They tumbled back to the floor.

Pattie broke free. She escaped, repeating, "He's not going to destroy my dream!"

Crayle, forced into a decision between Lalumière and Hekka, stood and traversed the nearest beam toward the Tower center. Toward the elevator.

• • •

Phoebe and Micmac's crawler halted, stuck between cross-members. Having no way to enter the battle, they drew their weapons, looking for shots at Lalumière and Pattie through the multitude of steel bracings.

• • •

With Crayle's team nowhere near, the diminutive spy returned to her work.

Just then, a dark clad figure approached across a steel beam.

Pattie turned, drew her Manurhin pistol, and painted the red dot.

Lalumière recognized the figure and held up his hand. "*No!* It is Épiphanie. Jean-Marc's birth mother. She performed with Cirque du Soleil in her youth. She will help."

The woman overcame the narrow footing and pelting rain with her exceptional balance and absence of fear. She arrived and crouched beside Lalumière. She pulled electrical tools from a belt and began to splice a lead for the nuclear football. The countdown to midnight by the French president would do the rest. After they were safely away. Except for one problem.

Flori regained consciousness and, aided by her black belt in Brazilian Jiu-Jitsu, deftly traversed a cross-beam and dove at Lalumière's former mistress. They crashed into the northwest crawler before Pattie could turn and get a clean shot.

• • •

Jack and Lenny's elevator descended, reaching the restaurant in short order. Tonight's patrons, who felt they had purchased the fireworks E-ticket, paid them little notice.

• • •

In the plaza, the police cordon was about to be breached and the French government was about to be lynched. The president made a command decision. Midnight would come early this year.

"Dix … Neuf … Huit … Sept … Six … "

• • •

Phoebe and Micmac, on the opposite side of the Tower from the action, aimed their best, but the darkness beyond, the effective transparency of the black-clad participants, intensifying rain, and the proximity of fireworks bundles precluded taking a shot.

• • •

As the president had hoped, the crowd picked up the count.

"Cinq … Quatre … Trois … "

• • •

To this point out of the action, Micmac and Phoebe leaned to either side and sought clear shots. The government-designed crawler's brakes, proclaimed viable with minimal usage and absent testing for side loads, gave way.

"No!" they screamed as their crawler plummeted.

• • •

"Deux ... Un ..."

• • •

A bright flash of light. A huge explosion. Not the bomb. Lightning. Thunder.

The storm system's center arrived. Hail pelted those on the tower and the crowd below.

The fireworks bundles received their electrical signal from the French president. As if in concert with the heavens, their performance began. All eyes in the plaza jerked skyward.

At the top of the Tower, the *whoomps* of the fireworks fired skyward deafened. The explosions. The crackling. The flashes of light. All distracted the crowd and the police.

Lalumière, recognizing his predicament, grabbed the football under his arm. Not a candidate for suicide, he intended to take his ball and go home. Careful not to look down, he prepared his crawler for descent.

Flori, Pattie, and Épi all scrambled along their beam, trying to catch up with him. Épi reached over Pattie to grab the Brazilian. Flori spun. In self-defense, she applied a grappling technique to her pursuers. Her grip was vise-like. But in the struggle, and pelted by heavy hail, her foot slipped.

The feminine cluster plunged into the darkness.

Crash! A woman speared through the restaurant's ceiling, collapsing a set table and scattering diners in all directions.

Crash! The next woman slammed into a champagne fountain, spraying bubbly everywhere.

Crash! The third hit a cable strung with festive decorations. It whipped around her neck, dangling her in mid-air.

• • •

Heading down, Lalumière witnessed the battle and its consequence. His worries for his lover were trumped by his resolve. Whatever awaited him on terra firma would be welcome. Oddly, instead of anger and hopelessness, he felt a fierce inner pride. *Water* and *height* within a week. He had accomplished a great deal. But his feeling of elation evaporated. He began to sweat. What had befallen his Sandrine? His Magdalena? His Pattie?

CHAPTER 40

Frequent bolts of lightning danced over the Parisian landscape, some starting fires. The flames worked in concert with a number of automobile conflagrations ignited to demonstrate the rage of the citizen mob.

Ten of the mob sought shelter under an urban-tolerant London Plane tree. Like a government foray into social good, a great idea until it fails catastrophically. The next bolt exploded the tree, sending the shelter-seekers flying—most impaled with wooden shards, some splashing into the Seine.

Politicians in the Tower plaza, accustomed to hiding behind lies and political spin, transitioned into a comedy in euphemisms. They executed a massive Chinese fire drill, ran in circles, and into each other. The only calm was embodied in Archbishop Zoran, who stood atop the circular stage, humbled himself to his knees, and prayed.

As quickly as it had begun, the storm moved east beyond the city. Unable to congratulate themselves for solving anything, the politicians turned their attention to the man in religious vestments. The mob, calmed, stopped its rampage to listen.

"As all can see, problems, even those from displeasure in the heavens, can be resolved. It requires an unselfish heart. We must be able to accept the best in humanity, and utilize those attributes to propel us all forward. We must remove the cancers, for they destroy the human spirit, without which we are doomed."

The voice of an elderly woman bored through the cacophony. "Zoran—I'm an atheist!"

"No matter your external manifestation. You have a warm heart, a fertile mind, and an eternal spirit. Religious or not, those facts are indisputable. Those three gifts are either of a supreme and generous God, or not. To neglect them, or misuse them, is sinful either way."

The crowd ceased chanting and shouting curses. They now pressed in, under the Tower, to hear his every word. Hungry for resolution of their dire circumstances, they forced the politicians into a tight, donut-like band about the stage.

While the throngs pressed closer to the archbishop, the politicians, whispering loudly into each other's ears, formulated a plan. Never able to come together on matters of national or international import, they took mere minutes to agree upon a strategy for self-preservation.

It was the president who led them from the plaza and into the sewers of old Paris. They scurried past the ubiquitous rat population, which peered at them, then each other, as if to say, "Our plague agonizing, but quick. Theirs slow, with a death more dire."

• • •

Beyond the scene, a tall man carried his special football as he clambered into a hearse. He felt dead. He had heard the archbishop's fiery words. Strangely, they provided him solace. The prelate had presided at his son's initiation into the Illuminé. His dark mood turned.

His son, Jean-Marc, appeared both frustrated and resolved. "That was our chance, Father. Give me the ball. I will join the crowd. Explode the bomb. I will give you your dream."

"You are a wonderful son. I couldn't have asked for better," Lalumière said, bleary-eyed. "No. The crowd will disperse. Nothing will change. But the time will come, and I will share—I must share—my future with you."

"First, we have a change in plans. We will not travel west to the CIA mortuary as originally planned. You've had a very rough day. Please try and relax."

As if led by the thunder and lightning storm, the vehicle of death headed east and out of Paris past Euro-Disneyland and into France's Champagne region. The landscape, drab with the season, rolled gently, providing a smooth ride.

"I have good news. All police surveillance on our château ended with the New York explosion, Father. We're going home."

The partition separating them from the driver lowered. The man, also Illuminé, turned, smiled, and pointed a silenced automatic. "I am Mr. Wohlford's Plan B."

"He's dead!" cried Lalumière.

Two shots rang out. The driver's head slammed against his seat back. Father and son jumped as his red effluence decorated them in a spatter pattern.

They saw the two holes in the windshield before the hearse slammed into an embankment. Jean-Marc jumped out the door.

Sporting a scoped rifle, Pattie Norbrunn approached. "Let's agree that you didn't run off and leave sweet little Pattie. And let's agree that I just saved both of your lives." She placed the weapon on the hearse's hood. The two of them tossed the driver's body over the bank and into the river. The bloody Somme, bloodier.

• • •

At the base of the northwest Tower leg, the remaining crew gathered at the pre-planned rendezvous. Jack held his abdomen as red drops dripped from under his parka.

"We'll make our way out," Jack wheezed. "I need some help. Thank God, you're all in one piece. The police and gendarme forces have been decimated by the economy. The ones they have are still at the … the … Convergence. Follow me."

He directed them across the Seine via the Pont de l'Alma to the Bateaux Mouches tour boat station. A boat crew, still in awe of the stark variety of aerial fireworks, huddled in a shelter from the cold. In spite of signs proclaiming that Acts of God, unstable sailing conditions, or unfavorable weather would preclude departure, the team bribed and threatened the men, coming to an agreement in short order.

A short ride and a drop-off later, Jack Sommers led them up *Rue du Vieille Temple*, Old Temple Street, to *Rue des Rosiers*, Rosebush Street. They turned right at the inviting Jo Goldenberg delicatessen. The team was hungry enough to eat the iconic red awnings, but the project leader pressed them onward. He stuck to the cement sidewalks, avoiding the uneven, narrow, and empty brick street.

Jack waved above, wincing as he did. "These five-story buildings are centuries old, but they and the narrow street protect us from any bothersome overhead surveillance."

Stumbling forward with the aid of Crayle and Micmac, Jack led the weary crew past a number of windows sporting Falafel sandwich signs. They stopped mid-street and checked both ways. No one tonight—save the team—in the Jewish Quarter.

Lenny pointed his tablet computer with an enhanced low-light camera at the various signs along the way. Intel sprang to the screen overlaying the visual. "*École du Travail.* Entire faculty and all the boys shipped off during the Nazi years. Hitler killed 'em all."

Although it pained him dearly to reach above his head, Jack knocked three times on the top of the doorframe, hitting a concealed pressure sensor each time. "An old colleague … owes me … a favor," were the words he threw over his shoulder. Before he collapsed.

His right hand raised to quiet the entry detection doorbell, a man creaked open the centuries-old, over-painted door. He stooped to peer at his long-time associate, Jack Sommers. "Ah, you are alive." Then, he glanced up at the others, then stepped back. "Please. *Entrez-vous.* You may call me Charleroi."

• • •

Back at the Eiffel Tower plaza, the archbishop concluded his words to the masses in record time for a man of the cloth. To the cold and huddled, he'd utilized his natural leadership abilities to whip them into a cheering, admiring throng. Everyone brought into abeyance by this Croatian cleric joined in. They understood the safety in association better than anyone. Some appeared unsettled when they heard, *"Zoran! Zoran! Zoran for President!"*

CHAPTER 41

The road east was open. The sight of the long, black hearse drew stares and sighs—an apparent expression of gratitude for not being the one in the back. In less than four hours, Lalumière peered through the dark-tinted side window and viewed the forest of the Vosges. His forest. Another half hour and Jean-Marc approached a billboard, pressed a clicker, and saw it swing to one side. Once he guided the hearse through the opening, the billboard swung shut.

"Take your time down the driveway. Let me savor the twinkling of sun through my trees."

The drive, long and winding, soon terminated beside a field of grape vines and an overgrown, iron-gated, walled compound.

"My son, you have not cared for the château in my absence. After all I accomplished."

No longer asleep, Pattie's eyes moved beneath closed eyelids. After all *we* accomplished, she mentally corrected.

"You are right, Father. Please understand that I have travelled far. To Miquelon to retrieve you and transport you to Victoria. And then to more meetings with the northern royals. And then to the Eiffel Tower. I need a little slack here."

"You are right. I am an ingrate. But I have travelled far, sacrificed my body and soul, and survived immense odds."

"You, too, are right, Father."

Lalumière caught his breath. "Stop! Something is wrong! The gate is open. You would not leave it so."

"Stay in the vehicle, Dad. Pattie and I will investigate." He removed a Sig-Sauer 9mm from his waistband.

"Jean-Marc. What are you doing with that firearm?"

"Self-defense, Papa."

"I'm little," the spy whispered to Jean-Marc. "You're tall. Stay behind. Watch my back."

She moved up to the wall, and then along it to the gate hinges. A large white van stood parked next to the château's entry. Two men, dressed in turquoise overalls, loaded case after case of Lalumière wine. A woman attired in cream-colored cargo pants and a dark green top, and no doubt the lookout, puffed on a Gitanes, argued with her cell phone, and paid no attention to the gate.

Pattie screwed a Brausch silencer onto the business end of her Manurhin semi-automatic. She waited until the men went inside again, transferred the gun to her left hand, and positioned it behind her back. She limped toward the woman, waving her right hand high in the air.

"Excusez-moi, Mademoiselle. Voulez-vous—"

Pfft. Pfft.

One of the remaining thieves toted another case out the door. Pattie, back to the wall, let him step into the van. She cleared her throat. He turned, paused, and stared at the petite addition to the scenery.

Not being one to risk a case of fine wine, she nodded at the woman on the ground. *"Elle a une maladie."*

He set down the case of wine to attend to his ill comrade.

Pfft. Pfft.

The third thief heard the commotion and ran to the door. He drew down on Pattie. A shot rang out. The man crumpled on the stairs, and then rolled onto the gravel. Still alive.

Pfft. Pfft.

Pattie turned. There stood Jean-Marc, smoke emanating from his barrel with a blank stare on his face.

"First blood. You've got the look. And thanks. Expect to get lucky. Tonight."

The young Frenchman glanced back at the vehicle bearing his father. Then back at Pattie. That he would be repaid for saving her life with sex did not register cleanly into his mental computer. He didn't need intrigue between himself and his father, but turning down this woman could be fatal.

She broke his reverie. "Come on, Jean-Marc. Let's get this wine back into the house. I'm starving, and I'll need some slosh to go along with the food."

"And the bodies?"

"You still have that guillotine? How 'bout some chopped steak?"

Chameleon-like, the son's face emulated the estate's sage-colored surroundings. "We will consume other food."

Lalumière entered his château. "I will prepare the meal." He waved at the dead thieves. "You two. Dispose of this garbage."

• • •

With the three bodies buried well into the forest and their white van driven down the roadway and over a cliff into dense foliage, the three gathered in the wine tasting room to prepare appetizers. Jean-Marc thin-sliced a wedge of cheese, while waving a special knife as he spoke. "Father, you and Pattie relax. Have some cheese, especially the aged parmesan and gruyère. I'll prepare our dinner."

"And what might that be?"

"Your favorites. The cheese followed by wisps of prosciutto and thin slices of provolone. You love Italy."

"I hate Italy and everything from it. I shall never return … and why do you serve me this … this … foreign food?"

"It's been awhile. It's all that's left. Everyone French is unemployed or on strike."

The older man groaned. "The world—or at least France—is coming to an end. Why, tell me, does it need a king?"

The two knew better than to respond.

Pattie carried a wine bottle into the Great Room. Placing it on a coffee table, she replaced the fleur-de-lis bouquet in an ornate vase with the football. She stepped back. "There. Focus. As children, we learn how to use the ball to win. And what does win mean in our frame of reference? To win, we must replace the French government."

"Right now, they would probably pay us to take their place." Sylvain Lalumière, the hermit lookalike, sauntered in and plopped onto the sofa. He'd brought toast that appeared to have come from a Lilliputian loaf and placed a combination of the cheeses on a slice. "Mmm. The Italians and the Swiss."

Finally, the son strode in with an 18th century bottle of Nordic water. "Had the archbishop not stepped in, the crowd would have devoured the sorry …"

"Yes. In one way of thinking, he got in our way."

"If we're smart, we'll manipulate him to our own ends. I just don't see how."

"Oh," Lalumière lamented. "If only Magus Crayle were here. You should have heard his brilliance in devising my plan."

"Had you followed it, you'd be king. Right now. But you changed it."

"You are grousing, Jean-Marc. In the beginning, after he had developed Chin's plan, he told me that he provided consulting and, no matter how excellent the plan, it could fail if not executed to the letter."

Before father and son could reach further into the enigma of their existence, Pattie's ringtone played Taps. She listened intently before returning the phone to her pocket.

The two men sensed the newborn tension.

"We've got to move. DGSE has gotten wind that the place is occupied. Probably the heat signatures of the thieves. We're still on someone's hotlist. Listen carefully. We haven't lost yet, and we're not going to lose." She glanced left. "Prince?" Then right. "King?" Rare for her, Pattie drew in a steadying breath.

Her demeanor caused Lalumière and Desrochers to sober as they leaned closer to her.

"Here's what we must do," she began.

CHAPTER 42

It was a matter of hours by car or train from Rome to the Cinque Terre region of Italy's Liguria region. The arc-shaped coastal area known as the Italian Riviera was centered at Genoa, eighty-five miles from the French border. Just beyond lay the Principality of Monaco. The two men were whisked incognito into the garage of a hillside villa. The Elder dressed in the garb of a successful business man while Archbishop Zoran chose a more servile, non-ecclesiastic appearance.

"My deepest congratulations, Zoran. You've nearly pulled off the coup of the century. Many centuries, in fact."

"It has been a long road, Elder. We are at the threshold."

"We've come too far to let up. We must redouble our efforts and press this to the end. No matter how devious and incompetent the previous American president, Magus Crayle's Blackstone Strategy has surpassed all of the scandals and cover-ups and more."

"How do you feel regarding what is about to transpire?"

Zoran settled into a sumptuous chair and reflected. "The Illuminé goes back many, many years. Always, it fought religion—organized religion. It maintained that great minds, rather than blind beliefs, provided the key to quality governance. Great minds solved problems. Lesser minds used guilt, divine pre-destination, and belief systems to avoid addressing the problems of the masses."

"We are about to change that, and you have become the catalyst. After all of our work to prepare you and to set the stage, tomorrow will be your, and our, biggest day."

"I wish it were so simple. There may be several days. There may be weeks. It has happened before."

"Worry not. As the Americans say, the fix is in."

"Not to throw a monkey wrench into the works, but this won't appear to be a fixed outcome. Am I right?"

"Again, Crayle provided the perfect solution. From Lalumière's Water Diamonds to the Blackstone Perfection. The puzzle pieces have all fallen together with the exception of the final one."

The Elder popped the cork and poured the champagne. He held up his hand to thwart any early moves by the archbishop, and dabbed a special litmus paper into each. "Ah, green. Thanks to the American spy agency's Science and Technology group, we may safely engage in a toast."

"Here, here!"

They quaffed their glasses in one gulp. Refilled. Another gulp. Before twenty minutes had passed, they were both asleep on a Louis XIV settee.

• • •

After a few hours, they awoke, refurbished. The archbishop poured drinks this time. Effervescent water from a nearby Italian spring. He presented a glass to the Elder before furrowing his brow. "Why me? Why did you choose me?"

"I will answer your question shortly."

"Still, I must thank you for your assistance in my promotion to Archbishop."

"Yes. A pity that your competitor, Bishop Uzelac, lost his footing and fell from his bell tower."

"And, in the process, sliced his carotid artery."

"A freak accident, no doubt." As time passed, the Elder's confidence that he was without limit increased with each move on the chessboard. "Remember, Zoran, that you are a spy. A mole. For Illuminé to succeed, the Roman Catholic Church must crumble."

"But how can I, a simple—"

"I have gone far beyond what you have witnessed. Tomorrow, there will be a meeting of the cardinals. A conclave. They will choose a new pope. I have placed *your* hat in the ring, as they say."

"But I'm young. Inexperienced. How—"

"The how is not important. You must become infallible for us to achieve mastery of the human race."

"How can anyone destroy a religion?"

"It will be a challenge to you, but I believe it can be accomplished. You will diffuse the church's strengths."

"But it's about human nature's spirituality. That's why religion exists in the first place."

"It's about questions … and their answers, Zoran. The pair of opposing factions are scientific proof … and blind faith."

"We've seen nothing but smoke and mirrors from the scientists. To this day, big bang or not, no one has proven where the substance of the universe came from."

"Precisely. How could space transform from the absence of anything, to the presence of everything, and to this big bang?"

The archbishop laughed. "I feel like the two-headed god. I have my intellectual, scientific head, and my spiritual head. And each asks questions."

"An excellent mind must constantly seek answers. Please. Continue."

"Let's say that Catholicism collapses. Where do the masses turn to express and sate their spirituality? Protestantism? Too bland. Too black and white. No wow factor. Islamism? No one wants to step back into the seventh century."

"Permit me to stop you, Zoran. Do you think for one moment that I would allow the remaining religions to survive?"

The archbishop's eyes widened.

"The Church has diverged from its grand purpose. It reasserts with every edifice, with every acquisition of art, that the masses are indeed the sheep and the Church their shepherd. Their master. Visibly, the shepherd's wealth grows beyond measure as the flock is fleeced."

"Please accept my next words in the spirit of an intellectual joust. Your statement exceeds cynical … but I can't argue the point. Forgive me for delving into your mind, Elder, but you seem to have drawn a direct parallel between governance and religion. You are saying that societies have evolved to power elites. Secular. Religious. It doesn't matter. Am I right?"

The Elder appeared quite pleased. "Bravo, my son."

Given the irony of the religious entreaty, the archbishop leaned back. He considered a chess euphemism. Time for him to deploy his queen. "What if the new pope … began liquidation of the holy treasures?"

"This is why I chose you."

They pushed aside the sparkling water, graduating to crystal glasses of single malt.

"As I warned. The most important event of our lives will be the emergency conclave. On December twenty-eighth."

"Tomorrow."

"It's the premier religious question on this planet. It must be decided *before* the new year begins."

"There are just four days left."

"The biggest surprise for you … and I take you into the strictest confidence. You, as I have indicated, are on the shortlist."

"But …" the archbishop blanched. "… I'm an atheist. It's—"

"Impossible?"

CHAPTER 43

A warm weather system swept into the north of the European continent, though it had not yet pushed into central Italy. With the dated heating systems fully engaged in the chambers, the electorate donned heavier mantles for warmth. The fascinating beauty of the elongated nave overwhelmed consideration of creature comforts, but it still paled against the seriousness of the task at hand.

The Cardinal Chamberlain, the man in charge, entered the quarters. His squat personage did nothing to diminish his strength of presence.

"Of course, you know where we are, why it is historically special, and what we are about to achieve. Since the time of year is late, and we must conclude our work prior to its end, I will be brief."

A few of the cardinals cleared their throats. Brief speeches in The Vatican's more than eighty-year history were a rarity. That Cardinal Secretary of State Pietro Gasparri had signed the Lateran Treaty, causing the tiny country's creation, was known to few. And no one recalled that the prime minister who'd signed for Italy had been none other than its future dictator, Benito Mussolini.

The Cardinal Chamberlain continued. "I have the list of candidates, but I'm certain it has been previously disclosed to you ..." He glared at his staff. "... and, consequently, you are familiar with them all."

A lone voice emanated from the throng. "There are but two candidates, Your Eminence."

An ungodly hush overcame the room.

The chamberlain sought out the voice's owner, but all attendees appeared the picture of innocence. He cleared his throat—there were to be no further interruptions. "This list is a starting point. You will confer, add others as you see fit, and then I will collect the completed list for validation and verification. Once done, I will present the final list of candidates to you, you will confer once again, and then proceed to the first vote." With that, the chamberlain stepped back. The cardinals began to engage each other in assorted cliques.

At the far end of the large room, two cardinals paced the floor.

"The man is three hours late. There is no time to lose," mumbled one.

A disturbance to their left caught their attention.

A man strode into the room, a Swiss guard still tugging at his vestments.

"I am Cardinal Smith. Unhand me. Or I'll have you damned."

Cardinal Fratze rushed to the American's aid. "It's alright. *Geht's guet*," he added in Swiss. The clown-uniformed sentry eyed the German cleric for a moment, then retreated to his post.

"I am Cardinal Fratze. The vote takes place in forty-five minutes. We must talk first. Where have you been? You were notified yesterday of the emergency conclave."

"In Marseille. Visiting the Notre Dame de la Garde site on the mount just east. The building was severely damaged by the nuclear explosion. November 15, if I recall correctly. Several of us showed the church colors and blessed those who did not perish. My return flight to Rome diverted me north to Paris. There were delays. It seems that baggage handlers have gone on strike and the pilots demonstrated their sympathy with a work slowdown, and by drinking more alcohol than usual."

"That's insane. There are few travelers, fewer jobs, and still they strike?"

"It's a regular thing. Built into the system. The union negotiators extract higher salaries for the same work. Then, from the newfound wealth, extract most of the difference for themselves and their abetting and abiding politicians."

"Never mind that now," said the German. "You can pray for all of their souls another time."

"There aren't enough hours."

"Like I said, never mind. We must win this vote."

"Should we lose, there's Hell to pay … really." The second of the pacing cardinals, Cardinal Alighieri, proffered a leather-bound notebook, opening it to a bookmarked page. "*Our* candidates."

The young American looked up. "There's only one."

Two nods.

"Please help me, I am new. What are the qualifications for a name to be entered onto this list?"

The Cardinal Chamberlain passed by, pleased that the unruly pair of cardinals had calmed. "I am so glad you've asked, young man," he said in an admonishing tone. Without answering, he continued on his rounds.

The young man turned to the pair of older men, who'd gathered on either side of him. He glanced left and right, engaging them both. "I am Cardinal Oswald Smith from America. Saint Louis diocese."

"Ah, yes. We know. A diocese named after the sainted King Louis IX. I am Cardinal Alighieri. Of Italy."

The younger man relaxed, then leapt to his feet. "I've hurried here. I need a …"

"W.C.?" The German, sporting a permanent grimace and having introduced himself as Cardinal Fratze, pointed in the direction of the Sistine Chapel, knowing the man would not gain entry.

The young cardinal hurried away.

"When he returns, he will need our help even more."

"We need him."

"Pray tell. Why is he key?"

The mischievous Cardinal Alighieri inserted a moment of silence. "I can tell you why he is the most critical man in this room—to the outcome."

The other man shrugged. "Okay …"

The first lifted his chin and slowly rotated back and forth, as if trying to detect an aroma. He scanned. Safe. He leaned closer and whispered, "I have taken account of the position of every cardinal. My tally is accurate. He's the tiebreaker."

"But he's not Illuminé! Not one of us!" came the hushed response. "You, my friend, are the devious one. How do we …?"

Alighieri closed the gap until his lips brushed the other's ear. "Seduce him?"

The other man's eyes turned to fire. "Yes."

"We play to his ego. What does he wish to have … more than anything?"

The other man sat back. "Seriously?"

"Seriously."

"He would like—you'll love this—for the pope to direct our Roman Catholic Church to divest itself of all riches. And actually feed the poor."

An unholy silence ensued.

Fratze curled his lips. "Then we have just the pope for him."

They shook hands.

One motioned the other close. "Here's how we do it."

CHAPTER 44

The mountains in the northwestern aspect of Italy were rather cold with snow patches and the occasional howling winds through west-facing valleys. On this blustery day, few braved the weather. Unlike the scruffy man ensconced in the fortified hillside structure, they remained sheltered of their own free will.

"Let me out!" The man shook the bars with every ounce of strength. "Let me out!"

"Quiet, my love. You should've mastered this by now."

"You mean after the Bastille, Château D'If, uh … Montserrat …"

"The last one doesn't count. It wasn't a formal incarceration. But you've hit my sympathy chord. Give me your clothes. Every last one."

"I need them. It's freezing in here." He slapped his arms at his torso for emphasis.

"They require washing."

It was true. The rancid-smelling togs of the hermit had replaced the new clothes he had donned at his château. He reluctantly disrobed, handing her the clothes.

"You are so tense, even for a lay person." She reached through the bars below his belly, reeling him closer. "Relax." The little nun bent to her knees and proceeded to relax her partner in crime. The pace of his heart accelerated for the next few minutes, warming him.

"Go lay down, Mitim. Under the covers. I'll be right back."

He lifted the polar fleece-type blanket, similar to those at his other residences, and punched in sleep number 92. In record time, the man who appeared ever more hermit-like achieved a deep sleep.

A rat-tat-tat-tat-tat rattled his cage. Pattie Norbrunn's present incarnation, Sister Magdalena, reversed her cross, and again dragged it across the bars.

Her prisoner leapt to his feet.

"Good! Your heart's ready. Time for the exercise yard." She nodded at the rusted door.

He pushed. No movement. Again and again, his heart raced. He leaned into it with his weight. Again. Nothing. He quit, expended.

She felt it necessary to remind him of her control over every aspect of his life. "Back away."

When he followed her command, she unlocked the door. He stepped into the stone passageway.

Since she maintained the only flashlight, she led them along the dank, dark hallway, him following in her footsteps. In ten minutes, they stepped through an arch-topped heavy door. Their hands went to their eyes to shield them from the blinding light.

They ascended stairs in a wall tower. She unlocked an iron gate, much more breachable than the cell door by modern methods.

"There's no one here?"

"No." Pattie swished along. "Piedmont, and with it the rest of Italy, is headed for Rome, anyway they can."

"Christmas has passed. Why?"

"The new pope, our pope, is to deliver a world-changing speech. Catholicism will change forever, my love."

"Then we, too, must go." He gestured with both arms, still nude.

"Did you know Napoléon was in this part of Italy?" She peered through a crenellation and pointed. "That valley, *Valle di Susa*, passes this way from France. These fortifications were built to keep him, and any other French, out."

"It has a name?"

"*Forte di Exilles*. Come. I want to show you a very special room."

He followed her along another dank, dark hallway. When she stopped, he saw the sign. "I see. All of these prisons are symbolic. Every such place you've taken me were residences of the Man In The Iron Mask." He sighed recognition, and resignation.

"Never forget who you are. You are Mitim." She gestured at the cell. "This is your heritage. This is you. You are imprisoned for the sole purpose of breaking free. To know what the original endured. Our failure in Paris was a setback. A learning experience. Did you learn?" Her head twitched.

"In how many places was this man imprisoned? How many more before I can meet my destiny?"

She had a ready answer, but his question evoked in her another question. What about *her* destiny? He broke her reverie.

"I want to leave. I am tired of this pathway to royalty. I want to visit all of Napoléon's places. Elba …"

Pattie experienced an epiphany. If not Rome, why not halfway? "Corsica?"

"Yes! *Yes!* His place of birth."

"Well, if you don't behave, this fort contains three possibilities for solitary confinement. And beyond our near-term adventure, there will be one more Mitim residence to visit. And that one will be the last. It has a lovely view of Cannes."

"The island, Sainte Marguerite."

"But not this trip. So relax."

"I will do as you say." Sincerity sounded absent from his voice.

She brought her fingers to her mouth. "Hmmm." She squinted at her watch. The hour-hand is between Joseph and Mary, and …"

He grabbed her wrist. "This is a religious watch. Where did you get it?"

"At Montserrat. Mother Superior wanted me to have it. Don't you just love how they used crosses for the two hands?"

Hopelessness attacked him once again. He stood naked on the ramparts of a fortress-prison where the original Mitim had been held captive—in ice cold weather with a serial killer. "I am changing our plan."

She moved closer, her tone softened. "No, no, no, my love. We have a place we must go, and we must arrive by the 31st, in two days, or our dreams …"

"*Our* dreams. What are *your* dreams? What do *you* really want?"

"You already know. I want you to give me a very special gift when you become king."

His voice portrayed both suspicion and apprehension. "What manner of gift?"

"France."

He glanced at her. His brow furrowed, his eyes pleading. Then, he expressed resignation. "Then, where do we go?"

"I'd love to tell you, but it's classified." She appeared sorry.

"Who do you take orders from?" He grabbed her shoulders and shook. "Who?"

"Stop! Stop!" She shoved him away. The heave of her chest calmed. "Alright. Let's figure this out. I need your help with this. It's not my husband, Randy. He's dead. It's not my boss, Neil. He's dead. Hmmm. Tell you what. I'll introduce you personally. By the 31st. How's that?"

He began to feel that hopelessness had levels. Degrees. And with each of her sentences, he sank farther. "There is something I must do first. After that, I will do as you say. Agreed?"

"Sure. Anything."

"Take me south. Take me to Genoa."

"Genoa?"

"The Genoese ceded Corsica to France just before Napoléon was born."

"I see where you're going."

"Ajaccio."

"Of course. Aircraft activity is limited to police and military because of the pope thing. We catch a ferryboat from Genoa to Corsica. We are so close. Why didn't I think of it?" Her expression betrayed no signs of her manipulative acumen.

"I know much about the most famous of French emperors. When we learned about him in school, I went deep into the library resources. He was born Napoleone Buonaparte of an Italian family. Later, when it became necessary, he changed his name to the French equivalent."

"Napoléon Bonaparte."

He nodded. "He was an enigma. In the years following the revolution, he became emperor."

"When your ancestors lost their heads? Sorry. But I see what you mean. He wanted and needed absolute authority, but he couldn't be king—without the bloodline."

"He was the first French emperor since …"

"Charles the Fat."

"All that history—it means little to the people of today."

"But we travelled the Route Napoléon to Paris. In our quest."

"Unlike the Corsican, we failed." The naked man turned morose.

"Not so, my Mitim. Some say that history repeats, others that it is always different. When they write about you after your death, historians and biographers will mention the similarities *and* the differences. You won't be the second coming. You'll represent a unique blend. The past … and the present."

"You always elevate my heart when it has reached a low."

His gratitude touched her. For a moment. "Let's move our thoughts forward. Let's say that, instead of king, you'll be Napoléon the Fourth, and I, your Josephine."

At long last, he smiled. "Angel, Anne-Isabel, Sandrine, Sybille, Pattie, Sister Magdalena, and now Josephine. How many more, my darling?" He turned for her response. In just those few seconds she had become, like him, naked.

Their coupling began quickly. Then, she pulled away, spun, and leaned forward onto a gap in the crenellation.

As Lalumière re-engaged, he thrust ever harder. They gulped chilled air, scorching their lungs.

"Once more!" he cried. *"Once more!"*

His final, emphatic thrust pushed them both over the limit. And over the wall.

Good fortune smiled down upon them now. They landed atop scaffolding in place for the never-ending restoration of such monuments. Finishing flat on his back with her on top, he caught his breath. She, likewise. He stroked her hair.

In just a few minutes, their breathing returned to normal. The mentally unstable spy purred, "They're not looking for you in Italy. Still, you must travel as my hermit charge. And I as the good Sister. Come!" She stood, extending her hand to him. "We must climb back into the fortress, travel to Genoa, and take the ferry to Corsica. Oh, Napoléon, I love you so!"

CHAPTER 45

A saddened Magus Crayle sat on the view deck atop their hotel. Exhausted, he was not yet ready for sleep. His eyes swept the City of Light from the tall office buildings of the west-end La Defense, across the Opera, the white Sacré Coeur basilica in the north, the Louvre, to the July Column marking the Place de la Bastille a few hundred yards from their location. Everyone had retired for the night, leaving peaceful streets.

The out of breath P.I. ran out onto the deck. "Check out the TV, Magus. The RAI channel is doing a piece on the new pope."

"Not interested, Lenny. I'm enjoying the view."

"This guy looks real familiar. That's all."

Crayle reluctantly followed him back to the room. He glanced at the flat screen. What he saw startled him. He walked to within three feet of the image. "It's him! Tell everyone! That's him!"

"What is it, Magus?" Hekka ran in from the kitchen.

"Yeah, what's with the racket? We're trying to sleep." Micmac and Phoebe entered from the bedroom. Her smile confirmed that the former UDT man had interfered with her sleep plans.

"I'll bet he's the one who grabbed Lalumière's bomb!" Lenny glanced around for agreement.

All eyes flashed to the screen.

Micmac broke the silence. "You're pullin' my leg. That guy in the white outfit—that's the new pope."

"I'm telling you, I bet he's got the bomb."

"Pope's save people, I've been told. If he took it, it was in order to save the people of Paris." Hekka deduced. "If he has it, I'm sure he's had it disarmed and put in a safe place. Since there are no more bombs, everyone is safe. We can return home now."

Crayle shook his head. "There's been something wrong all along. There's a piece that either Rorschach didn't have, or didn't restore. Let's put what we know together."

"Do it, Mag."

"We have two megalomaniacs: Chin and Lalumière. Above them, the mysterious Elder. Off to the side, there was Jack's boss, Neil Wohlford."

"Jack's on our side, right?" Lenny sought reassurance.

"Jack takes orders. He's an implementer. I don't think he goes off on his own. Right now, he's a question mark."

Phoebe asked, "Lalumière? And his son?"

"Lalumière's disappeared. Alive, dead, we don't know."

"And ..."

"Jean-Marc?"

Holding his abdominal bandage tight with both hands, Jack hobbled in. "Saddle up. I've got a place in the mountains where we can catch our breath. Different country. You'll love it."

"But—"

"Now, Lenny. *Rock and roll!*"

• • •

Jack had been able to clear his jet under the airspace restrictions. The few-hour flight from Paris-Orly afforded them a modicum of additional rest. By the time they reached Jack's destination, he knew they had to let everything out. The villa came stocked with every manner of booze known to mankind. Without exception, they took advantage.

• • •

Still clad in a wine-stained toga from the previous night's let-it-all-out bash, Hekka Poppi personified the reason American Indians preferred to forego alcohol.

The Italianate kitchen mixed dark, heavy wood with handcrafted and painted tiles to embody rustic. That there was still a crystal water glass in the cupboard was beyond miraculous. Nothing like the sturdy old-fashioned glassware with which her mother had stocked the ranch, it performed the only function necessary at the moment.

Plopped into the last of the Nordic water, her Alka-Seltzer tablets created their guaranteed fizz. The sound—given her condition—was akin to heavy metal Metallica played through the villa's $20,000-per-pair JBL Synthesis S4700 speakers and a cranked amplifier.

When the sound completed, she plodded through the double glass doors onto a 500 square foot veranda. Lake Lugano. It spread to her right to its eponymous city and beyond. To her left, the lake proceeded across the Swiss border to the Italian town, Porlezza. Jack had remarked that he'd once sailed the lake steamer to the town to purchase a beautiful pair of shoes and a knit sweater for his wife for a mere $30 U.S.

Hekka smiled that he, at one time, had a love like hers.

"Did I mention the shoes and sweater last night?" came a voice from behind.

"You did, Jack. I bet Marilyn still has them."

"Y'see that little patch across the lake? Campione d'Italia. It's Italian, surrounded by Switzerland. They didn't want to play ball when the Swiss Confederation was formed."

"Independent people. They didn't want to change their ways or compromise. I understand that."

"There's a casino. A big one. It's where I proposed to Marilyn …" He teared up.

"This is not my business … perhaps she will take you back."

"She began to think that way. That maybe I wasn't such a jerk-off."

"Then there's hope."

"Until Malibu. I'm afraid that was the final nail."

She didn't understand the words he'd used, but she got the meaning. "Then there will be someone else. Someone new. Perhaps someone close. I don't know. I just feel that."

He hung his head. "Hey. How 'bout that new pope?"

She skipped over the deflection. "I see happiness. For you." She quaffed the remainder of her drink, touched his arm, then stepped inside.

The rest of the team had risen and taken up residence on loveseats, chairs, and bean bags. The television was on, the sound muted.

"We've been suitably out of touch for a few days. All we know is that Paris had a precious moment after we left."

"It was that religious guy calming the crowd."

"Yeah, the one we met in Croatia."

"The archbishop."

"Hey, look!" cried Lenny, pointing. "There's the new top religious AWG!"

"AWG?"

"All White Guy."

"Look at his outfit—even his car."

The figure, waving to the crowd, touching some, came closer in the video.

"It's him alright."

"Yeah," authorized Lenny. "Zoran's the new pope."

Jack whistled, then took a seat at a card table covered in deep blue felt. He hoisted a card deck as if performing a bicep curl. He shuffled.

Lenny moved to the other side with the comment, "Gin Rummy. Deal."

Jack sighed. He placed several cards face up on the surface, calling out each new suit. "Acorns, Shields, Roses, and Bells. It's J-A-S-S. Yass."

"I'm in."

"The game's quite complicated."

Before the P.I. could whine, a knock sounded at the door.

"I'd get it," said Lenny. "But you're the oldest in the room." He nodded at Jack, who considered pitching him off the patio into the deep lake. The knock came again. Louder.

"Alright." He limped to the door, holding his abdomen. He peered, nodded, and cracked it open.

A thirty-ish man, clad in what appeared to be a clown suit, stood before him with a clipboard. He looked up from the board. His accented English had an Italian flavor. "*Mi scusi.* I believe you are in the wrong room, Mr. ..." He referred back to his notes.

Already irritated, Jack slipped. "Sommers. Jack Sommers. I reserved this room. *Ich ha es Zimmer reserviert,*" he translated into Swiss-German. "*Ho reservato una camera,*" provided the Italian.

The man smiled, then produced a silenced Beretta.

Pfft. Pfft.

Blood spurted from Jack's chest. But he didn't budge. The clown fired again. And again. Same result.

Jack grabbed the man's wrist and, rotating his own body, yanked him into the room. At the last second, he rotated back, flinging the bony first joint of his index finger into the man's windpipe.

With a crack, the airway collapsed. Then, the man.

As the bloodied project manager went to shut the door, he glanced at the woman who stood transfixed across the hall. Her hands at her mouth, she couldn't utter a sound.

Jack smiled and shrugged. "It's okay. We're with the circus."

Inside, door closed, he checked the man. Dead. Then his pockets. "No ID. No anything. We've been made. I'm guessing Italians."

Lenny shook his head. "No, Jack. My dad brought me to Europe when I graduated high school. He said, 'Let's see the Vatican.' I said, 'We're Jewish.' He pointed at a naked statue of a man, at his tiny genitals. 'See? There were Jews in Rome.' "

"Wonderful." Jack took command. "Everyone! Saddle up! We're gone!" As they all packed in a rush, he whispered to Lenny, "What's the rest?"

"Long story short. This guy," he said as he gestured at the body. "He's wearing the uniform of the Swiss Guard."

"So?"

Crayle entered the dialog. "They guard the pope. Someone wanted to take us all out. They must believe we're still in the hunt for Lalumière's final bomb."

"Rome?" asked Phoebe.

"No. Next door. The Vatican. But maybe both."

"You can tell about a man by his shoes," Hekka said. She pulled off the clown's wooden shoes, and peered inside. "There is carving. Just one word."

All wanted to know. "What?" said Crayle.

"Ljuta."

"Everybody out of my way." The diminutive private investigator pushed through and grabbed the shoes. "Vatican … pope. Ljuta … pope."

As if to enhance the discovery process, Crayle laced his fingers and pulled them down onto the crown of his head. "Is this man, Zoran, really the head of all the world's Catholics? Or is he just another Illuminé plant?"

Then, Hekka. "And is he giving us a warning … or begging for help?"

CHAPTER 46

They had driven all night, arriving at Milan's train station just in time to see two nun's arguing with a man in a ticket window, trying to cancel at the last moment and receive a refund. The taller one was adamant; the shorter one pleaded her case for a peaceful resolution.

"Push me over there, Lenny," Jack ordered. "Excuse me, excuse me," he shouted as the P.I. spread the crowd with an aggressive effort. Jack motioned the smaller of the nuns over. He whispered his solution to their problem. In five minutes, the nun's emerged from the ladies' bathroom, attired in street clothes quite similar to those of Hekka and Phoebe. The latter two emerged clad as nuns, tickets in hand. Phoebe muttered something under her breath about managing her language.

"Hey, guys, they forgot their valise." She opened the alligator-skinned container atop a trash receptacle. "Oh." It was filled with condoms.

Lenny's hands dipped in and out, creating a waterfall of foil packets. "Does this mean we're … screwed?" He laughed an instant before Micmac's hand covered his mouth as eyes darted their way.

"Not funny, Lenny. They give them out now." Micmac's knowledge of Catholic tenets was limited.

"My faith was shaken for a second."

"You're Jewish."

"We have big enough dicks for these." He held them aloft again.

Phoebe squinted at the print. "Small?"

Jack needed to restore order. "Knock it the fuck off, you two. And there's no fucking Vulgarity Vase, so I am fucking safe."

"What's this?" Hekka pulled a zippered ballistic nylon bag from the case.

Phoebe snatched it. "A donation receptacle." She held it up for Jack to see, then tossed it into his lap.

"Arn … ungh …" He face lit up red. His suppressed need to express himself with vulgarities generated indecipherable grunts. Familiar territory.

Then, something new.

His body shook, convulsing wildly, then he collapsed onto the floor. Serious. His heart stopped.

Micmac hammered his chest.

Nothing.

Again.

Nothing.

Crayle intercepted his third attempt in mid-air. He reached down and depressed an acupressure point with his finger.

Jack restarted.

Along with the others, Crayle breathed a sigh of relief and smiled. "Ling."

• • •

The ride to Genoa's train station and on to Corsica's northeast corner by ferry proved uneventful, even pleasant for the two fugitives. The seas remained calm, but they carried a darkness, as if awaiting an impending storm.

Lalumière's nun hailed a taxi. Not having mastered the unique Corsican language, she explained in Provençal French that they required a round trip to the primary town and birthplace of Napoléon. Once having checked that box, they needed to be transported aboard the ferry to Civitavecchia, port city of Rome.

The taxi driver stared. "You are not from this place. If you were, you would know there is no such ferry."

The nun pointed to the heavens. "There will be. Just get us back here by sunset." Before he could argue, she handed him three one-hundred Euro notes. "*Moitié*. That's half."

The winding highway through the hills of the island to the opposite end provided them additional time to rest.

The driver, anticipating they would be hungry and certain they'd been unable to eat the ferry fare, pulled up to a restaurant as soon as they entered Corsica's main town, Ajaccio.

Later, as they exited to the taxi, Lalumière seemed to brighten. "I have wanted to make this pilgrimage my entire life. Thank you, my love." He planted a brief kiss.

The driver's eyebrow raised. While they'd been inside, he'd made a call.

Sunglasses allowed the nun to observe the driver through a tinted window. She checked her watch. "We have just enough time for a run-through. Then, we must proceed to the mainland."

"Sandrine … uh … Sister Magdalena. There is nothing in Italy for me. And this is the place that presented the most famous of Corsicans to the world." He waved his arm at the town and surrounding hills. Then, at the sea.

"Don't you want to visit the Vatican?"

He whispered, "I am Illuminé. As you have reminded me in the past, we don't believe. You must remember that the Catholics are the only religion with their own country. They are our worst enemy."

"Didn't Napoléon believe?"

"He was the best. The best French general, the best leader. If he believed, it didn't get in his way. He was true French."

"I've got news for you. A year before he was born, Corsica belonged to Genoa. It's no surprise that he was born with an Italian name. He took the French version later, when it suited his needs."

"You make this up. He was French through and through. We will see his birthplace. I will feel his …"

"Vibes?"

"Yes. Vibes."

Sister Magdalena waited a couple of minutes for Lalumière's glow to subside. "Change of subject. The pope announced that he will destroy the elitist Illuminé, Mitim. And the French, after what he accomplished in Paris, are feeling a resurgence of faith. In just these few days since Christmas."

"It won't last. My people have grown weary of the Church and its empty rhetoric. Believe, believe, believe. And to what end? Peace? Ha! There has been no lasting and final peace for all these centuries. And protection of the innocent? More have been killed in the name of religion than not."

She sat down beside him and placed her hand on his back. "You're not getting this. Your enemy, until now, has been the government. And its ideological socialism. The pope can replace them with his own ideological Catholicism. Note the *ism* in each of those words. They both end badly."

Lalumière turned to look at her, his face alive with passion. "But he is Illuminé. I am confused." He dropped his head into his hands.

"I'm a spy, darling. I know about these things. The new pope is either still Illuminé, and the most significant spy mole in world history—he could destroy organized religion—or he's a double agent, a religious man all this time. We—I mean you—can't take the chance. If we don't take him out, then, as of the day the Conclave concluded, our dreams went up in smoke. Literally."

"Oh, my God."

"Would you stop saying that?"

He sat back, hands on his thighs, resolved. "We shall do this—travel to Rome. But I have one condition."

The new smile drifted from her countenance.

"We must make a little stop … on the way." He leaned to her and whispered in her ear.

She stared at him, disbelieving. "You can't be serious."

The driver drove them uphill, then left, then right. He pulled up to a quaint house, quite old. A teenage boy stood in front next to a sign, which proclaimed *Napoléon Bonaparte's Birthplace* in large script. He led them inside, asked them not to touch anything, then stepped back outside.

Once the young man departed, she turned to Lalumière. "Make something out of nothing. I think we're being had. They do this sort of thing all the time in Kansas."

"We're not in Kansas." He glanced around at the artifacts, in awe. School books, writing instruments, an old mandolin, a corporal's insignia. A truly somber moment. His emotional bonding conflicted with the mood outside.

"We got another one," the boy chuckled to the driver. "We'll split the money when you return. At the Irish Pub."

Behind him, Sister Magdalena intoned, "*Bisogna fa di forza legge.*" Necessity makes its own virtue.

The young man turned, surprised by her presence, and her usage of the Corsican proverb.

The nun beckoned him inside. "I would like for you to explain something. In the bedroom. Please." She smiled.

The boy, a semi-devout Catholic, couldn't believe how he felt. A surge of sexual energy. From a nun's smile.

By the time the pair of tourists had re-entered the taxi, the possibility of sharing at the Irish Pub or anywhere else had been put to rest. Pattie was so adept, even Lalumière was unaware of what she had done. At the conclusion of their return drive to the docks, the boy's co-conspirator met a similar terminal fate.

As Lalumière's young compatriot promised, a ferry awaited them. Its sign read *Civitavecchia*—the Ancient City.

"I shall remember those two. Do you see now, my darling? As with the rest of we French, Corsicans can be as vital as life itself."

Peering back from the ferry, she wondered at what point she had misplaced her mental compass.

CHAPTER 47

Before anyone could take a seat, Micmac caught their attention by waving his arms like a cheerleader. "Listen up! This private car seems fancy shmancey, but it's a lot more. All of the window glass and the outside walls and doors are double-bulletproof. In addition, the floor is IED impregnable. We are safe. But a good defense is not enough." He produced a remote control. "On command, the skylight rotates open and fires up to five surface-to-air missiles. In addition, should we so desire, a pair of M134 mini-guns—my favorites—will put 8,000 rounds-per-minute into play. The ornate bench seats along the sides are actually ammo bins."

"You built this, didn't you?" asked a knowing Hekka.

"I must confess. I accomplished this mobile safe-house at a remote factory, totally underground, along with senior members of the Science and Technology Directorate's Special Transportation Division. We not only designed, but we built the whole thing right there."

"Uh, that would be the STD's STD," Lenny opined.

Phoebe resisted "what else haven't you told me" and asked instead, "You built a custom railway car underground, and you somehow got it to Italy for us to use?"

Proud of his work, Micmac smiled.

Phoebe glared. She pointed to the bottom right corner of a dark wood wall panel at a gold leaf signature. *MacKay*.

While the team sat around the periphery of the rail car's lounge area, the wounded and recovering Jack lay in the bedroom with Flori attending to his needs. "Come on, now," she purred. "Another sip." She pressed a straw between his lips. "It's good for you."

"What kind of gin?"

"Your favorite. Bombay Sapphire. And Schweppes Diet Tonic Water—for your waistline."

He took a long pull and enjoyed the flavors, anticipating the impending numbing effect. He glanced over at his number two, whose eyes remained locked onto his tablet computer. "Lenny, boy. Give us a rundown on the nukes so far. The explosion timeline. Can you do that?"

Lenny pecked, then sat back with arms folded.

"Give me the f … f … the freakin' intel." He reached for a cane, but not for mobility—because it contained a firearm.

"Just teasing, boss. Here we go. Fasd, Iran: October 22. Xinjiang, China: November 4. Beijing, China: November 13. Marseille, France: November 14. Hey, how about that? Exactly four months after Bastille Day."

"Lenny!"

"Paris, France: that one we skipped the first time. New York, USA: November 22. Paris, France again: skipped again. How'd I do?"

"Terrific. Now go out on the back deck, make your peace with your god, Satan, and jump."

"He didn't mean it." Flori smiled.

"Yeah. The boss is just out of sorts, as they say."

Jack made a serious move at Lenny, but pain and lack of strength caused him to topple onto the floor. Crayle and Micmac, who had just entered, replaced him on his bed. "Flori? Take care of this guy. He needs sleep. We'll process the intel."

Flori was already on the way. She closed the door, shutting out what became a lively discussion.

The train descended the Apennine Mountains into a valley. In less than an hour, it entered a picturesque city alongside a winding river, coming to a halt at a large station.

"Our train will refuel and replenish here for the next hour-and-a-half. C'mon, gang. Let's get some real food."

The team proceeded away from the station and down a cobbled road too narrow for traffic.

With Lenny pushing the chair and Jack directing with hand signals, the troupe passed the beautiful *Duomo Santa Maria del Fiore*, and approached a square. The look of a crowd ahead was menacing. The square, *Piazza della Signoria*, was abuzz with protestors, some yelling and gesturing, some pushing and shoving. Jack's apparent malady prompted them to ignore him and his team. Keeping to the piazza's periphery, they skirted the cacophony and arm-waving and passed the *Palazzo Vecchio*, guarded by a copy of Michelangelo's David. Its clock tower, of the same gray stone masonry as the castle, seemed tall enough to provide the time to the entire province.

"This is the place," said Jack, nodding ahead. The team felt, as much as heard, his memories.

Phoebe turned his way with a smile. "Marilyn, huh?"

"Did you propose here, boss?"

Jack paused. Briefly. "C'mon. Let's eat."

They entered *Ristorante Il Bargello* that, uncharacteristically devoid of customers, allowed them to observe the happenings in the square outside while eating—as Jack would argue—the world's best pizza.

"Alright, listen up. You were partially right, Lenny. Marilyn and I were here, but not for romance. It was the first time I'd ever seen someone shot … up close."

"Her?" asked Hekka.

"Yeah."

"Boy, I can see why she has it in for you," Lenny concluded, bobbing his head up and down.

Jack took a long breath, then glanced at Lenny. He seemed to resolve something in his mind. Something that took Lenny out of focus and brought his own earlier days to the forefront. "Yeah."

Crayle checked his timepiece. "Time to get back. Let's all stay out of trouble. We can't miss this train."

Jack left a generous tip and the troupe departed. They had taken a much needed break and their nerves had retreated. Not one of them was green. Not anymore. They all knew that mortal danger couldn't be far. It never was.

Skirting the mayhem, the team re-passed the castle and cathedral, following a different narrow and cobbled roadway back to the station. They were all armed, but the size of the unruly crowd made defense from any manner of serious threat impossible.

"There's where I bought her a cute little purse." Jack indicated a family-run leather shop. "I snuck a brand new Beretta Nano inside." He sighed. "Nine millimeter love, I called it." He dropped his head. "She never got to use it."

In minutes that seemed like hours, they made their way back into their custom railcar. Full of food and wine, each picked a place in the lounge and fell asleep. Crayle slipped into the bedroom. Right away, he saw Flori's exhaustion. "Get some sleep. I'll see to him." He nodded at the door.

"*Obrigado*," she said, thanking him in her native tongue. "The room is sound proof and isolated. He should sleep well." She pecked the dormant project manager on the lips and left.

What Crayle had in mind next had been a long time coming. Too often, he and his associates, and now his lover Hekka, had been dispatched into enigmatic quagmires. Each time, the project manager had been at the controls. The time had arrived for transparency on Jack's part.

Crayle pulled up a burgundy chair, backwards, and sat for what seemed like hours. He gazed at the man who had caused him, and those he'd grown to like and to love, nothing but heartache.

"So, Jack. Is what I have seen the best you can do? What else?" The more he doted on the subject, the more enraged he became. He'd reached his limit.

Magus Crayle rose and latched the door.

Having first set the brake, he dragged Jack's near-lifeless body into the wheel chair. He slapped the man. Once. Twice. "Wake up!"

Jack Sommers began to come around. His eyes peered through what seemed like a veil, trying to focus on his interrogator. He gagged against the putrid rag Crayle had just stuffed into his mouth.

The former spy and mathematician pulled a device from a bag. He grasped the pistol-like grip, pushed it against each of Jack's wrists, and fired. The gun spun tie-wraps around both forearms, fastening Jack to the chair.

"You may wonder why I'm being inhospitable … with the restraints and gag. I've reached the end. I've been attacked more times that I can count, and I have placed others at mortal risk … and for what?" He returned to his reversed chair.

The older man, coming around, struggled. The pain from his wound caused him to cease.

"I'm tired of being everyone's toy. A pawn being moved by multiple hands. On multiple chessboards. Really … really … tired."

Jack made a few muffled sounds, sounding more like sumo wrestler grunts than complaints or pleas.

Crayle opened a necktie case and removed a pistol. "I realized this room would be sound-proof. For those private moments. And comms. To be on the safe side …" He removed a four-inch cylinder, screwing it onto the weapon's barrel. "I will phrase my questions for either yes or no responses."

More muffled sounds, louder—still indecipherable.

"There is no 'f' in yes or no, Jack. Head movements will suffice. Are you ready to begin?"

The project manager shook his head. "No!"

"Did you know Neil was Illuminé?"

Nothing.

Crayle poked the silencer in the older man's belly wound.

Muffled, pained noises emanated.

"I say again. No 'f' in *yes* or *no*. Did you?"

Jack stared into the steel blue eyes. Eyes that should've been laid to rest long before. The Serrano amulet caught his eye. Resigned, he shook his head.

"Lalumière?"

No.

"Any of the players, including Pattie Norbrunn?"

No.

"Anyone else at the CIA that you suspect of being with them?"

No.

"Good. This last bit—it's perhaps the most important. I've come to feel that relationships are very important." He paused. "Did you and I work together before … before my crash?"

Silence. Jack squeezed his eyes shut.

Crayle could recognize pain. Anguish.

"It had to do with your wife, didn't it? The one I met in Malibu. Uh …"

"Mmh … mm … mmh," Jack replied.

"Marilyn?"

Jack nodded affirmative.

"Yes. Marilyn." The next pause seemed to last forever. "Switzerland?"

Before Jack could respond, the train decelerated dramatically, throwing Crayle against a nearby wall. A second later, he hit the floor hard.

The brake on the wheelchair snapped from the force. The chair accelerated at Crayle. With Jack's 200 pounds of additional weight, it gained momentum.

At the last second, Crayle rolled.

Jack slammed into the wall.

"Emergency stop!" Crayle pulled himself up and, with a flash of his wrist, enabled his Kershaw folder, severed the tie-downs restraining his adversary. "Something's seriously wrong."

Jack tore away the gag.

Before he could commence a verbal rampage, Crayle slapped a hand over his mouth. "The sound proofing! We can't hear what's happening outside!"

The other man's jacket hung on a wall hook. Crayle reached inside, grabbed the P229 automatic from its shoulder holster, and shoved it into the former CIA operative's hand. "Weapons ready! I'll check outside!"

"And I've got your six, Magus," came Jack's bitter sounding voice.

Crayle slid to the wall next to the door.

Jack took aim.

The man, operating with a mélange of his former memories and an incomplete sense of his tactical abilities, pried open the door an inch to catch sounds.

Flori's attempted hard knock became a soft tap with the inward motion of the door. Her normal sexual intonations had turned to out-of-breath excitement. "Protesters. Stopped the train. Attacking this car. It expresses wealth."

Crayle glanced up. The skylight was coated, but translucent. He made out the figures stomping the light, trying to break the bulletproof glass. Others pounded the roof with feet and fists.

"Make a hole!" Micmac pushed through and yanked open a wall panel. It revealed levers and switches. He pulled the one on the left.

A horrific sound emanated from the shell of the car. Then, screams. Bodies seemed to fly from the car's surface.

"A little voltage." He returned the lever to its off position. He pulled another.

They heard cries and groans through the doorway opening. Through one-way windows, they saw the out-of-control mob running in all directions, away from the car.

Micmac shut that lever with a wry comment. "Synthesized fart."

The train lurched.

"Thank you, Gadget Man," Crayle said, followed by an "Amen," from Jack.

Micmac threw a two-finger salute and exited, his arm around Flori's waist. If Phoebe's glare as they entered the parlor could've made a noise, it would've seeped in through the closing door.

The excitement had been too much for a man in Jack's condition. When Crayle turned, he relieved Jack of his weapon and re-strapped his hands. "Our previous conversation was productive, but interrupted."

"Just kill me and get it … mmph … mmph." The gag had been reapplied.

"Good. I'd offer you a drink, but …" Crayle poured three fingers from a bottle of the Italian liquor, grappa. He took a sip, then tossed down the rest. At this point, he required *yes* questions. "So you were dangling me from strings while you were being dangled. Marionettes manipulating marionettes?"

Before Jack could respond, Crayle saw in his eyes a recognition that he hadn't been gagged to prevent others from hearing him cry for help. It was because his master spy chose not to deal with exculpatory dialogs, just answers. He nodded.

"The Elder has killed tens of thousands of people through his puppets. Through you. Through me. Any idea why?"

No.

Crayle refilled his glass. "Why are we going to Rome?"

Silence.

"This is end game, isn't it? This Elder, whatever his motives, is the embodiment of *evil.* And despite all our faults, by some irrational rationale, we are *good.*"

Silence.

"A situational Armageddon. He is godless, and we are the army of a Supreme Being, who proclaimed himself, in various texts, as great and good. I'm a mathematician, among other things, but I can't for the life of me—literally and figuratively—deconstruct this. Can you?"

Jack provided no more answer than a shake of his head.

Crayle stepped over to a writing desk, opened a humidor that sat atop, and extracted an honest Cuban cigar. After suitable preparation, he held it up, pointed the pistol, and triggered a long flame from the silencer, searing the cigar tip.

Jack's body relaxed, but not his mouth.

Crayle removed the gag.

"You fucking son-of-a-whore. Untie me, you—"

"Easy, Jack. That's ten bucks in two seconds. Shall we run a tab, or do you realize that you are out of a job? Without income."

"You … you … mmph … arnh …" He struggled to no avail with the new set of tie-wraps.

The man known as Magus Crayle pushed open the door and hailed Flori. "Jack's looking for you. It seems he's into bondage." He saluted the project manager and rejoined the party. Flight attendant turned train stewardess, Flori, rushed in to liberate Jack and tend to his requirements.

CHAPTER 48

It was the most unusual aircraft landing that the control tower superintendent ever witnessed. And it happened that Capodichino International Airport, a mere 1.87 miles north of Naples, had seen some crazy happenings. He had been advised by his superior's superior that he needed to get this particular unmarked cargo plane on the ground, and then to electronically eradicate it from the system while it taxied to a remote location, awaiting reload and takeoff at a moment's notice.

Once in position, the wheels were chocked by crew, and the four engines spun down. The rear ramp lowered to accept a Ferrari-red, stretch limousine that appeared from nowhere. Name badges with one of the middle r's missing gave it away as of Chinese manufacture. Without rolling down any of the blackened windows, the driver backed it up the ramp, which closed behind. A half-minute later, the ramp lowered again. The limousine proceeded to the airport exit.

"None of this happened," the superintendent admonished his team in Italian.

One of the more youthful and ebullient air traffic controllers started to speak.

Thrusting his hands in the air, fingers pressed white against thumbs as if holding precious pinches of salt, the superintendent exclaimed, *"Eh!?"*

The ensuing pin-drop silence evinced the notion that the order had come instead from a Mafia don.

Within the limo, Chin's trio of daughters—Black, Red, and new Beige—had taken seats in its well-decked-out aft cabin. The vehicle and driver were necessary since Chin issued standing rules forbidding his daughters to leave the Dragon Building unless under specific orders. In addition, he assured that their education excluded the fine art of driving. The driver, whose masculinity had been permanently depleted, served also as their bodyguard. He was armed, although the young women excelled in various forms of martial arts.

Red daughter was perplexed at their situation. "That we are this far from Father is very strange. He seems to be changing."

"He has achieved his wishes. He is master and emperor of the new China. He has much work to do. There will be many changes."

"Do you think you will remain his favorite, Black?" asked an innocent new Beige.

"I don't think of such things. I think of seeing to his wishes. His needs."

Red daughter had turned away as if to view the passing scenery. In the window's reflection, she observed her facial muscles ripple her jaw line.

The driver—short, swarthy, and replete with a Beretta model 92 pistol—spoke over the intercom. "This is an interesting vehicle. It belongs to a Neapolitan crime family whose don salivated at the opportunity to acquire perfect one carat diamonds as payment for its rental. Ah, I am sorry. *Buongiorno*."

"Buongiorno," replied Black. *"Come va?"*

Red smiled, but was privately disgusted that Father had chosen Black to learn basic Italian for this purpose. On the good side, this mission would afford many opportunities for her opposition to have an "accident" in this country, thus removing Red's major thorn.

"We go north for your next transportation. It will be superior to our roadways, which are packed with the faithful. You will find the garments requested by Mr. Chin in the small trunks at your feet. You are college students."

Black checked. For her, there was a cardinal and gold sweatshirt from her American alma mater. Red's was blue and gold. They glanced at each other as would enemies.

"Oh! See what I have," exclaimed new Beige. "Notre Dame!"

Red was not happy. "These are ridiculous for cover, but will suffice for this leg of our trip." She chose a decorative pillow, placed it between her head and the window, and drifted off.

"We could shop in Rome for more appropriate clothing," new Beige concluded as she paged through a travel guide.

"No. We must focus. We must find Mr. Crayle. We must take him, willing or not, back to Hong Kong."

"How will we find him?"

"The man he is after expressed to Father that he fears for his life. We will go to him. And wait."

"Are we to protect this man from Mr. Crayle?"

Black considered the question, and her answer, carefully. The new Beige daughter was a couple of years younger than she and Red. Still, her life would be in equal danger, and she should be read into the plan. "When we have our man, we must see that this man—the one in fear—is dead."

That last word brought Red around. She changed the subject. "You realize, Black, that Father must choose White daughter for his empress. Her's is the imperial color."

Black saw the implication immediately. But, no. Father was dedicated to never defiling a woman as would be customary in the post-nuptial ceremonies. Never. Still, it unnerved her more than she would have anticipated. She glared directly into Red's eyes. "You must never mention this again."

• • •

The train made brisk passage south through the inland hills and valleys of middle Italy. The gross ineptitude of the national government, and the consequent devastation, spread like an economic cancer. Small protests in Siena and other towns were visible, but insignificant. The more violently demonstrative crowds had already migrated north to Florence, and west to the capitol city.

The only two of the Crayle team who weren't taking the opportunity to sleep sat on one of the long ammo containers masquerading as 18th Century sofas.

"What if China and France aren't the end game, Hekka?"

She appeared to ignore his question. "My father thought that hot dogs were a white man's plot against Indians. Like the alcohol that made us act crazy, the hot dog would make us fat and lazy. We would lose our warrior spirit."

"Is that why, when I first met you, you wore buckskins?"

She nodded. "When I went down from our mountain valley to school, I stopped at the Walmart to change. He didn't know. He believed I represented our proud heritage at the white man's college."

Crayle's interest was piqued. "Go on."

"At school, I was not who I appeared to be."

"Like the pope?"

"No. Not him."

"Who, then?"

"The Elder."

Although Hekka was no operative in the classical sense, Crayle examined her every word for the wisdom inevitably contained. "You may have something. Rorschach restored my China memories, then my French. But I learned nothing more of the man in charge. This Elder."

The discourse awakened Jack. He chimed in. "It comes down to motivation. It always does."

Crayle remembered the turncoat motivation trio, MIR. Money. Ideology. Revenge. "We know it's not money. To front this operation, the Elder must have plenty. So far, we've assumed that it's ideology. Because of the Illuminé. If not, then it was truly diabolical of the Elder to gin up the old secret society, co-opt powerful people all over the world, and then set in place the Blackstone. I don't know."

"He had help," said Jack.

The three words hit Crayle like gut punches. He spun, facing the project manager. "Alright. He has money and, if we discount ideology, that leaves revenge."

"Revenge needs an impetus, a reason."

"And a Tango." Hekka laughed. "I got that word from Micmac. It means …"

Phoebe rubbed the crust from her eyes and laughed. "We know. A target."

"Revenge is an aspect of ego. Like power."

"Maybe that's his motive, Magus. Not revenge. Power."

"But over what? Whom?"

"Let's go over his game pieces." Jack collected items from the table before them. "The pepper is China, and the salt is France. No more alike than night and day." He removed the lids.

"Or Yin and Yang." Hekka had learned a few other things at school.

"Pepper and salt," Jack repeated. He tossed a smidgen of salt in his hand. "He uses Lalumière to move the diamonds to Chin." He poured the diamonds over the pepper shaker. "The Frenchman is single-minded. His Tango is the government of France."

"Let's assume he's done that. Either Mitim dies in the process …"

"… or, like Chin, survives and takes power. But what's the Elder's prize?"

"Maybe he keeps it up until he has the world. All of the old monarchies restored to power."

"Not likely, Jack. Once in power, they'd go straight to status quo. Not one of the ego-centric European monarchs would give him the time of day."

"It's something else, then. Power?"

"I don't believe so. Power is an addiction that snares the narcissist, sociopath, or psychopath. Those who don't care whom they hurt."

"Or how many." Jack offered. "And dopers. My dad told me that dopers don't care about hurting people … or anything else. Even kids."

"Enough for the moment. If anyone gets an epiphany, share it immediately. We'll reconvene. For now, get some rest."

The others took his advice, leaving Crayle with his thoughts. They turned inward. As if invoking the spirit of the late Doctor Rorschach, he began an internal dialog. "How could I now, after my crash, be unselfish, care about right versus wrong, and have a firm grip on reality? The difference between now and then, a *simple* car crash. Two complete opposites in one man." He mulled over that notion. Simple? Not a chance.

CHAPTER 49

The trip from Corsica included rough seas, meaningless to a depressed man. Sylvain Lalumière, seeing no real hope nor any tangible plan for his accession, lapsed into a funk.

With Neil gone, Pattie now took orders from the very top. While she had been read in on what was to occur next, her orders were to keep him in the dark. Still, she knew he would be re-energized when he learned of the grandiose night in store.

The distressed Lalumière and his CIA handler arrived hours later at the Italian port city of Civitavecchia. That, and the subsequent 50-mile train ride to Rome's Termini central station, proved inconsequential.

The hermit turned to his companion. "Perhaps, of all your names, I should choose Magdalena—the modern day Mary Magdalene."

That notion remained sequestered in a very guarded segment of her mind. "Please. Call me Sandrine. And follow me … it's not far."

She led him through streets where men and women sat on curbing. Some stared at passersby, some just stared. The normally effusive Romans appeared lost. He followed her into the ancient Roman Forum, past relics and crumbled columns to a special site.

The beaten man was at once captivated. He examined the football-shaped object he'd carried since the debacle that Paris became, then placed it next to the tomb of the Roman conqueror, Julius Caesar. It proved a far more supple seating appliance than the stones nearby. Over and over, he read the words inscribed on a plaque, understanding none of it.

ARA DI CESARE

DEPOSERO LA SPOGLIA DI CESARE NEL FORO, LA DOVE E L'ANTICA REGGIA DEI ROMANI, E VI ACCVMVLARONO SOPRA TAVOLE, SEDILI E QVANTO ALTRO LEGNAME ERA LI ... ACCESERO IL FVOCO E TVTTO IL POPOLO ASSISTETTE AL ROGO DVRANTE LA NOTTE. IN QVEL LVOGO VENNE ERETTA DAPPRIMA VN ARA, ORA VI E IL TEMPIO DELLO STESSO. CESARE, NEL QVALE EGLI E ONORATO COME VN DIO.

Sandrine, fluent in all dialects of the French language, struggled with the Italian translation.

CRYPT OF CAESAR

"Deposit the naked body of Caesar in the Forum, at the ancient palace of the Romans, and accumulate above tables, seats and how many other timber-items are there ... access the fire and all the people assist at the ROGO—I don't recognize that word—*during the night. In that place, come erect at first a crypt, you and the temple of the same Caesar, in which he is honored like a god."*

"It seems as though he's here with us, doesn't it?"

"I understand why you brought me to this place. Caesar conquered Gaul just as I wish to do."

"Precisely."

He turned to her. "Why have I failed?"

"The answer is quite simple."

He turned back, staring at the stone crypt. "Spare me the sordid answer."

"At any point prior to his conquest of your ancient forebears' land, he was not finished. And so stand you. Your quest is incomplete. You aren't finished," she said.

"Here in the grand Forum I sit. Caesar accepted the gratitude of all Romans in this place. When he returned victorious, the place was packed. It is empty, Sandrine."

"He didn't seek their approval. He achieved it through sacrifice and his other-worldly skills. And when all was said and done, they revered him. Remember what it says, my Mitim: *honored … like a god*."

For once her magic proved inadequate. She would punt now, and try again later. "We need to take a timeout and regroup. Absent Neil, we no longer have CIA support and, by the looks of the jackets Crayle's team wore, France's spy agency is on their side, as well. No matter."

"No matter? *No matter?* Everyone is on their side. I have lost. *We*, my precious Sandrine, have lost."

"Look on the bright side. Because of Crayle's team and exceptional luck, we were unable to conquer Paris. When we troupe into Versailles someday, with the roads lined by all manner of grateful countrymen, the City of Light, intact, will be ours. Don't forget, Paris is the *Île de la Cité* of old. The Romans called it *Lutetia Parisiorum*—the beginning of it all."

Lalumière mused. "Yes. In 250 B.C., it was a mere settlement of the tribe, *Parisii*. On the islands, then the banks of the Seine. Defensible. I believe you are right about Paris, but what can we do? Now the president calls me, Mitim, a traitor, a destroyer of France. His so-called Convergence created an unholy alliance with the Catholic Church. Leaders, religious and secular, are aligned against me."

"Perhaps I can help," said a voice from behind the tomb. A man stepped out of the darkness. He wore a dark overcoat over a contrasting garment.

At the sight before him, Lalumière gasped.

"I believe you have recognized me, Sylvain. I am Illuminé."

"No! You can't be!" His heart palpitated.

Sandrine interceded. "I'm afraid so, my Mitim."

"No! You're the … "

"Pope?" The Dalmatian, formerly known as Zoran, smiled. He glanced at her. "In your vernacular, you might describe me as … a mole."

Mouth agape, Lalumière stared.

"Come, Sylvain. We are about to implement Plan C. The Elder has asked me to assist, and has provided a new pope to that end."

The pope took one step closer to the Frenchman. "Before we proceed down the Forum way, past multitudes of stones and columnated edifices, there's one thing you've forgotten."

Lalumière appeared horrified. "And that would be?"

The pope pointed behind him to the item the Frenchman had used as a stool. "The bomb?"

• • •

Finally, after all the battles, the train pulling the somewhat battered covert ops car pulled into Rome's Termini station. There were a few straggler protesters, but most had moved into the city center to seek a recognizable seat of power. Leaderless, they spread everywhere, sometimes fighting over the lack of direction.

The team, however, had specific direction. It knew how to coordinate. Its mission was clear. Find and diffuse, or find and destroy, the bomb.

"The NSA can pick up even small amounts of radiation from their special satellites, Magus. With the radiation-absorbing sponge, Chin's people have all but eliminated that aspect of a nuclear device."

"That's wonderful, Micmac. How do we find them?"

"Intel from the president indicates that Pattie has a chip embedded in her person. It has a strange name. Vestige. Have you heard of it?" He grinned.

"Real funny. The problem is, you have to start with a pickup point and go from there."

Hekka stepped in front of the two men. "Does Termini Station count?"

CHAPTER 50

Picking up the Vestige trail had been far easier than anticipated. And Rome possessed a surfeit of steel building girders, sign posts, and traffic light standards. Within a few blocks, the team arrived at a giant stadium south of the train station. An ancient stadium. Familiar to everyone.

As usual, Lenny opined. "Everyone wants to play in the Super Bowl. No one ever wanted to play here." He scanned the team for acknowledgment of his witticism, but found no takers.

Crayle consulted with Jack before speaking with the team. "Lenny and Micmac. Whatever is going to happen will happen here. I'm tasking the two of you to search the catacombs of the Colosseum. Its underbelly. I wish I knew what to tell you to look for, but I don't. The rest of the team will search from the top down. Remember. Our primary mission is to acquire and disable the bomb. That's number one. If we can take out the principals on the other side, that's secondary, although it would eliminate further bloodshed if we were to get them all. ROE time. If you get a shot, take it."

"Extreme prejudice," Jack confirmed.

"Aye, aye," Micmac acknowledged as he led his P.I. minion into the darkness of the stadium's outer shell.

Crayle viewed a map on his smart phone. "This way." He led Hekka and Phoebe up a stone stairway. Corridor-like, damp, and cold, it provided no clue as to what might loom ahead.

Several minutes elapsed before they reached the first level. They stepped out onto a walkway that skirted the Colosseum and took in their first view of the ancient artifact.

"That's not normal." Crayle pointed to recent construction below.

What they observed was a rectangular platform, approximately twenty feet by thirty feet. It appeared to be secured to the stonework sides of the Roman structure by four gangways, perhaps four feet wide. Because of the lateness of the day, it was difficult to discern objects at the platform's center.

Phoebe raised her CIA-spec binoculars. "It appears to be a table in the center and … I think I see movement … someone waving … to us."

"It's a setup," Crayle observed. "It's also our only option."

They found their way down the stadium-like stonework to just beyond the platform, noticing that the structure was held aloft solely by the four gangways, one exiting diagonally from each corner.

Approaching with trepidation, Magus Crayle, Hekka, and Phoebe took seats on one side. Their chairs seemed to lock in place.

They heard a click, and the table produced a cold glow. They reacted, not to the glow, but to the men. The glow illuminated Sylvain Lalumière and son, Jean-Marc, at the table's end to their left. Upon digesting that visual and its implications, they scanned right. Across the table sat the individual who had beckoned them in the first place. Their host. The tall, thin man wore a regal-appearing purple and gold robe.

"In the event that you might not recognize me, I am the heretofore mysterious and faceless Elder." He allowed a moment for the magnitude of his presence to sink in. "As you can see, the platform suspends us over the catacombs and affords us a coming together to resolve our differences."

Phoebe leaned to Crayle. "Where's Jack? Out of the action once again?" She grabbed the table as if to push herself away. Her chair didn't budge. The others tried. The chairs were locked in tight such that the three team members could not climb or crawl out. Solid sides prevented anyone from accessing a weapon.

Phoebe rubbed the table, and made a face. "This feels funny, like it was molded from something greasy and soft."

"Ah, yes. Another useful creation of your Gadget Man. C-4, I believe you call the substance. Your chairs are locked into position and, as an extra precaution, are connected by proximity devices should you consider effecting an early departure." The Elder tilted his head back a notch to emphasize his lethal-if-necessary control over the meeting. "I am certain, Mr. MacKay—whom you refer to as Micmac—would appreciate what I've accomplished with the seating arrangements."

Crayle analyzed the situation. He realized the need to scramble the Elder's presumption of control. He slammed his hands on the table, causing everyone to jump. "How do you know him? How do you know his backstory?"

The Elder was unrattled. He continued in a deep, smooth, measured tone. "Mr. Wohlford, somewhat above him in the hierarchy, knows—that is, knew—his capabilities. It should be no surprise at this point in the game that I possess a dossier on each of you." The Elder clasped his hands, resting them on the table edge. "With all that has been restored to your memory, Mr. Crayle, do you understand what this is all about? Do you comprehend why Chin agreed to furnish the nuclear weapons?"

In silence, Hekka and Phoebe observed the battle of wits and intellects between the two men.

Crayle had his opportunity to engage. "It was his compulsion to become the reborn emperor of China, wasn't it?"

The Elder produced a brief smile. "More than 2,000 years ago, toward the end of the original Ch'in empire, a great stone was unearthed. Any guess as to its nature, Mr. Crayle?"

"Jade?"

"Very rare black jade." The Elder tilted his chin and smiled. He pondered whether the American would consider a game of chess.

Crayle considered his response. "I suspect that the jade was carved to Ch'in's specifications and …"

"Please relax and I will relate my exquisite story. The perfect jade stone was hidden. Purposefully. Under the Terra Cotta Warriors at Xian. In a sense, they guarded the stone for over 2,000 years."

"And it was you who uncovered it?"

"My charitable organization, the International Children's Rescue Foundation, opened an office in Xian. A search of ancient records related to one of my favorite subjects, China's first emperor, revealed that a team of twenty men had disappeared after the five-acre burial chamber had been filled in. Curious. Furthermore, the legendary black jade had not been listed in the burial manifest, nor did it appear in any writings after the death of Ch'in Xihuangdi."

Crayle searched the upper reaches of the Colosseum for answers. "Let me guess. Chief minister, Li Si, had forgotten to include it. He realized that the terra cotta warriors couldn't protect the carving if it wasn't already included with Ch'in and the warriors in the burial space. So, he commissioned a special ops team to put it in place, without disturbing the site. A work of art, so to speak."

"Well intimated, Mr. Crayle. You've recalled the size of the entombment no doubt from your earlier stay with Chin Yao-wu."

"While I strategized his conquest of China?"

"Of course. Please indulge me further. The best is yet to come. The covert tunneling on my behalf was, itself, a work of art. The team of workers found and retrieved the stone in just three months. Fully intact. Not a scratch."

"I don't suppose those workers notified the press about their success."

"Uh, no. The removal of the stone left a chamber beneath the treasured Warriors that would have been subject to cave in, and discovery. As it turned out, the excavation team filled that void perfectly."

Crayle saw a man of position, of power, but also a supremely ruthless and narcissistic man. "Then?"

"We evacuated it to Beijing. Following one of my state visits, we transported it to my home. Monaco."

"Then?"

"It seems the artist had carved Ch'in's figure in full battle regalia onto the left aspect of the large crystal. The other half he left untouched. Perhaps he planned to add an empress at an appropriate date. Whatever the reason, it never occurred."

Crayle stared into the darkness as if corroborating the Elder's brilliance. "I see. So you struck a Devil's bargain with Chin. He provides the nuclear devices for himself and Lalumière, and you carve him into the Ch'in black jade. He displays it to his admiring public, and his credentials move to a loftier level."

"*Pre-ordained*, you might say. And, one might say, Chin had been seduced by a crystal."

"A Crystal Seduction."

"Well put, Mr. Crayle." The Elder seemed quite pleased and open. "At this juncture, do you have any questions for me?"

"Something's been bugging me. I understand Chin's goal, and I understand Lalumière's goal. You, however, are still one hell of an enigma. So tell me, what's your why?"

The Elder regarded Crayle, wanting to believe he had, at long last, achieved the end game. He knew better. "I've either observed or researched what organized religion has accomplished throughout the millennia. Inquisitions. Oppression. Land grabs. Political killings."

Megalomaniacs, Crayle observed to himself, travel only in their own minds. All else … mere props on their canvas.

The man continued. "Joan of Arc, first a heretic burned to ashes, then a saint, as it pleased the popes. Don't get me wrong, Mr. Crayle. I've seen the other side. The false science of global warming. Other misbegotten science throughout history killing millions. No good can come without a good heart."

"And mind."

"I was pleased to have known and worked with the previous Magus Crayle, the supreme strategist the Central Intelligence Agency created—manufactured—from the good and honorable man seated before me. The experimental process changed the original into someone who would produce results no matter the consequence. All accomplished by manipulating your brain. Once past her nymphomaniacal proclivities, one has to admire the brilliant scientist of the mind, Monika Rikki. Don't you agree, Mr. Crayle?"

"It wasn't just the memories of the strategic planning that were removed. Long before, the memories of my childhood and everything to that point, they were removed, weren't they?"

"Well done. Please continue."

"It makes sense. You took away who I had been, including my moral compass. You replaced it with the means to plan these operations. When you were finished with me, you ordered my death. You didn't plan on my survival against all odds, and you didn't plan on Rorschach restoring the plans. Last, you didn't count on my character, my sense of honor, burrowing their way back to the surface in an attempt to rectify what I, under your manipulations, had done."

"Bravo."

"And you didn't count on my team."

"Bravo, again."

"So, I'll ask once more. What is it? What is your why?"

"Another seduction, Mr. Crayle. An additional crystal seduction."

"With the memories I have intact, that means nothing to me. But there's something else, isn't there?"

The Elder laughed and shook his head. "My, my. You never quit." He pushed back from the table and eyed them all. "Odd as it may sound, I have come to like you who sit before me. All of you." His face, for the ensuing seconds, portrayed the contrary emotions of remorse and resolve. "All of you … it is such a pity. You are all required to die."

CHAPTER 51

"I for one was seduced," came a voice from the darkness. A white-clad figure strode into the open. He eyed the Elder, who had been, until now, in complete control. "A minor suspension of disbelief, and the faithful believe that I was, like Chin, pre-ordained."

"The advent of The Innocent to the party is, itself, as if ordained—if you will pardon the religious reference," commented the Elder.

The new pope nodded his acceptance of the usage, and took a seat.

"Pardon us if we don't stand." A bitter Crayle clenched, then released his jaw. His eyes drifted back to the Elder. "The deal you made. You offered the completed stone to Chin if..."

"If he would play ball, as you say."

"He would provide the football-shaped nuclear bombs and receive payment from Lalumière, including a profit, of course, so he could acquire his own bombs. And if he succeeded, you would provide the perfect centerpiece for his new palace."

"Bravo, Mr. Crayle. I caused the right side of the stone to be carved and, following Chin's accession, it has been placed." The Elder wore smug like he owned it. He proffered a gold-cased tablet computer, depicting the carved black jade in full HD on a central altar at the new palace.

"That's not all." A tall woman with flowing bright red hair entered the scene. She wore a black Chanel suit and spike heels. Her brightly colored Hermés scarf set the American taxpayers back $5,000.

"Ah, Dr. Rikki, my long lost psychiatrist."

Not sure whether he was religious or not, Crayle felt himself in a gathering of demons. Angry, he lashed out, "How's my good friend, Dr. Rorschach?"

"His last word was, *Ahhhhh!*" she breathed, unaffected. "Subject Crayle, we needed to know what you would be able to recall regarding the Blackstone Strategy, and which of us—as far as you knew—were involved. Your survival of the poorly engineered car crash …" She glanced at the Frenchman. "… was heaven sent." The atheist doctor smiled. "Simply put, your plans were perfection, and we got greedy. We already possessed all of your strategic thought processes on record. In our Illuminé archives. I sought the requisite verification that they were lost to you. That led us to the memory recovery program." With that, she curtseyed, then left the way she'd arrived.

"Why the attacks? Why try to kill me when you could have done so at the Quarry hospital?"

"I weighed the risks. The risk-reduced implementation of your perfect plan versus scientific curiosity. Curiosity lost. I had Neil order Jack to spirit you to Hong Kong. He told Jack you needed answers."

"Then it wasn't so I could interrogate Chin as I was told."

"No, Mr. Crayle. Your meeting with Chin merely allowed Lalumière's hit squad time to reposition beyond the boundaries of the United States. We chose French assassins such that they, if captured or killed, would not lead to Chin. It was what he required before he would agree to his part."

Crayle attempted to turn the tables. His glacial blue eyes bore into the Elder. “I and my team foiled you for the final time in Paris. The French government has survived intact. You have lost.”

“Conditions in my neighbor country worsen by the day. The time for change in France remains long overdue. We had hoped for a king, with emperor our second choice. The French government is in hiding since the Christmas affair—and, evermore, the public demands their heads. We …” He nodded at the pope. “… have struck a deal.”

“Yes. You see, there is a surviving aspect of French monarchy such that he who holds another black crystal—in this case, a 100-carat, perfect diamond of that hue—holds the throne. Never a problem, the crystal has been lost since the revolution in 1789.”

“No!” A lone thin figure emerged from the shadows on gangway one. As she stepped closer, Crayle recognized the figure, then the face.

“Ling! Get back!” Forgetting the consequences, he struggled to break the chair’s confinement.

She stepped onto the platform and faced Lalumière. “Father—Emperor Chin—will have no more of this violence. I tracked you here to retrieve the remaining football, as you call it. You will receive a full refund within thirty days.”

Not confined by one of the special chairs, Lalumière abruptly stood, his chair upending behind him. “It’s mine. My quest is not yet complete.” He grabbed the ball from the table.

Ling started toward him.

“Get back, Ling!” Crayle repeated. “The table’s C-4!”

Late to the party, she realized that she perceived less of the situational intel than required. She retreated.

The Elder continued. “You have no quest, Sylvain. Your coronation will commence shortly. Having completed the ceremony, my people will transfer you to Paris following tonight’s fireworks. At that time, you shall enjoy full support of the outgoing, elected government.”

The man realized his role as the glorified Mitim neared its end. He staggered. And lost his grip.

Jean-Marc deftly turned in his chair, fielding the football before it could strike the platform and bound into the bowels of the stadium. "Father. This is too important. You must not drop the ball."

Lalumière leaned against the table edge. Something changed. It was his mind. "This may be a trick. The nuclear bomb is my strength."

Before anyone could digest the man's ranting, the sound of something rolling over an uneven surface echoed in the stadium. They all turned as Red daughter and new Beige guided a gold throne with red velvet cushioning across gangway two. Even in the darkened lighting, it proclaimed royalty.

"One other thing," said Ling, ignoring the new arrival. "Emperor Chin has commanded that I return Mr. Crayle—and his team, if he wishes—back to Hong Kong."

The Elder shook his head. "He knows us all. He knows our alliances. He knows the entirety of our strategy. A return to Hong Kong will not happen."

Ling's phone rang. It stopped all conversation. "Black daughter," she answered. "Oh." She turned to the group. "Something big is happening. Red? Beige? We must return to Hong Kong. Immediately." Controlling her accelerating breathing, she turned back to the Elder. "Please send Mr. Crayle as soon as possible. It will not go well if we must come again for him." With that, she and her two sisters departed.

The *what just happened* looks pervaded the group. A sigh refocused their attention.

Lalumière, re-invigorated, seated himself on the throne. "It fits perfectly."

Recognizing that he had lost control of the dialog, the Elder rose. "What is going on here?" He motioned at the third gangway. A noise, as if someone had fallen. Then, *"Ahhhhh!"*

A ghost of sorts trundled, cane in hand, toward them, a golden hat-box tucked under his free arm. The apparition came into focus. A white lab coat. "I haff chust shtepped in a … a … *ahhhhh!*"

Faces blanched. Hearts stopped. Eyes saw, but didn't believe.

Crayle answered the obvious question. "He's dead."

When the doctor had restored his calm, his accent disappeared. "Not so fast, my dear subject Crayle. Thanks to the thieves who pilfered much of the gravel above my hospital, there was not enough left to crush me. And your problems were not *my* fault. It was that …"

Another rumble, this time from gangway four. Two men pushed a wheelchair toward the throng.

Rorschach caught sight of the seated man. *"Ahhhhh!"*

"Jack!" cried Phoebe.

"Omigod!" Hekka followed. "My brothers!" She struggled to free herself.

The trio stopped. Jack flung off his lap blanket. He lifted a pistol. The two former paratroopers behind snatched up sniper carbines velcroed to the back of the chair. Jack spoke. "Magus Crayle is coming with me. I've been pulled back in. Neil's old billet," he lied. "Take *us* on … you take on America."

"You will not shoot me, Mr. Sommers," the Elder observed. "Head of state, and all."

"Nor me, for obvious reasons," added the pope.

Crayle assessed. He, and those for whom he cared, needed time. "It's a standoff. You all know it." He remembered misdirection, and pointed at Lalumière. "The ceremony?"

Shrugs all around. They realized. Once more, Magus Crayle was right.

Those not restricted to their seats gathered around the throne. The white-bermed Doctor Rorschach, clutching his gold box in both hands, appeared as would a ring-bearer at a wedding.

"I envy you, Sylvain," said Illuminé's Elder—the Prince of Monaco. "I will attend the ceremonial counterpart in Paris. Our countries shall forge an indelible pact, which we shall establish before you depart."

Lalumière's excitement caused his chest nearly to burst. Still, he understood the Elder's implicit admonition. He would have to agree to this pact, whatever it was, or his reign would be short-lived.

The pope provided a string of words in Latin, then English. "May you go with God."

"But—"

"Go with God, Sylvain. Trust me."

"Kneel," ordered the Elder.

"Where?" Lalumière's heart palpitated.

The Elder pointed down.

"Oh."

The pope elevated his scepter. "I give to the new Kingdom of France, it's first king. Louis the Nineteenth."

A hush fell over those assembled.

Rorschach extracted an item from his box. He stepped forward with the bejeweled gold crown.

"Check for wires, Louis," a frustrated Crayle quipped.

The pope intercepted the symbol of the royal head of state, and placed it on Lalumière's head. "Rise, my Liege."

The man who appeared every bit an aging, wasting hermit rose to meager applause.

The Elder cleared his throat. Heads turned. "We're not quite finished."

The glow left the king's face.

"There must be a queen."

"But—"

"Before we continue, I'm sure you're wondering about the empty chair to my right." He turned and spoke to the shadows to his left. "Please join me, my dear."

Lalumière anticipated. "The voluptuous Doctor Rikki again, I presume."

The Elder smirked, then shook his head. "You've all been introduced."

A young woman stepped from the shadows, passed behind him, and took the seat.

"Thank you … Father."

CHAPTER 52

Of all the surprises in one night, this one topped them all.

The Elder leaned to her and kissed her forehead. "You may know her as Angel, Anne-Isabel, Sandrine … or even as Pattie. But to me, she's my little Gretje. You could not possibly know her history. She is the great, great granddaughter of the infamous, but quite successful, Mata Hari. Perhaps the grandest female spy in history."

"Gret-ya," Crayle repeated. "Perhaps history's greatest spy, murderer, and psychopath."

She smiled and recalled having left the letters RLP on a fogged mirror in Zurich, self-proclaiming as Randy's Little Psychopath. Comfortable with Crayle's assessment, she stared into Lalumière's eyes. "He loves me, Father. I know he does."

"An alliance of state, my daughter." He glanced over his shoulder. "You should know this, Mr. Crayle, if only for a little while. I was stricken by her mother's intellect, and her sense of humor. But it was her natural sexual allure that drew me in. A dalliance? Perhaps. But the product of that relationship, this young lady before you, always deserved to be a princess. Tonight, we skip that step. She has waited far too long."

Lalumière perked up. "That is why you told me not to sleep with her when I met with you at your castle. It wasn't that she was dangerous. You wanted your daughter pure for our impending royal marriage. Now, I understand."

The Elder, teeth clenched, barely controlled his anger. "I told you not to sleep with her *because* she is my daughter."

Pattie, now positioned next to the pope for the ceremony, ripped off her velcroed vestments to reveal an elegant long gold lamé dress above gloss black high heels. Doctor Rikki stepped forward from the shadows to adorn her ears and neck with sparkling jewels.

"Why that little … mmph!"

Crayle slapped a hand over Phoebe's mouth.

Heads shook and bobbed. Only then did Crayle notice. A bright red dot scrawled back and forth across the table, zig-zagging toward himself and Hekka.

Three feet away.

Two.

He glanced up. The light flickered through the field of snowflakes that began to fall.

"Hekka!"

She noticed. They fought their restraints as the dot sought a target.

Her brothers picked it up. They traced the laser, highlighted by the snowflakes, to the Colosseum's top row.

A friendly moon showcased a figure.

Two shots rang out.

The body tumbled the entire distance, bounding off the numerous rows of seats, and finally thudding onto the platform next to the new king.

Hekka's younger brother moved, as he had been trained, to verify the corpse. Using his rifle barrel, he pushed it over.

"It is Thierry Jacquard," said Lalumière. "The third and final of the triplets. His brother, Jerome, killed your father, Miss Poppi. That *your* brothers took his life is, I believe, the justice you have sought. The circle is complete."

At first amazed by the new calm monarchic demeanor, Crayle saw into the man who had been his nemesis for so long. He turned to Hekka, grasping her hand. "I'm sorry. That man …" He gestured at the body. "… placed the bomb on the Queen Mary 2. Tonight, he must've been trying to square his two brothers' failures."

She squeezed back.

They snapped back into reality when King Louis-elect turned to the Elder. "What was that you said? Your daughter? The American spy?" An errant image popped into his mind. Pattie in her nun's habit with small crime scene corpse outlines denoting confirmed kills. He shook his head to clear the image, nearly losing his crown.

"You understand the conditions …" said the Elder to the Frenchman.

Regaining his composure, the new king uttered the words, "I accept."

The pope confirmed the new queen's ceremony with a second gold crown he'd kept hidden in his valise, just in case. "The proper process includes a greeting, opening prayer, the Liturgy of the Word, readings, psalms, gospels, and so forth that we will bypass due to the inclement weather. Still, you are required to consent and exchange vows. If you both nod affirmation, I have the power to waive that requirement, as well."

The two nodded in silence.

"I pronounce you husband and wife—married in Holy wedlock. You may now exchange a kiss."

The delighted Pattie deployed her dimples and pressed her lips against Lalumière's, her glance into her father's eyes lingering. She considered making the kiss *very* French, but quashed the notion.

"In closing, it is with great honor that I proclaim you king and queen of the Kingdom of France."

They bowed to their eclectic audience and the king retook his seat. His queen hopped onto his lap. "Pictures?"

Needing no further cue, the City of Rome's New Year's fireworks commenced.

"12:01," proclaimed the pope.

The Elder whispered into the king's ear. "She is our pact. Our indelible pact. As the Americans say, *We're good.*"

The man in white jerked upright as if he had just unearthed a revelation. "I must leave now. I must prepare for my miracles."

The pope strode across the fourth gangway and proceeded to the top of the Colosseum. There, he was assisted into a glacial white carriage, perhaps two hundred years old. It seemed to levitate west over the vast city. Spotlights focused on the transit, tracking progress while keeping the thick suspension cable invisible.

Lightning, which had not been expended by the storm over Paris a few days prior, now flashed near and far, along with the requisite trailing thunderclaps. The pope, now adorned with white gloves, waved. It was at once holy and unholy. The vision became progressively smaller as the carriage approached the Vatican, crossing St. Peter's Square.

All was fantasy-like, save the still-confined Crayle team, the explosive table, and the five megaton nuclear football. Their attention returned to their reality. They'd lost sight of the carriage as it crossed toward the Vatican.

No one saw the next bolt select the carriage as the perfect conduit to the obelisk grounding structure centered in St. Peter's Square.

• • •

Lost in the catacombs, Lenny continued his search. Having experienced similar in Paris, he ignored the flashes and crashes from the storm and fireworks. In his quest, he was uncertain what to expect, but determined to follow his nose. He rounded a sharp bend, weapon at the ready, and encountered a dead end. Huge stones formed a wall in front of him.

To his left he spotted an old stone wheel, one with horizontal grooves cut into its circumference. Believing that it might open a secret passage, he grasped the shaped rock and gave it a twist. No movement. Certain that it may have been centuries since it was last turned, he leaned into it. Finally, a response. Water seeped in through a gap created by the twisting action.

In the distance behind, he heard the familiar voice of Micmac. "Lenny. If you've found something, don't touch it 'til I get there."

"And share the glory?" he muttered to himself. Encouraged, he forced harder. Persistence was a key attribute of successful private investigators, his father had said.

The water incursion evolved from a trickle to a flow. Rapidly, it covered his shoes. As it rose in his little chamber, he tried to close the discovered valve. No luck. The ice-cold fluid rose up his socks like water climbing in a toilet reservoir, but with no end in sight. He grabbed a timber and tried to wedge it shut. The stone's decrepit iron shaft snapped. It tumbled away, nearly taking out the P.I.

He ran to higher ground, toward Micmac, as he heard the wall give way behind. In the tunnels, the crash sounded more like thunder. Up close. Real close.

In seconds, the Tiber River's influx reached flood stage. Too late, Lenny remembered a school class regarding the Romans and their Colosseum. Often, they would flood the base level in order to stage mock sea battles. He had just broken a water valve that no Roman plumber could fix. He ran, climbing and stumbling over the uneven channel as the water chased after him. He needed to warn the others.

• • •

Above, the interplay reached a crescendo.

"All in all, nothing matters," said the Elder. "Because all attempts to stop your team have failed, Mr. Crayle, I must do it myself." He, followed by his daughter, stood.

Not being of sound mind, little Gretje decided to provoke a little fun. She reached down to the table's edge, and flipped a hidden switch.

Crayle, Hekka, and Phoebe fell backwards, rolling out of the chairs and tumbling onto the soaked platform.

No explosion.

"The table is disarmed!" Crayle yelled. The trio jumped to its feet.

Firearms appeared from the strangest locations. But no shots were fired. There was something else.

A roar beneath them, like the Niagara Falls of gushing water it was, prevented a bloodbath. Distant at first, the rumble built to a threshold. The Tiberian water entered from a side tunnel, flinging a sopping Lenny and Micmac to one side. It filled the arc-shaped channels below and reached the platform in seconds.

The Elder and his daughter scampered for the nearest crumbling walkway.

The water ascended, one foot per heartbeat. The platform shook from the force. Gangway one collapsed.

Like a billiard table aboard the Titanic, the platform wobbled and swayed. Maintaining one's balance—impossible.

Gangway two broke free.

Everyone fell, grasping hopelessly to the slimy surface.

One-by-one, good and evil, they slid into the flooded channels.

"Help, Magus!" Hekka's cries whooshed into the distance.

The overwhelming currents pulled them along convergent channels toward an exit tunnel. There was no possibility of grabbing any of the criminals. Staying alive trumped all else.

Past the triumphal Arch of Titus, the floodwaters flushed them across roads and into the ruins of the ancient Roman Forum, bouncing them off relics and columns.

Above them, the New Year's fireworks popped and screamed, supplementing the battlefield feel.

In mere minutes, the 252-mile long Tiber lowered enough to stem the tide. Survivors grasped artifacts and pillars, climbing to safety.

Gasping for air, Crayle clambered atop Julius Caesar's stone crypt. He caught his breath. "Everyone! Check in!"

"Micmac!" came from one direction.

"Phoebe!" came from another.

Silence.

Crayle's heartbeat ramped.

"Hekka." The voice came from directly behind him.

He spun, clutching her tight to him, silently giving thanks.

She pulled away. "Where are my brothers?" She called their names, but the young men's voices were stilled, or out of earshot.

Crayle joined in. *"Jack!"*

No response.

"Lenny!" Hekka called.

Nothing.

"Anyone. Can you see the football?"

Three answers, exactly the same. "No!"

"Wait." He clamped his eyes shut. "It's a nuclear bomb. It wouldn't float."

Groans greeted his deduction.

"Lalumière? Jean-Marc?"

"No."

"Elder? Pattie?"

Same response.

Crayle climbed to the top of the protective crypt surrounds. As the water receded, it produced no answers.

Hekka shivered. "I'm freezing. Magus, let's try interlocking our jackets."

"We can't stay here," Micmac yelled.

"Where can we go?" Phoebe added to their quandary.

"Only Jack knows."

"We can build a fire." Hekka began to look for anything dry.

"In the Roman Forum?"

"Wait! I see Phoebe and Micmac now, Magus. Over by those columns."

The other two waded to their location through the waning flood waters, mud, and loosened artifacts. Out of breath, Phoebe spoke. "We've gotta find Jack."

"And Lenny," Micmac added.

Phoebe shook her head. "After what happened back there, it's probably only Jack by now. In a wheelchair."

"Yeah. We need to catch up with them. Shouldn't be too tough."

"We're done here," Crayle assessed. "We're done."

• • •

They marched away from the Forum. Now on the modern-day street above the receding floodwaters, they located and followed tracks from Jack's chair that hadn't yet filled in with mud. Fifteen minutes passed.

"There!" Phoebe yelled. She pointed to a black speck in the distance.

The team broke into a run more like a trudge. Another speck appeared.

"That's Lenny right in front of him. Hands on knees, out of gas."

"Jack's gotta be exhausted, too. Anger can only take you so far."

From the distance, came a too familiar apology. "Sorry about that."

Phoebe, worn out and happy to be alive, didn't even reach for her Glock. "Hey! Wait up!"

"My lieutenant," Jack smacked Lenny on the back of the head, "broke the ancient Roman water valve." He hit him again, followed by, "STFU!"

"What does that mean?" Lenny asked, in his most annoying tone.

"It means Shut … The Fuck … Up!" Jack snarled.

"Five bucks!" Lenny retorted.

Before Jack could exact revenge, the others arrived. A saved-by-the-bell Lenny formed in behind his boss and began to push.

The fireworks over the city entered the grand finale. The team watched in wonder as two shadows, Jack uttering a string of graphic and creative obscenities, and Lenny, providing a running tally, led them through the night.

Together at last and alive only by a miracle, the team followed Jack's lead across Rome, across the now shallow Tiber River, and along a narrow street to the left of the Vatican's Saint Peter's Square. Through the snow they saw kneeling masses in the square, seeking deliverance from the lightning spectacle they had just witnessed.

Unsure of the fate of the new pope, the team pressed on. The curved colonnade on their right demonstrated the magnificence of the Vatican. At the same time, it presented a physical demarcation of Rome—and the rest of Italy—from the Roman Catholic city-state.

Lenny pushed left through an entry area to a door. He guessed at verbiage on a brass plaque below a sign announcing *Residenza Paolo VI*, and buzzed into the elevator. Oddly, there were no hotel staff members in sight. Arriving on the second floor, they rolled down the corridor to a room.

Jack fished into his wet sponge of a pocket and produced a master key. "It's okay. It's one of our safe rooms."

CHAPTER 53

Lalumière's gone. Again," Crayle moaned. "And his son. And the spy. And the football. Gone."

"But what about that pope?" Lenny mumbled, teeth chattering.

"No one will be able to tell the masses that their hero, the new pope, is most likely an atheist. But with him in place, this Elder has a lot more power now. I don't remember this aspect from the Rorschach restores."

"We didn't do any Croatian or Italian restores, MC."

"Lenny, fire up the computer. Let's see if we can find any involvement by me with Zoran. Before my crash."

• • •

Jack provided team members a time-out before exfiltrating the Roman madness. TV and room service at the Rezidenza Paulo VI were both excellent. Although the room lacked spaciousness, the six found all the comfort they required. Lenny ramped up the TV audio.

The Italian television commentator's excellence in English was only exceeded by his elation. "The world's new pope addressed the city this morning. Late autumn, early winter rains had flooded the Tiber, making passage under Rome's bridges impossible. Today, the first full day of Pope Innocent's reign, waters have receded to the passable levels of late September. Hundreds of watercraft are celebrating the new pope's first miracle."

Crayle turned to Lenny. "In actuality, your tactical maneuver with the Colosseum's water network is what lowered the river levels. I think the pope is taking credit that is rightfully yours."

"Yeah, P.I. Get out there and take a bow." Phoebe motioned at the panoramic terrace outside. It faced over the Vatican's south colonnade, across St. Peter's Square, and bore a direct line of sight to the pope's chambers.

Lenny started up from his seat against the wall.

Jack caught him with a single word. "No!"

CHAPTER 54

The rest at the Rezidenza enabled the team to travel. Dark-windowed vehicles in which passengers could only see out aided by special goggles indicated transport of *persons of interest.* Jack's jet was its usual self sans one component: flight attendant Flori. When the team viewed the flowing red tresses of her replacement from behind, their minds went to the oversexed Doctor Rikki.

She turned. "I'm not Monika, but I do get asked." She smiled.

The pilot turned on all the burners as ordered by Jack. The winged capsule headed west.

"This is January 1, MC. If we fly fast enough, we'll end up in last year."

"No!" chorused the depleted remains of the team.

"Sleep, Lenny. That's a direct order."

"Yes, boss."

• • •

They didn't touch down on the previous day in the previous year, but when they did, they were whisked in similar vehicles to stealth helicopters, and then to an anonymous location.

"Debrief time?" Crayle posed to Jack.

"You'll see."

In minutes, they found themselves once again beneath the ground in a cathedral.

"More medals, boss."

"You'll see."

A door to the far side of the room opened. In strode the same man as in their previous visit to this place. President of the United States, Kimbel Stones.

He noticed that Magus Crayle and Hekka Poppi stood together. And Phoebe Bransfield and Mick Mackay.

The president snapped his fingers. Bells chimed. "We'll forego the medals this time … I'm running late. But I do have time for this." He scanned the two couples. "You're getting married."

After the initial shock, and despite their individual toughness, emotions poured.

"You proposed to me that night in Malibu. You remember?"

As usual, Hekka's question was direct. Crayle smiled. "And the answer you whispered into my ear …"

"Yes."

Phoebe turned to Micmac. "And you proposed when you declared that groupies, other than myself, were a thing of the past. A commitment if ever there was one."

Micmac decided to play. "I don't remember that you said yes."

"It was the little love tap. That was yes."

The president broke in. "We can stipulate, at the presidential level, that both parties are in agreement. Ms. Bransfield?"

Phoebe nodded.

"Mr. MacKay?"

Micmac nodded.

Before the president could continue, Lenny's whine alarm, in abeyance until now, went off. "Fine. You're all paired up and happy, and I'm standing here alone. Fine." Moping and pouting battled for supremacy.

Phoebe reacted. "If we could trust you not to screw it up, you could be the ring boy."

"Oh! Oh! Thank you! Thank you! I'm really happy for all of you." Lenny hung his head. "Looks like I'm the only one … who keeps his … *freedom!*"

Everyone's jaw dropped, including the president's. The P.I.'s dancing and finger-snapping echoed in the hallowed chamber. Under the circumstances, how could Lenny still be Lenny, they asked themselves.

"Not so fast, you little twerp!" A slender figure emerged from the darkness. "No way you're gettin' outta this."

Lenny, in disbelief, lapsed into silence.

Alona appeared before him like a poker player who'd just been cheated. She pressed her lips together, then forced them to one side. Like the attorney inside, she contemplated her next words.

The P.I. began to speak.

"As your attorney, I advise you to keep your mouth shut."

As if afflicted by a newfound wisdom, he remained quiescent.

"Lenny Lipschitz, will you marry me? … the answer … better be …" She glared into his eyes as if accumulating the seconds of silence for a future, egregious penalty.

"Yes." The little man's eyes watered. "Yes, yes, yes!"

He threw his arms around her. It took a moment for her countenance to resolve what had just transpired—for reality to sink in. They kissed.

Crayle turned to the side and whispered, "Nicely done, Jack."

"She's got work to do," he whispered back.

Lenny and Alona's enduring kiss had to be broken up due to the president's busy schedule.

As the newly engaged pair turned to face the team with big smiles, Jack cried out. "Ahhh!" Everyone spun his way. He collapsed, writhing on the floor.

Standing behind him—someone he hadn't seen for awhile. His ex-wife, Marilyn. Dressed in red with matching lipstick and signature Hollywood sunglasses, she blew wisps of smoke from the tip of her cattle prod. "We're even," she announced. She helped the damaged CIA off-the-books project manager to his knee. She smiled, crossed her arms, the still-smoldering prod waving ominously. "So, you gonna propose?"

His nervous system still in disarray, her ex-husband nodded in both directions.

Lenny, too, was shocked. Not about Jack's predicament, but that his new fiancée had turned her normally mousy brown hair into a vibrant Copper Penny.

She tossed her trench coat aside with a "How do you like it?" She rotated before him, exhibiting her white wedding gown.

"Don't do it," Lenny admonished.

"Do what?" She twirled.

"Don't ask me the *fat* question."

She began pummeling the P.I. until he ran to a confessional, vainly trying to open the door.

"You're Jewish," cried Alona. "Go in there, and the whole place goes up!"

She was the first to laugh. Then the contagion spread. Lenny would be married this day, and Alona would be his ideal partner. She looked about, as if searching for someone.

"Hey! Where's my Matron of Honor?"

The other women, realizing that they were all deep underground in an ornate covert cathedral, stared at her.

"Not to worry," came a sultry voice from behind. An attendant wheeled in the voice's owner.

Phoebe recognized the woman at once. *"Flori!"*

The attendant pushed the young Brazilian woman between the group and the president. Upon setting a footbrake and reaching down to the gurney's frame, he pressed a rocker switch. The gurney, plentifully adorned in flowers for the occasion, rotated the wounded flight attendant to a standing position. As a Scotch plaid blanket fell away, the team saw that she wore a full gown of deep burgundy velvet. Beautiful.

"I want a Matron," Alona croaked. "You're not a virgin, are you?"

The team laughed, then covered their mouths as Flori feigned offence.

With all necessary parties in attendance, the president commenced. "I've never done this before, so I've asked an old friend for a little help. We met years ago while I was on vacation. In fact, this fine man was a college student, and also my tour guide."

Surprised, questioning looks.

From the far right, in walked yet another surprise. A man dressed entirely in white. Jaws dropped. Crayle did a double-take.

"Zoran!"

"Oh, my," escaped Hekka's lips.

"Whose side is he on?" Lenny exclaimed.

"Shut up, Lenny," chorused the team.

The lights came down to the point where the cathedral flickered to the electronic candles adorning the walls. Computer-controlled reflectors focused the glow like a soft spotlight on the cast of characters.

The president cleared his throat, then raised both arms. "Yes, ladies and gentlemen, I've called in a favor. On my tour, Zoran stumbled into a river. He banged his head and went unconscious. I was able to pull him out."

"Bless every one of you," said the pope. "Please. If you will, line up in pairs, as appropriate. We shall begin."

"Wait!" Lenny shouted. "We're Jewish, You're not. This'll never hold up in court." His attempt at humor was met with a scowl from both pope and fiancée.

"You'll never make it to court if you don't shut up," she admonished.

"Yes, ma'am."

"Alright," Jack's voice echoed off the walls. "Let's get this done. *Rock and roll!*"

The pope performed the ceremony within the twenty minute time-frame agreed upon by he and the president. The two shook hands, waved their goodbyes to the team, and departed.

The newlyweds exited down a holographic gauntlet of rice-throwing FBI, NSA, and military men and women. Through large steel tunnel doors, they came upon what appeared to be a hotel resort's valet area replete with three vehicles.

"Come on, Alona. There's my big black Buick!"

"Jack, Jack, Jack," Phoebe cried. She ran to the gloss black Porsche 911 she had driven in France and Monaco. She turned to Micmac. "This is beyond fabulous, Mick. Jack is just …" The smile on her husband's face gave him away. "You … you …" She punched him hard in the shoulder.

"Ouch! We're an item, Phoebe. Save the physical for the bedroom."

Crayle and Hekka looked into each other's eyes and smiled. Before them, no more than twenty feet away, sat Jack's red Cobra. Beer cans attached.

"It's yours," came his voice from behind.

They turned. Crayle spoke for them both. "You're a gem, Jack Sommers." He held out his hand.

Jack placed his Kershaw folding knife into Crayle's palm.

Flipping open the blade, Crayle cut the cans loose.

Hekka smiled.

Their gazes returned to each other. Then, in the same instant, both broke for the driver's side.

"I'm driving," Hekka yelled.

"I'm more qualified," cried Crayle.

The small caravan exited via an underground tunnel, proceeded through a forest on a dirt road, then through a mammoth iron gate that opened as they approached, and onto U.S. Route 13 south. They all beamed as they headed for the 23-mile-long Chesapeake Bay Bridge-Tunnel. Next stop … no-one knew. Or cared.

• • •

A woman watched the exodus through high-powered binoculars as the entourage sped away. She, too, smiled. It brought her dimples into play. She remembered what had happened after the flood.

A young couple had ignored their parents' admonitions and had eloped to Rome.

"Are you liking your date with me?"

"A trip to Rome for New Year's Eve? You've got to be kidding. This is the best, Tommy. And the fireworks last night …"

"You mean me?"

She blushed.

"Hey!" He ran to the side of Via Appia. "Look what *I* found."

"What is it?"

"Check it out." He spun to face her. "A football!"

"We'll be back in Kansas in plenty of time for the Super Bowl. Give it to a kid."

"Now, you're the one who's kidding. Here." The young American stepped back five paces.

His girlfriend just shook her head. A waste of time to argue. She took three steps back, and held out her arms. She couldn't help but giggle. "Everyone's dream. Playing football at the Colosseum."

He stretched back his arm.

"Catch!"

He stopped. His fiance's face had turned ashen. She stared directly behind him. At a diminutive, ragged-looking individual whose head seemed loosely affixed to her body. Scarred, bruised, and dimpled. With a gun.

"I'll take that," she said.

EPILOGUE

Chin is complete, I believe. Although it is merely a crystalline substance, the black jade figure from the Ch'in era in 200 B.C. symbolizes the empire's emperor. He has that, he has the military, and he has the people. Well done."

"Yes, my dear. While the jade is beautiful, meaningful, and quite artistic, France's Louis the Last possessed a 100 carat, perfect, black diamond as his symbol of selection."

"You don't know, do you?"

"Know what?" She continued to carve aged cheese slices and bite-sized triangles of Brie. "There." She slid the blade across her lips, licking it clean. "Oh!" Her brow furrowed. She examined the knife. Lalumière noticed the blood.

"I cut myself, Mitim. Come see."

He moved away.

She tilted her chin. A smile, slow in coming, mutated to a laugh.

It was the tipping point for the man known throughout France as Mitim, the Man In The Iron Mask. He was certain that he would stay with her to the end. "I shall publically be made Louis. The XIX. And you … Marie Antoinette. The second."

"I think Marie misspoke when she said: *Let them eat cake.* We are king and queen for Chrissakes, albeit in Italy. Hey, let's pretend we're in exile."

Lalumière wasn't sure about the gleam in her eye. "What would you say?"

"I'd say: *Let them eat shit.*"

They chuckled. Caressed. Made love.

• • •

Pattie was first up on the edge of the bed. "Cigarette?"

Lalumière observed her. Then he remembered his unanswered query. "You didn't know, did you?"

"About …"

"The stone. The King Louis stone."

This time she deployed her dimpled smile full force. In a singsong voice, she replied, "I know where it is."

• • •

Magus Crayle was finally home. Like him, the rest of the team had its fill of travel to exotic locations for awhile, and enjoyed their respective honeymoons at their homes in the Big Bear Valley. He had taken a moment away from the cabin and his new bride to cross the grounds to the dock. And to reflect. The undulations of the dock beneath his feet mirrored his life.

Without warning, a boat sped by, hurling waves at the shore, oblivious of the consequences. He assumed a wide, balanced stance. The dock jumped and rolled, then calmed once again. Slowly, he shook his head and returned to his purpose. The means he chose to express himself would have surprised no one.

"I know you won't have the opportunity to hear my final internal dialog, Doctor Rorschach. In a way, I'm sorry that the cave in at the Quarry Hospital destroyed your work. Your research could have produced incredible benefits, and they could have assisted those of us in the spy game immeasurably. But in the wrong hands, and with the wrong attitudes and goals, they could have been devastating. Not just to our country. To the world. I'm going to destroy your computer. I'm going to live on with the memories I have. I'll need to forget that I had a personal life before all this happened. Perhaps Lenny will help track it down. I hope anyone who has been harmed will somehow forgive me."

He could almost hear the doctor's constitutional outcry, "Ahhhhh!"

"In addition, I have decided that it will help me in my recovery to enumerate those who have entered my life, and describe what I believe to be the seduction—and that's precisely what it was—that brought us all together. So, if I have your permission, here goes.

"Lalumière was seduced, not by wealth or fame, but by his heritage. That heritage required, in his mind, the reinstatement of the aristocracy of his ancestors, and the elevation of himself and his son, Jean-Marc, to royalty status. He had to return France to a monarchy or an empire, and that's where I came in. That he played the role of The Man In The Iron Mask to do so—that was an inspired alteration to my plan. Status: presumed alive; whereabouts: unknown.

"The man's son, Jean-Marc, wished to please his father. The penalty for his participation was the violent death of his birth mother, Épiphanie, in Paris. Status: presumed alive; whereabouts: unknown.

"Chin Yao-wu sought to be the second coming of Ch'in Xihuangdi, China's first emperor. To accomplish his task, he conspired with the Illuminé Elder's choice for unelected leader of France, Lalumière. He required mini-nukes for the operation, and Chin's General Li filled that billet. The bombs were to be divided between himself and Lalumière. Status: alive; whereabouts: Hong Kong Palace.

"General Li's seduction was the chance to become the top military man in China and to become number two in the government. Money and fame. He also grew to covet Black Daughter. Status: alive; whereabouts: Hong Kong Palace apartment.

"Annie Ling—Black daughter—a captive since the age of thirteen. She harbored sincere feelings of devotion and commitment for her nominal Father, Chin. His very wish was her command. Status: alive; whereabouts: Hong Kong Palace.

"Jack Sommers spent his "retired" life just following orders. He didn't ask questions, but over time became enamored with the team. Close. It took him awhile, but he finally found his way and his meaning. Status: married again; whereabouts: Big Bear.

"Neil Wohlford felt French to his very core, because he was. He became a deep cover spy implanted into the CIA and later co-opted by the clever Elder. He was seduced to become the number two man in the Illuminé, perhaps the second most powerful man in the world, with the option, if he could pull it off, to replace Lalumière as the next king of France. Status: dead; whereabouts: Arlington.

"Pattie Norbrunn grew to be seduced by her dual life: Embassy travel agent and wife of the Deputy Chief of Mission—and CIA spy. Her lineage dating back to the Mata Hari spy of World War I provided genetic continuity. She played multiple roles in Holland and the regions of France to the hilt. But for the grace of God, she could have become the queen or empress of France. This grand seduction and the psychopathy engendered by her multiple personages were her undoing. Status: unknown; whereabouts: …"

"Right behind you!"

ABOUT THE AUTHOR

Novelist Dennis Bowen has a long-standing commitment to international affairs, and has traveled to more than 60 countries. Given his martial arts training, classified defense and intelligence community background, and wartime service with amphibious forces, it's not surprising that he pens thrillers. *The Crystal Seduction* follows *The Water Diamonds* and *The Blackstone Perfection* as Book 3 in his International Thriller Series. When not traveling the globe to research his next book, he resides on the Southern California coast.

http://www.twitter.com/DBowenThrillers/
http://www.facebook.com/#!/Dennis.Bowen.90
http://www.dennisbowen.com/

THE REDROCK QUARANTINE

BOOK 4:
International Thriller Series

Available: Spring 2015

CHAPTER 1

The unseasonably warm day peaked at 8 degrees Celsius. The man and woman, who sat across from each other, felt the chill as the sun descended and cast shadows from the ancient fortress across the bay. The woman, wearing a red polka dot top, pulled the lapels of her parka tighter. The man observed. Her butterscotch-toned skin glowed in stark contrast to the pale-complected patrons of the harbor terrace restaurant.

She glanced into her guide book. "The fortress is called Suomenlinna. The Finns built it to defend against the Russians."

"They may need it."

Onlookers made no effort to conceal their curiosity about the woman. Her flesh tones and waist-length, silken black hair set her apart, even among tourists.

"This is a beautiful place. I'm glad you've helped me to experience things like this."

He noticed a fleeting expression of sadness. Neither one of them would ever forget what his insertion into her life had cost. Her father. He reached across the table for her hand.

"Hekka, I don't remember my parents, but I do remember one of the lessons they taught me. Rather than grieve, perhaps we should consider ourselves fortunate to have had such wonderful people in our lives."

She nodded. "A good thought. I concede that I was most fortunate with respect to my father. But my mother …"

"Helsinki is our starting point. I'll do whatever it takes to help you. Until we find her, or what happened …"

"You're here with me and for me. I love you, Mr. Crayle."

"I'm yours to the end, Mrs. Crayle."

"If my mother is dead …" Her voice broke. "… I need to know."

"We'll find out. We will solve your mystery as we solved mine."

"Father would have wanted this as much as I must have it."

She changed the subject. "I believe Finland is a good place, and my mother's people and their culture are good." She made a water-ladling motion. "The sauna with the rocks diffused our jetlag."

"I'm not sure about the blood-sucking cups. I'm glad we passed on that treatment."

Hekka sampled the Finnish fish stew. "I read about this in my travel guide. They call it Kalamojakka, Magus. It's wonderful."

He scooped some into his spoon and tried the mixture. A flock of seabirds taking flight caused him to jump.

"Those people of yours, Mr. Crayle, cost us our Christmas together."

"Lalumière, Pattie, and the rest are not my people. They never will be."

He tossed down a shot of vodka, then glanced at her.

"I'm not sure about this, but here goes." She felt the burn.

Crayle knew he needed to diffuse the serious topic. The alcohol helped.

"About Paris. Didn't you feel that starting Christmas Day atop the Eiffel Tower was special?" He remembered how she'd fought like a seasoned operative high in the Tower. He knew Hekka had been determined to protect him, whatever the cost. She'd sought an end to his demons so they could live in peace.

"It was to die for." She laughed, a rare occurrence.

He followed suit. "I believe we're safe now."

Feeling the effects of the customary vodka shots with every bite of food, she laughed again. "I wanted to see Santa Claus and his reindeer fly by."

He refilled their glasses as she forked a sausage into her mouth. "This is delicious, too."

"It's Rudolph."

She froze. "Reindeer meat?"

"Rudolph is terrific. I've learned enough of your Serrano culture to know that we must thank him for providing our sustenance."

They clinked glasses. "A toast to Rudolph," they chorused.

She pointed across the harbor. "Over there, where all those stalls are with white tops. On the jet, I read that it's called the Kauppatori—the shopping square. Take me there, Magus. I want to shop."

So intense was their focus, they didn't notice a group of young men attired in Adidas warm-up suits, approaching along the quay.

As if to alert him, Hekka pointed.

Crayle's head spun. His body tensed. Then, he exhaled. He shook his head. It was different now. He joined her for a final glimpse of the setting sun, a huge orange disk settling into the sea beyond the harbor's breakwater.

Hekka smiled her minimalist smile. "The sun is so bright and warm, it seems it would boil the sea."

The athletes passed by them, but the last one, quite tall, pulled up behind Crayle. With the hint of a French accent, he whispered, "Do you remember me?"

Before Crayle could answer, the man slammed a ball on their table.

Crayle recalled what he'd witnessed Christmas Eve atop France's Eiffel Tower. This ball, covered with a honeycomb material, was no ordinary rugby ball. It was Sylvain Lalumière's five megaton nuclear device. Made in China.

"Before you make any decisions, look at your wife's blouse."

Crayle turned his attention to the polka dot fabric. Something looked wrong—out of place. Then, he had it. One of the red polka dots. It moved.

"She's not our target. You are. You must come with me now, or …"

Crayle recognized a laser-sight dot from his days as a CIA operative. He knew he could take a bullet for her, but never the other way around.

"Now, Mr. Crayle."

A shocked Hekka Poppi Crayle followed her husband's gaze to the fabric that covered her breast. She knew what the mobile dot portended.

Crayle stood and departed with the tall man. He glanced back at Hekka. The dot vanished.

They approached a van. Crayle felt a pinch in his neck muscle. As cold fluid streaked its way into his heart, the face of the woman who'd seen him through battle after battle—and whom he loved with all of his being—blurred to black.

The unconscious Crayle felt nothing when the other young men tossed him into the van. He didn't hear Hekka scream.

Spring 2015

THE REDROCK QUARANTINE

From International Thriller Writer
DENNIS BOWEN

www.ingramcontent.com/pod-product-compliance
Lightning Source LLC
Chambersburg PA
CBHW020258030826
48979CB00026B/1386/J

* 9 7 8 0 9 9 6 0 4 1 2 0 1 *